MR. GRIN

THE BRADDOCK & GRAY CASE FILES

H.P. BAYNE

BAYNE INDEPENDENT PUBLISHING

1

EVELYN HARLOW LEANED on the balcony railing, gaze travelling over the street below.

It wasn't a real street, but as director of the Kimotan Rapids Historical Museum, she'd been proud to help make it appear that way. Though the city had numerous museums, no other came with a to-scale, indoor street styled as one from the turn of the past century. Boomtown KR, they called it.

During the day, they were often busy with school tours or families. Few got to see it the way Evelyn did now, stretched out below, quiet and empty. She'd silenced the sound effects already, a tape loop containing the noises of horses' hooves and neighs, carts clattering along rough road, clanging from a forge and the incoherent din of numerous human voices in conversation.

While most staff members loved Boomtown KR during the day, they avoided it at night. Evelyn had heard the talk, both from her staff and from countless members of the public. But if the museum was indeed haunted, she had yet to meet the ghost responsible.

Evelyn didn't believe in ghosts. She didn't believe in anything she couldn't see with her own eyes. While she tried to avoid saying as much to her employees, not wanting to insult anyone she otherwise respected, it could be hard to keep a neutral front. It was easy to let one's imagination run wild in a museum like this—especially after hours when the place fell silent. Free of sound effects and the movement and chatter of the public, every creak and crack became evidence of a restless spirit rather than the settling and shifting of these life-size buildings and their contents.

Stories had circulated, too, about the sightings, about a woman in a long Victorian-style dress and a man in a newsboy hat who never showed his face. Evelyn put this down to, at best, exhaustion and, at worst, pranksters. One maintenance man had a habit of concealing himself in unexpected places and jumping out at colleagues.

From where Evelyn stood on the "Red Lion Hotel" balcony—behind which sat her office—there was nothing to be frightened of. Not now that prankster John had gone home for the evening, anyway.

Evelyn inhaled through her nose, taking in the smell of the place. It held that certain indescribable scent only found in museums. The smell of *old,* she'd called it as a child. Oil, dust, timeworn leather, the overpowering medicinal odours from the pharmacy on the other end of the street—all of these things combined to create this place's unique scent.

After twenty-two years here, and many more as a frequent visitor before that, it was the smell of her second home.

Evelyn turned at the sound of movement behind her and spotted Bob Lindberg, her curator, at her office door. She and Bob had worked together a long time, so long they'd attempted a romantic relationship twice in the past after their respective marriages had ended. Evelyn hadn't yet ruled out a third try but was reluctant to bring it up with Bob after the last time.

"Sorry to bother you," he said. "I'm sure you're readying to head out the door."

"In a few minutes. What did you need?"

"Hoped to talk to you about something." Bob entered the room and approached Evelyn, joining her on the balcony. His yet-unasked question lingered on his face, but he left it there for the moment as he gazed onto the street below. "It's nice when it's like this, isn't it? Once everyone else goes home, I mean."

Evelyn smiled, as much at Bob himself as his observation. One of the reasons Evelyn had agreed to date him in the past was because he loved history as much as she did. He was the only person in her life she didn't feel stupid with, making comments like the one she was about to.

"It's like you can really feel the people who might have walked on streets like this back then, isn't it?"

Bob shared in her grin. "Thought you didn't believe in ghosts."

"Ghosts, no. Memories, nostalgia, feelings, yes. Many of these buildings—the façades, anyway—were actually in use somewhere at one time. People walked in and out of these doorways doing business or going to work. And all the items in our collection, those were really possessed and used by someone."

"Many someones, in quite a few cases," Bob said. "I know. It's pretty amazing when you think about it."

"Still haven't told me what you need." Part of Evelyn hoped Bob might have come here to attempt to renew their on-again, off-again relationship, or even just to compliment her on how she'd done her hair or dressed today.

Instead, his expression became serious—and not in a good way. "Not quite sure how to say this. Some of the staff members are nervous. I guess they're not sure how to approach you with it either."

Evelyn sighed and pinched at the bridge of her nose. "I don't know why they always go to you with their concerns. I mean, I'm a nice person. I've never been a lousy boss."

"Of course," he said quickly. "You're an amazing person. That's not the issue."

"So what is?"

Bob gave a shrug, although the way he pressed his lips together in a frown told Evelyn he was plenty in the know.

He took a moment to respond. When he did, he spoke with deliberation. "I think they feel you're a little ... hard to approach about some things."

"Some things, being ...?"

He grimaced. "Some things being ghosts."

Evelyn's frowned. "Oh lord, Bob, not again."

He gave another shrug, more pronounced this time. "Just passing along their concerns."

Evelyn held back the eye roll. "Okay. Which one is it this time? The woman in the dress shop or the man in the hat?"

"Neither, actually. It's something else."

There it was. The moment she'd been dreading. Not enough the place was inundated with stories about the two supposed spirits she'd already heard about; someone had come up with something new.

She said nothing, leaving it to Bob to explain in his own way and time.

"It's the dummy," he said.

"You mean John?" She asked the question with a smirk, tongue-in-cheek as it was meant to be.

While Bob grinned his approval at her quip, the humour faded quickly. "Not this time. I meant the ventriloquist's dummy. The one from the donated collection."

The collection in question had come in a couple of weeks ago. Bob had dug right in, documenting and labelling everything so he could get it out on the floor as soon as possible. The items had belonged to a man named James Holmes who recently passed away after a long lifetime of collecting unusual artifacts. Among his collection were a pair of well-maintained Model Ts, a closetful of Victorian-era clothing and a famous—or rather infamous—First World War-era ventriloquist's dummy named Mr. Grin.

It seemed Mr. Grin was causing some concern.

Evelyn couldn't help it. She chuckled.

Bob raised his brows.

"I'm sorry," she said. "I'm not meaning to make light of anyone's concerns. It's just, I wondered how long it would take before someone said something."

"What do you mean?"

"Well, it's not the nicest-looking thing, is it? Puppets are generally cute these days, but they looked pretty damn creepy a century ago."

Bob gritted his teeth in apparent agreement. "Creepy is right. The thing has the face of a corpse. And that grin." He shuddered. "It's like it's plotting something. No wonder people took to renaming it Mr. Grim over the years."

Evelyn chuckled. "Are you sure it's just the other members of staff who are spooked by this thing?"

Bob smiled. "Okay, not just them. I'm not crazy about it either. Thing is, though, it's more than the way it looks. Constance said she came in this morning and it had moved."

Constance Neudorf, head of the security team of two. During the day, Constance and a second person looked after security for the museum. At night, the cleaners kept an eye on things until they finished their work. After that, the security system—an alarm and a series of surveillance cameras—did the rest. So far, there'd been no need for on-site staff after hours, and Evelyn was happy to keep it that way. The less she had to request of the board, the better.

If there was a benefit to ghosts over human visitors after

hours, Evelyn thought, it was the lack of added expense. "Maybe we can ask it to help with cleaning."

"Don't let Constance hear you making light of it," Bob said. "She was freaked right out."

Evelyn turned serious. Bob wasn't in the mood for jokes. "Okay, you're right. I shouldn't make fun. Moved how?"

"It was outside its case, she said, and the door was wide open. If that weren't bad enough, the eyes were wide open."

Despite not believing in ghosts, Evelyn shivered. Without thinking about it, her hands came up to hug her arms. She stopped herself before moving to rub away the chill. "Probably John. Seems about his speed."

"Yeah, he was my first thought. Talked to him about it, even. He insists it wasn't him."

"You believed him?"

Bob nodded. "I did. He's a goofball, but he's always admitted to being responsible for previous pranks—even when someone's been genuinely frightened."

Though Evelyn hated to admit it, Bob was right about John. If he had done it, he would have fessed up. "What about the cleaning staff?"

He gave a snort. "Carmelita and Flo? They get their work done as soon as possible so they can get out of here before it gets too late. They work here because it's a paying job and because they like the staff and their bosses. Being here after hours creeps them out."

Evelyn raised her brows. "They told you that?"

He gave a noncommittal shrug. Evelyn pressed her lips together. Another secret kept from her.

Leaning against the railing, he gazed from one side of the street to the other without appearing to focus on anything in particular. "I don't know, Ev. Maybe we should consider putting up a camera to monitor the thing."

Evelyn wanted to laugh at the idea of watching a lifeless and aging ventriloquist's dummy. But her views on the paranormal seemed to be precisely why she was dealing with a staff who refused to confide in her with their fears.

"They're really that afraid of coming to me with these things?" she asked.

Bob faced Evelyn with a kind smile, one suggesting he was about to speak a truth she wouldn't want to hear. "You're a skeptic. People don't want to be told they're crazy or seeing things or making stuff up. When people are afraid, they want to know someone will listen." His gaze returned to the museum space below. "That's why I thought the camera might be a good idea. It would show we're taking staff concerns seriously."

Evelyn read between the lines: he'd meant to suggest it would show *she* was taking staff concerns seriously. Though she hated to admit it, he was right.

"We have some money left in our annual budget," she said. "We could certainly purchase a new camera. John can mount it for us."

Bob's relief was obvious, his posture easing and the muscles in his jaw slackening. Evelyn felt badly for causing this level of unease in a man she considered a friend, if not something more.

"We could just as easily repurpose one of our existing cameras," he said. "We have the one already mounted above the doorway leading into the collections space. If it works for you, we could ask John to adjust it so it zooms in on Mr. Grin instead."

Evelyn liked the idea of using an existing camera and indicated so with a nod and a smile. She'd hoped to reserve the remaining budget for new Christmas decorations at the end of the year.

"I like it," she said. "But no need to bug John with it. I can do it. I've adjusted the camera in question before when John was away. I'll take care of it before I leave this evening."

More relief from Bob. His shoulders dropped an inch or two. "Fantastic. I'll let Constance know first thing. I'm sure she'll be relieved. I won't say anything to our cleaners. They haven't mentioned Mr. Grin yet, and I'd rather not be the one to bring it up."

"Good idea," Evelyn said. The fewer people who found reason to fear Mr. Grin, the better.

THE COLLECTIONS AREA was separate from Boomtown KR, located through a door at the end of the street. Above the door, a single camera was positioned to catch the movements of everyone in or out of this area.

The camera was one of five set up in and immediately around the museum, all of which fed into a small security office with a series of monitors, one for each camera. Evelyn entered the security suite and scanned the monitors until she found the camera in question.

Bob edged into the suite behind her and pointed at the monitor. "This one. If you zoom in, you'll be able to see the dummy in better detail."

Evelyn resisted telling Bob she already knew this. He'd come along to try to help, politely refusing her suggestion that he head home for the night.

As she used the remote switch to focus fully on Mr. Grin, she found reason to be grateful for Bob's offer.

The door to the dummy's glass cabinet was wide open.

"What the hell?" she muttered.

Bob leaned closer to the monitor and squinted. His index finger tapped at the screen. "Is that the door to the cabinet?"

"Yeah. It's been opened."

"I walked through there only a few minutes before coming and talking to you. It was closed. I'm sure of it."

Evelyn didn't mention Bob's poor eyesight. He'd likely missed seeing the open cabinet while walking past. A staff member easily could have left it that way—the cleaners knocking something while wiping the glass or even John performing another one of his pranks.

Sure, it was creepy, but it wasn't paranormal.

Not possible.

"If we rewind the recording connected with this camera, I'm sure we'll discover there's a perfectly logical explanation," she said.

Bob reached for the computer keyboard, but Evelyn waved him off.

"Not now," she said. "It's late. We can deal with it tomorrow. I'll go close the cabinet, and then we can head home."

"I'll go with you," Bob said.

Evelyn considered arguing but decided against it. She couldn't explain why, but the idea of having Bob accompany her to Mr. Grin's cabinet was something of a relief.

Bob played with the camera controls, zooming in a little on the cabinet in question. Evelyn stared at the monitor, studying the dummy seated within.

In Evelyn's mind. Mr. Grin bore a passing resemblance to Howdy Doody, although this particular puppet had been created quite some time earlier. Despite its age, Mr. Grin was well-designed, possessing a body that could be shaped via its wire skeleton and a face that moved through hand motions made by the puppeteer. Its head swivelled; its eyes and mouth opened and shut. According to period photographs, Mr. Grin had once possessed a mop of dark hair, but that part of him had been lost to time and a lack of care.

Most notable about the puppet was its smile—a lengthy, toothy grin extending well beyond natural proportions. While in Evelyn's experience, it was normal for ventriloquist dummies to have unnaturally large mouths, this one went beyond even that. It didn't close all the way, keeping its row of teeth on full display. Rather than boasting a friendly or a happy grin, this dummy bore a grimace—one that, as Bob had suggested, belonged on the face of a dead body rather than a toy used for entertaining children.

Evelyn had to admit, nothing much about Mr. Grin seemed particularly entertaining, even less that would be appealing to kids—today's kids, at any rate.

Evelyn and Bob made their way from the administration area upstairs down to the museum space. They walked side by side through Boomtown KR until they reached the doorway leading to the collections area. There, Evelyn led the way across the room to the display area in which a variety of old-time children's toys were arranged, each with a numbered plaque to guide visitors to short write-ups posted on the wall.

She sought out Mr. Grin's location as she walked.

Bob seized at her arm, fingers gripping her flesh. "Evelyn."

She drew up short, stalled midway across the collections floor. Her eyes fixed on Mr. Grin's display case.

Empty.

It took Evelyn a long moment to formulate a coherent thought, another few seconds before she found the words to voice it. Even then, she was unable to come up with much. "It's gone."

Bob nodded dumbly.

"Where?" she asked.

Bob shook his head, his gaze flitting around the room.

In searching for the missing dummy, she put a temporary pause to her disbelief. Plenty of time to consider it later—that somehow, in an otherwise unpopulated museum, an inanimate object had somehow not only opened its cabinet but had vanished from sight.

"It has to be John," she muttered as they searched. "Has to be."

"John went home two hours ago." Bob spoke in a monotone as if he, too, were struggling to move beyond a state of shock.

"Someone else then. There must be someone here besides us." She stopped, eyes flashing wide as she snatched at Bob's sleeve. "What if whoever did this is still here? Bob, we might have an intruder. We should call nine-one-one. No, we should check the recording first. Come on, let's—"

"Evelyn." Bob's single word came out tight. His eyes were locked on something in the distance, nowhere near the toys display. He followed up by pointing with his left index finger. His hand trembled slightly.

Evelyn tracked Bob's fixed stare, finding he'd settled onto one of the Model Ts from the same estate as the dummy. There, behind the wheel, sat Mr. Grin. His eyes, lids at half-mast, seemingly settled on a non-existent road.

"What the hell?" Evelyn muttered. No one else was here, she was sure of it. No one to move the dummy in the short space of time it had taken to walk from the security suite to this spot.

"What am I going to tell the staff?" Bob asked. Evelyn wasn't sure if he meant the question more for her or for himself.

She wanted to check his expression to see how he was doing, but she couldn't drag her eyes from Mr. Grin.

The Mr. Grin which needed a concealed string around its neck to keep it upright in its cabinet. The Mr. Grin which was somehow managing to sit up unassisted in a slick leather car seat.

Evelyn gave it a minute, taking the time to squelch the anxiety she had abruptly come to share with her colleagues for this creepy-looking doll. Bob, too, stood glued to the floor, a stone statue at her side, once in a while managing a breath.

"I suppose I should go and get it." The words came from Evelyn's throat almost of their own accord, slow and thick. She didn't want to go over there, definitely didn't want to put hands on that thing. But it needed doing, and she couldn't in good conscience ask Bob to do it. Not when he was giving off all the vibes of an impending panic attack.

Summoning her courage, she reminded herself there was no such thing as the paranormal, no way for a dummy to control its own movements and magically relocate from within a locked cabinet to the driver's seat of a classic automobile. There had to be a human hand in this somewhere. A very-much-alive human hand. Just because they hadn't seen anyone didn't mean they weren't here somewhere.

She'd put the dummy back in its case, lock it back up. Then she and Bob would return to the security suite and review the recording. The camera should have captured the moment the dummy was taken. They would see the back of someone—maybe even a profile or a full face if they were lucky enough. If it wasn't someone they knew, if it ended up they had an intruder, she and Bob would lock themselves into the suite, summon police and wait there until they arrived.

Plan sorted, she felt a bit better. Evelyn was an organizer. She found her strength there, and it didn't fail her now. One deep breath, eased out slowly. Then she left her spot, headed for the Model T and the dummy inside.

All good. She could do this. She *would* do this.

She believed it.

Right up until the point Mr. Grin turned his head to face her.

2

It was an unusually warm April evening, warm enough Dez Braddock didn't bother slipping into a jacket before stepping out onto his back deck to check the progress being made by his new barbecue.

His family had chipped in together to buy it for him for Christmas, and he'd been itching to break it in ever since. His wife, Eva, had managed to rein him in twice already, convincing him it was ridiculous to stand outside in frigid weather while monitoring a grill. Today was different, with the snow all but gone and the day's temperature having reached nearly twenty degrees Celsius—pretty incredible for Kimotan Rapids in April.

No one argued when he dug out the burgers from the deep freeze and suggested calling his brother, Sully, and their mom over for a meal. Naturally, Sully would bring his girlfriend, Sarah, so Dez made sure to throw on a chicken breast as well. She didn't eat a lot of red meat.

The days were growing longer, the sun's remaining light ensuring Dez didn't need to flip on the deck lights as he lifted the grill lid to check the burgers. They were sizzling nicely, the sound and the scent making his stomach rumble with anticipation. He scraped each from the grill and carefully flipped them, leaving the chicken to cook on this side a little longer. Done, he closed the lid and returned the metal flipper to its plate.

It was too early in the year to take the deck furniture out of storage, so Dez had carried a canvas camping chair from the garage instead. While the temperature dropped as the evening progressed, he barely noticed. Being both six-foot-six and encased in a solid wall of muscle, he didn't get cold as quickly as most people around him —most notably Eva and their nine-year-old daughter, Kayleigh.

Eva had turned up the thermostat inside. This meant Dez would happily sit out here as long as possible with his new grill and enjoy the atmosphere of his backyard and the surrounding Kimotan Rapids neighbourhood.

The patio door separating deck from kitchen slid open. Dez lifted his gaze from the yard to see his brother had arrived. At six feet, Sullivan "Sully" Gray was built lean, his own muscle more compact than Dez's. He appeared far different from Dez in other ways too, possessing dirty blond hair to Dez's coppery red, grey eyes to Dez's green, fine-boned features to Dez's more-square angles and a full beard to Dez's carefully maintained stubble. The differences made sense given they weren't blood; Sully had joined Dez's family as a foster kid at age seven.

Their differing genetic makeup meant nothing to Dez, hadn't since shortly after he'd first met Sully. Dez grinned a greeting, receiving one in return as Sully slid the door shut behind himself. They were close, always had been. Lucky thing since they now worked together as well.

"Hey, Sull," Dez said. "Sarah with you?"

"Yeah. She's inside with Eva, giving her a hand with some veggies. We brought dessert."

Dez leaned forward hopefully. "Cheesecake?"

Sully nodded. "Cherry."

Dez's gave a contented sigh. "I love you."

"Sarah bought it, actually. She knows it's your favourite."

Dez sat up a little straighter and twisted to peer through the kitchen window, the one over the sink. He caught Sarah's eye through the glass, shared a smile with her and gave her a wave of greeting. Then he focused his attention on Sully, his lips quirked. "In that case, I love her more."

Chuckling, Sully checked out the grill. "How's it working for you?"

"Awesome," Dez said. "If I wasn't already happily married, I'd propose to this thing."

Sully laughed, managing to look pleased with himself at the same time. Dez was pretty sure he'd been the one to pick it out, probably with plenty of help from a knowledgeable salesclerk. Sully possessed as much expertise with gadgets and tools as Dez did with Sully's particular, and highly unusual, brand of knowledge—and that wasn't much.

Sully could communicate with the dead, a fact which left Dez with a certain unease. While Dez liked learning things—part of the reason he enjoyed investigation—some types of knowledge he wished he could give back. How Sully coped with carrying the load he did, Dez couldn't fathom.

Thankfully, with no current cases of a paranormal persuasion, they didn't have to worry about that for the moment. Dez changed his mindset to something more pleasant. "How are things going with Sarah these days?"

Sully took a few steps to the railing, passing a hand over the surface and checking the results before leaning against it to face Dez. "Going well."

Dez leaned forward, settling elbows on knees and knitting his fingers. "How well?"

Sully's lips quirked. "Really well."

"So?" Dez dragged the word out, letting his expectation bleed through. He wanted more, and Sully damn well knew it.

"So?" came Sully's response.

Of course, Sully was king when it came to playing elusive.

"Do I have to beat it out of you?" Dez growled.

Sully held up his hands in a show of surrender. "Okay, okay. I know what you're asking. And no, I haven't asked her yet."

"What are you waiting for? I mean, it's not like you're asking her to marry you." Dez leaned further forward, so far the back legs of his chair lifted an inch or two off the ground. "Hold on. You're not asking her to marry you, are you?"

"Not yet." Sully paused there, heaving a sigh. "I don't know, man."

The sizzling noise from the barbecue reminded Dez he should check the burgers. He gave Sully a moment to gather his thoughts while he lifted the lid and inspected the cooking food. The beef would be okay on the grill for another minute or two, so he left the burgers alone while he flipped Sarah's chicken breast.

Finishing the task without a response from Sully, Dez gave in to impatience. "What don't you know?"

Sully folded his arms across his body, hugging himself. "It's a lot to ask."

Dez joined him at the railing, ensuring its strength with a hand before leaning there himself. "How d'you figure that? You love her, right?"

Sully nodded.

"And she loves you?"

Another nod.

"And everything's going well in the physical sense?"

Sully's smile was unmissable. "No complaints."

"So then, what? What could possibly give you reason not to ask her to move in with you? And please don't tell me it's because you don't want her living in your dump of an apartment. You promised me you were moving out of there soon. And Bulldog said he'd be happy to help out whenever Emily needs something."

Emily Crichton, Sully's neighbour, was well into her eighties. While as sharp as a thirty-year-old, her physical health wasn't in peak form these days. Twice within the past couple of months, she'd fallen in her suite. Thankfully, Sully had been nearby both times. Extra-thankfully, Billy "Bulldog" Bird—a helpful and compassionate guy who had known Emily for a few years—was happy to fill Sully's current role, ensuring the childless Emily had someone nearby to help her out when need be. It didn't hurt that Bulldog loved her homemade coffee cake.

But while they had a solution to ensure Emily was taken care of and had someone trustworthy to rely on nearby, Sully still wasn't where he needed to be.

"Sully," Dez prodded, giving him an elbow nudge as added incentive to provide an answer.

"The type of work I do, I don't know how much I want to expose Sarah to."

And there it was, the real reason Sully was dancing around taking things to the next level with Sarah, the woman Dez was certain was destined to be Sully's forever relationship. Dez had had a feeling that somewhere at the heart of Sully's reluctance, his unusual gift must lurk.

"Explain that to me," he said.

"Your burgers are going to burn."

Rolling his eyes, Dez but stepped away long enough to lift the lid once again and shovel the burgers onto a piece of foil to the side of the grill, away from the direct heat. He left them there for now instead of plating them. They'd be okay for the time being while the chicken breast finished cooking. That done, he faced Sully.

"Burgers are fine," he said. "Talk."

Sully cast Dez an uneasy side eye before turning his gaze toward the kitchen window. Through it, Sarah and Eva were carrying on a conversation, sharing in a laugh as they worked side by side at the counter. Sarah had fit in easily and immediately with their family, and Dez wanted more than anything for Sully to secure every chance at happiness he could with her. Not only because she'd become one of them, but because she'd proven to be someone who had Sully's back. And if she had Sully's back, it meant Dez could take a step back from his nearly lifelong job of doing it himself.

Unfortunately, Sully had a bad habit of brooding. While a super-smart guy, he occasionally made stupid, off-the-cuff decisions which put his life at risk while overthinking the good things which came his way.

Sully didn't change posture, instead lowering his head so his chin disappeared into the zipped neck of his jacket. "The things I do, the things I see, they're with me all the time."

"Yeah, so? She knows that."

"Her knowing about my world is one thing. It's something else for me to make this her world too."

Dez raised a brow. "Have you bothered to ask her what she thinks?"

Sully frowned. An answer without need of words.

"That would be a no," Dez concluded. "You think she'd appreciate you making decisions on her behalf?"

Sully at last met his eye. "If you had a choice, you know damn well you'd give back all the paranormal knowledge I've basically forced onto you."

"Only way I could give it back would be through not knowing you, which isn't a sacrifice I'd ever make."

Smiling, Sully gave Dez a nudge. "Thanks, bro. But you know what I mean."

"What I know is you're about to sabotage yourself out of the best thing you've ever had with a woman. What's more, she deserves more credit than you're giving her. Comparing my response to ghosts with hers isn't fair when she deals with it a hell of a lot better than I do. As far as everything else, you ended your last serious relationship at a time when your life was legitimately and permanently in danger. Other than what we occasionally run into on the job, that danger's gone. Anyway, Sarah doesn't need you to protect her any more than Eva needs it from me. Sarah's a strong lady, Sull. Don't be a doorknob about this."

Dez had more to say—he usually did—but he was kept from sharing it when his phone rang in his pocket. The ringtone was the one he'd programmed for his and Sully's boss, Lachlan Fields.

Damn it. Lachlan didn't tend to make social calls.

"What's going on?" Dez asked upon answering.

"What are you doing right now?"

"Finishing grilling some food for supper. Why?" The one-word question dragged out, no way Lachlan would miss Dez's lack of enthusiasm.

"Job came up."

Double damn it. Dez dropped his head and gave it a shake. "Can it wait until tomorrow?"

"Ours isn't a nine-to-five, Monday-to-Friday gig, Braddock. You knew that signing on. No different from your previous job in policing."

Dez knew it, all right. But there had been a difference. He'd worked patrol, his shifts set out in advance and the only variations due to overtime he put in when needed. With Lachlan, it was like being on call twenty-four-seven. Ordinarily, Dez didn't mind, except it seemed as if Lachlan managed to call whenever he was busy with family rather than sitting around doing nothing.

Dez usually didn't whine about it, hating the way he sounded if he did. But he couldn't help it this time.

"I know we're not in a typically scheduled profession," he replied. "Doesn't change the fact I'm in the middle of something."

Sully, who knew Lachlan's ways equally as well, took the flipper from Dez and went to check the meat. Dez left him to it while he did what he knew he'd have to—focus on Lachlan.

"Sorry, princess," Lachlan said, the tone coming off amused rather than gruff. Dez was pretty sure the man got off on annoying his associates. "I'm going to need you to extricate yourself. Your brother too. He there? He's not picking up his phone."

Dez put his hand over the mouthpiece at the base of his phone and smirked at Sully. "Hey, buddy? He wants you too."

At the grill, Sully froze, then turned to Dez with eyebrows lowered to match his frown.

Dez moved his hand and put the phone onto speaker for both their benefits. "Yeah, Lachlan," Dez said. "He's here."

"Good. This might end up being his type of job. Had a call right before I dialled you. Curator over at the KR Historical Museum. Guy by the name of Bob Lindberg."

"And?" Dez said once Lachlan had gone a few seconds without adding to the explanation.

"Hold your horses, Braddock. I'm checking my notes." Papers rustled in the background. There had been a time when Lachlan's memory was what one might call photographic. Since suffering a severe head injury a few years back, his ability to recall details short-term wasn't what it had been. Ask the man about a case from twenty years ago, though, and Dez knew he'd better make sure he was sitting comfortably; it was bound to be a long and detailed story.

The paper sounds on the other end of the line ceased and

Lachlan's voice returned. "Okay, here it is. Couple of months ago, a local collector named James Holmes passed away. His estate's still being settled, I'm told, but one thing already sorted out pertains to a number of historic items he bequeathed to the museum. Couple of Model Ts in the mix as well as a few pieces of furniture and clothing. The item causing concern is an old ventriloquist's dummy. Bob sent me a photo, and let me tell you, creepy doesn't begin to describe it. Give me a sec and I'll send you a photo."

Dez waited more than a sec. Lachlan was a brilliant investigator, but he was exceedingly slow when it came to learning new technology. He'd bought a brand-new, state-of-the-art smartphone recently, and he still barely knew how to work even the most basic features. Dez had located an online manual for him and could now only hope Lachlan would be open enough to giving it a read.

Another long moment passed before Dez's phone's screen showed an incoming text from Lachlan. Dez opened the app, located the message and tapped it—and immediately wished he hadn't.

Looking back at him was the scariest damn doll he'd ever seen.

"This … thing … is what you're calling about?" Dez said.

"So you got the text?"

"Yeah, I got it. It looks like a corpse. What the heck is it?"

"Told you. A ventriloquist's dummy. I don't know much about it. The way I figure it, that'll be your job."

As he left the grill to check the photo himself, Sully met Dez's gaze. His brows shot up as he eyed the screen. By the time he refocused on Dez, he appeared as thoroughly spooked as Dez felt.

"You're saying this is my kind of job?" Sully asked. "Why?"

"I was about to get to that, if the two of you will let me

continue." Lachlan carried on without awaiting further response. "Seems this thing has been working full-time at creeping out staff at the museum. Several concerns have been raised about things happening around there, most notably the dummy moving of its own accord. Not only has it managed to open its own cabinet, but it somehow managed to relocate itself yesterday once the museum had closed."

"Sounds like a practical joke to me," Dez said. "Something as spooky-looking as this would be a perfect object for someone looking to mess with their co-workers."

"Which is exactly what Bob tells me the museum's director believes. Problem is, he's insistent no one else was there last night. Only he and the director, Evelyn Harlow, were present. The place had been locked up by then as well."

"I've been there before," Sully said. "The place is huge and crammed full of stuff. There's a chance someone—even a member of the public—found somewhere to hide after closing."

Dez tilted his head at the direction Sully's thoughts seemed to be travelling. "And then came out to move a dummy around? Why?"

Sully shrugged. "Just thinking out loud."

"And you're pretty much on the same track as Ms. Harlow. Problem is, police were called in last night along with the museum's security team. They searched the place top to bottom and came up empty. If someone was there who shouldn't have been, Bob insists they would have been located."

"What about surveillance cameras?" Dez asked. "Depending on location and positioning, those might have picked something up, right?"

"Sure, but there's the other issue. Camera in question—the one trained on the dummy—malfunctioned at the moment in question. Whether someone moved it or whether the dummy ran across the room on its own, it should have showed up on camera. Unfortunately, the feed simply cut out."

"What are they wanting from us exactly?" Sully asked.

"Couple of things," Lachlan said. "From Evelyn's perspective, Bob tells me, she'd like you to find out who's responsible for what's going on at the museum and put a stop to it. If it's a member of the public, they need to be caught for security reasons, obviously. And if it's a staff member, Evelyn intends to see to it they're disciplined. If Bob's right, though ..."

Lachlan trailed off, giving Sully a statement to finish.

"You need me to deal with it," he said.

"Bingo," Lachlan replied.

3

Sully stared out the passenger-side window of Dez's SUV as the city moved past. His stomach had been making noise since they'd left Dez and Eva's, protesting the rapid pace at which he'd been forced to scarf down his meal.

He turned from the window to eye his brother. Unsurprisingly, Dez seemed less bothered by having eaten too fast, his years in policing having made him something of an expert at feeding himself on the run. His expression suggested he was having more trouble digesting their upcoming job than he was his burgers.

"What's up?" Sully asked.

"Good question." Dez took a moment to meet Sully's eye before giving his attention to the road. "I really hate dolls."

Sully smirked. "Well aware."

"No, like *really* hate them. Remember that thing Mom's friend gave her for Christmas when we were teenagers? The toddler-sized thing with no face?"

Sully remembered, all right. Well enough to draw a laugh from him. "God, it freaked you out."

"Hey, it would freak you out too if you woke up to find it

standing next to the closet doors watching you sleep." Dez shuddered.

Sully struggled to hold the snicker in check but failed. Dez's eyes bored into the side of his head.

"Hold on," Dez said. "*You* did that?"

"You slept pretty heavy back then."

"You told me one of your ghosts did it."

Sully shrugged as he smiled. "Hey, you were a lot bigger than me. Way you freaked over it, I figured I'd get beat up if I told you the truth."

Dez backhanded Sully hard in the gut, turning Sully's laughter into a gagging cough. "I'm going to stop this vehicle eventually, you moron. And for the record, I'm still a lot bigger than you, and I'm happy to mete out an IOU on that beating."

Sully rubbed his sore gut as he chuckled. Dez might be big, but Sully was fast. If he could make it to the front doors of the museum, he'd be safe. Dez wouldn't beat on him in front of clients.

Probably.

To be safe, Sully decided a slight change of subject was in order. Better to discuss the clients' doll situation than their own historical one. "Any thoughts going into this case?"

"Other than wanting to refer these people to one of the other reputable PI agencies in town?"

"I was thinking more along the lines of how best to handle it," Sully said. "Sounds like the clients are at odds over the cause of their problem."

Dez shrugged, eyes remaining on the road. "No different from any other investigation. We interview the witnesses, get their take on the situation, search for additional evidence and decide for ourselves once we've compiled enough information."

"Interview them together or separately?"

Dez answered without missing a beat. "Separately. Always

best to do it that way when possible. Lets people share info the way they want without worrying about what the person next to them thinks or having to contend with someone jumping in to offer up their own version of events. With two competing points of view here, it's even more important."

"Might not be competing points of view on events themselves so much as on the cause of them. People whose beliefs don't include the paranormal sometimes bend over backward trying to explain away the unexplainable." A statement based on years of observation on Sully's part. While he had near-daily proof of the existence of a world beyond the five senses, most people didn't. That said, most people experienced unexplainable events throughout their lifetimes. Sully found it amusing how those who claimed to be scientifically minded and highly rational promptly discounted anything they couldn't immediately explain, including by readily suggesting they must have been suffering a hallucination when they saw a ghost. In Sully's view, the line many people had drawn between science and ghosts was far too wide. All modern science had once started off as something unproven and even radical. Why should ghosts—which, after all, were simply a manifestation of human energy—be any different?

He'd had the discussion a few times in his life with non-believers. Rarely did it go down well.

"Given both the director and the curator are meeting us, we could save time by each interviewing one," Dez said. "But I'm more inclined to have both of us present at each interview, at least at this stage. Better you and I both come away with a full view of the case."

"Works for me," Sully said.

The Kimotan Rapids Historical Museum was located over two floors inside a massive converted warehouse on the city's east side. Sully hadn't been there since grade school, back when his class had a tour there. He'd enjoyed it, might have ordinarily wanted to go back to see it again. Except he'd spent the entire visit with the creeping sensation of being watched. Without a doubt, the place was haunted. While his ability to see ghosts was limited to those who'd died by homicide, he nonetheless possessed a heightened ability to sense all manner of spirits. Not being able to see them could be as unnerving as having them pop into view.

Now he was older. The anxiety he'd felt as a kid had faded as life had granted him more experience in dealing with the spirit world. Whatever walked the museum, he could handle it.

Of course, he'd never dealt with a possessed doll before.

"Should we ask to see the dummy before we talk to them or after?" Dez asked.

This time, it was Sully with the response at the ready. "After. Definitely. Depending what's going on with this dummy, I might come out of this really drained. I'd like to hold off until we've had a chance to get all the background we need."

Dez gave a too-rapid nod. Sully smiled. Anything to delay the inevitable.

SULLY DIDN'T KNOW whether he could put it down to his distraction technique, but by the time they pulled into a parking spot outside the museum, Dez seemed to have forgotten about the closet-door doll incident. Sully imagined his big brother had found enough to occupy his thoughts right here and now without jumping back into the past.

As Sully and Dez made their way from the SUV to the museum's front entrance, Sully spotted the figure of a man backlit inside the entry hall. Impossible as it was at first to pick out any features, Sully wondered whether he was already looking at a ghost—until he felt Dez's arm stiffen next to his. Despite his abiding fear of them, Dez wasn't usually able to see spirits.

"Not a ghost," Sully said. "Don't worry."

"Not yet, anyway," Dez replied.

As Sully and Dez reached the glass front doors, the man inside pushed one open for them.

Dez took this as his cue to quicken his pace to the entrance. "Evening. I'm Dez Braddock."

"Bob Lindberg," the man said as Dez and then Sully brushed past him, leaving the cold behind as they stepped indoors. Once all three were standing inside, door closed to seal in the warmth, Bob extended a hand to shake.

"Sullivan Gray," Sully said once Bob turned to him. "Most people call me Sully."

"It's a tremendous pleasure to meet you," Bob said. "When our situation came up here, I remembered having seen you on television. I hoped you might be available to help with our problem. Thank you so much for coming." He switched his gaze to Dez. "Both of you."

Giving a wave as indication to follow him, he led the way down the hall toward the inner portions of the museum. "Evelyn's in her office and will meet with us there, if that's all right with you."

"We'll want to speak with each of you separately," Dez said. "Just the way we do things—especially since we're told you have differing views on what's going on."

Bob gave an amused-sounding huff of breath. "Yes, I thought it best I mention that when I spoke with Mr. Fields. Didn't want him to think Evelyn shares my beliefs."

"She's a skeptic," Sully said.

Bob spared him a glance, accompanied by a nod. "Dyed-in-the-wool, as they say. She's a wonderful person, but she has no patience for what she sees as silliness." He stalled, halting his steps and spinning back toward Sully. "No offence meant, of course. I most certainly don't believe what our staff and I have personally witnessed counts as silly."

It struck Sully this might be the ideal moment to gain Bob's observations without Evelyn's presence. "You mentioned to Lachlan you've been having issues with this dummy you recently added to your collection?"

Bob nodded. "He's called Mr. Grin, so named by the ventriloquist who worked with him during the First World War. Warren Malcolm and Mr. Grin were a well-known act throughout the country, touring town halls and concert venues to great success. Once the war started, they took their act farther, performing for soldiers both at home and overseas. Mr. Grin's seen more of the world than I have. Then tragedy struck, I'm afraid."

Dez crossed his arms as he eyed Bob. "What happened?"

"In July 1917, someone broke into Mr. Malcolm's residence. During the resulting scuffle with the intruder, Mr. Malcolm was severely wounded and Mr. Grin stolen. Mr. Malcolm died of his injuries within a couple of days. The incident was in all the major papers of the day, both here and abroad. Despite a massive manhunt and a significant reward offered, no one ever found the culprit, nor did they learn who it was."

Bob gave a sad smile. "One wonders if the break-in had happened during modern times whether it might have been possible to solve it. There are unquestionably better resources these days than they had access to back then—DNA, for one."

"Even now, forensics don't solve everything," Dez said. "But you're right. Tools available now might have made a difference. You mentioned Mr. Grin was stolen. Obviously, he's since been located. Nothing was cleared up when he was found?"

"It wasn't as straightforward as police no doubt hoped. Back in the mid-eighties, the city decided to renovate the old downtown train station. Not the current station, but the one in use far earlier."

"The one converted to a casino?" Sully asked.

"That's the one. Anyway, they were clearing some junk from the basement level—old boxes, unclaimed suitcases and trunks and the like. Well, imagine their surprise when inside an old steamer trunk, they found Mr. Grin. Remarkably, despite his age and the fact he hadn't been preserved or cared for in any way, he was in near-perfect condition. The workers who discovered him told local media they were fairly creeped out by their find." Bob chuckled. "I can't say I blame them. Imagine opening a trunk to find *that* face grinning up at you." He glanced from Sully to Dez. "I'm assuming Mr. Fields showed you the image I sent?"

"Sure did," Dez said. "Can't say I disagree with your opinion on its appearance. So even though they found this trunk, it didn't clear anything up? I mean, there wasn't any identification with it or anything? Nothing inside to indicate who it belonged to?"

Bob shook his head. "Unfortunately, no. The trunk wasn't marked at all, and nothing was inside other than Mr. Grin, wrapped inside a wool blanket."

He paused at the ding of a cellphone. Bob patted down his clothing, then pulled a cellphone from the front pocket of his jacket. He gave the screen a once-over and thumb-typed something before returning the phone to the same pocket.

"Evelyn," he told Sully and Dez. "Wondering if you're here yet. Come on." He made a motion with his head for them to follow. As they walked, he continued with the earlier conversation. "I mentioned the trunk already, right?"

Sully and Dez replied in the affirmative.

Bob smiled his understanding and took it from there. "Well, as the trunk was believed to be part of an open cold case involving a homicide, police took charge of both it and Mr. Grin.

I believe the trunk is still in police custody, though I can't say for sure. The dummy, too, remained there for a couple of decades, until the advancement of technology meant police could try DNA testing."

Bob pushed through a door leading from the main lobby area of the museum, the sign above the doorway reading "Administration."

"As I understand it," he continued, "samples were taken from the trunk, the dummy and the blanket. Unfortunately, the only identifying evidence found came from those who located the dummy in the train station basement. Nothing else usable was found."

Dez paused in the hallway, forcing the others to a halt as well. "Given the dummy's part of an open homicide investigation, police would normally hold onto it. But they released it. Why?"

Bob leaned up against the wall. "Since so much time had passed, the Kimotan Rapids Historical Society expressed a concern for the preservation of Mr. Grin. While it had survived quite well in the trunk for some reason, it deteriorated once in police custody. The wig, for instance, fell off at one point and was lost. The Bakelite portions were cracking in places. Some discussions were had between the society and the KRPD, and police finally decided to hand the dummy over to the society. Eventually, the KRHS auctioned off Mr. Grin to raise money for a conservation project they were involved in—with the caveat he be properly cared for and preserved. He ended up in the hands of a local collector named James Holmes—the collector who bequeathed Mr. Grin to us when he passed away a couple months ago."

"So you've had it a couple months?" Sully asked. "I thought you got it more recently."

"We've only had him for two weeks, give or take a day or

two. It took a while for Mr. Holmes's estate to be sorted out. Mr. Holmes, as I understand it, didn't have children, but his brother's kids caused a few problems for the executor, attempting to make claims on the estate. In the end, Mr. Holmes's wishes as far as the items for the museum were carried out, enabling preservation of those pieces. A few items left out of the will are still there in the house, I'm given to understand, and the property is still being dealt with. Most of the remaining items are of a more macabre sort."

Sully tilted his head as he regarded Bob. "Macabre how?"

Bob quirked up one side of his mouth. "Mr. Holmes had a penchant for collecting items connected to well-known crimes or hauntings."

Sully grimaced. While some people were attracted to those types of things and actively sought them, he couldn't imagine wanting to possess items of such a nature. Having recently dealt with a haunted car, the last thing he'd want would be to willingly put himself in contact with possessed items. Yet, it was likely that was precisely what he was about to do.

The sound of a door opening down the hall caught his attention. A moment later, a head popped from one of the doorways. An attractive middle-aged woman with blonde hair and impeccable makeup peered back at him. As their eyes met, her lips lifted into a warm smile.

"I wondered where you'd got to," she said, leaving the doorway and heading toward them, arm outstretched for a handshake. "I'm Evelyn Harlow, the museum's director."

Sully and Dez took turns meeting the handshake and introducing themselves.

"I understand your opinion on recent events differs from Mr. Lindberg's," Dez said.

"Please, call me Bob," he said.

Evelyn raised a brow at her colleague. "Bob, what have you

been telling them?" A twinkle in her eye and an amused undertone told Sully that while she might be skeptical, she wasn't obnoxious about it—at least not the way some people were. She might have already sorted Sully into the "flake" category, but she wouldn't be rude or offensive about it. At least he hoped not.

"We hadn't gotten around to a whole lot yet," Bob said. "I was mainly filling them in on the history."

She nodded at him, then regarded Dez and Sully. "It's a fascinating story, isn't it? Whatever you make of it, whether you believe in the supernatural or not, we were thrilled to be able to add Mr. Grin to our collection. I was keeping an eye on the cameras, so I know you haven't had a chance to see him yet. Perhaps this would be the opportune time."

Sully did his best to force a smile.

4

As Evelyn led the way through the museum's public area, she provided a running narrative of the place and its contents.

Sully enjoyed history in theory, but it became a different beast when he came face to face with ghostly evidence of it. While it was common for people to leave fingerprints or hair behind on items they'd once owned, what many didn't realize was how spiritual energy could be left behind as well. Sometimes, items cherished by deceased people still carried pieces of them, memories that replayed and could be read by those sensitive enough to pick up on them—residual hauntings, Sully had heard them called. And sometimes, the items came with the souls of deceased people themselves. That was when active hauntings occurred.

Picking up on spirit energy, Sully tuned Evelyn out as he trailed behind her through the Main Street area of the museum. While at least some of what he sensed was residual, Sully's awareness snapped onto hauntings of an active sort as soon as he walked onto the makeshift street.

He quickly locked onto the presence of two ghosts—one male, one female. Neither was visible to him, meaning neither had been the victim of a homicide. The female struck him as merely curious, playful even. The male was darker, less pleased with the constant comings and goings of the living. How the male spirit had ended up here, Sully wasn't sure, but he'd likely ridden in on one of countless objects on display in this portion of the museum. Might be the ghost was antisocial even before he'd been carted in here. Finding himself in a very busy museum was probably like hell on earth.

Sully turned at a nudge from Dez and caught a pointed, raised-eyebrow look—a clear indication to pay attention to whatever their new clients were saying.

"Some of our staff as well as many visitors have described two spirits in this part of the museum," Bob said as he passed a building fashioned into a horse stable, complete with a fake Clydesdale. "I'm not sure if you can pick up on anything yourself?"

Bob was hunting for something—affirmation if Sully was any judge. Sully gave him what he seemed to be after, describing what he'd sensed while adding he was unable to physically see either.

Bob frowned. "I had the feeling the male spirit wasn't happy having people around."

"Not your problem," Sully said. "If a spirit chooses to stay behind rather than cross over, they have to accept the world's going to go on without their participation in it. I believe in being respectful of earth-bound ghosts, but they need to be respectful too. It's a two-way street. He's decided to stay, so he'll need to deal with the outcome of his decision—both the positive and the negative. If he ever makes himself impossible to deal with, I can see to it he leaves."

Sully had said the last part for the benefit of the spirit. While he didn't like to force ghosts to cross over, he had managed it in cases where they were actively trying to harm the living or other spirits around them. Similar to living people who committed crimes against others, there came a point where a ghost forfeited their right to make their own decisions. Their right to decide their fate ended when it encroached on the rights of others to exist in safety and peace within the same world.

At least, that was how Sully had come to think about it.

"What you do, it must be fascinating," Bob said.

"It has its moments," Sully said. And it did, particularly when he got to watch as a spirit crossed over into the light. But each job started as this one was—as an unknown. No telling what he'd find once he peeled back the layers.

Though Evelyn seemed happy to speak about the museum, she hadn't commented on the ghost aspect of the requested investigation. Sully waited until she and Bob were facing away before shooting Dez a raised eyebrow and tweaking his head in Evelyn's direction. He left the thought unspoken, but Dez showed he'd read it anyway, signalling his understanding with a nod.

Sully smiled. While the best part of working with his brother was the unwavering support and unfailing backup, the second-best part was their ability to communicate without speech.

"Bob mentioned the ghosts," Dez said to Evelyn. "But you haven't said much about it."

She cast a glance toward Sully, giving an apologetic smile before answering. "Not everyone is as convinced about these things as some members of my staff. I suppose I've always been the sort to require more convincing. Hard to believe in what you can't see for yourself."

"I know it's hard to believe," Dez said. "I can't see the things Sully does. But that doesn't make them any less real."

She glanced over her shoulder at them. "I can't argue as to what others see. But I do like to eliminate other possible explanations before settling on the paranormal as a cause, is all." She eyed Bob before facing front once again, continuing to lead them through the building. "We do, after all, have at least one major prankster on staff."

"John wouldn't tamper with our security tapes," Bob replied.

Evelyn shrugged. "Or it could be intruders. I know police didn't find anyone, but there are plenty of places to conceal oneself in here. Who's to say?" She shuddered. "Whole thing makes me nervous, to say the least—the thought some stranger might be inside right now, hiding somewhere and waiting."

Might be she was right, but Sully suspected Bob's impression was likely the correct one. He'd know for sure soon enough.

At the end of the Main Street, to the left of a train station and concealed from the street by a chapel, stood a doorway marked "More Exhibits."

"We keep various collections in here," Evelyn explained.

She seemed to have fallen back into tour guide mode. Sully suspected it calmed her, focusing on the work she knew and loved and the normalcy of it.

"At Christmastime, we set up the old Parsons department store display in here. You know, the one they used to put up in the store each Christmas? Have you been to see it since we started putting it up?"

"My wife and I brought our daughter last year," Dez said. "It was pretty cool."

Sully recalled they'd asked if he wanted to go, but he said no. Nice as it would have been to check out, anything that had been around that long carried the possibility of coming complete with a ghost or two. Hard to enjoy a holiday display while being stalked by spirits.

As he passed through the doorway, Sully felt the two ghosts from the Main Street area fall away, suggesting they were rooted to that space. Just as well since he realized he'd have his hands full enough in here.

He felt it the moment he entered the exhibits area. The sensation grew as he followed Evelyn and Bob nearer a large display featuring classic toys.

It was the feeling of being watched. More than that, it was the feeling of cold, hard hatred.

A chill slithered down Sully's spine.

"Mr. Grin is right up here," Evelyn said as she walked, directing the statement over her shoulder for Sully and Dez's benefit.

Bob's lips pulled into a humourless smile. "Some people have taken to referring to him as Mr. *Grim*. The name seems to suit him better."

Sully was inclined to agree. The photo hadn't done the dummy justice. Mr. Grin was larger than Sully had anticipated, its head nearly the size of a human adult skull. Its lean body, although folded into a seated position, appeared to be at least three feet in height. A slim black tuxedo, although worn and faded with age, gave the appearance of even greater length.

But it was the face to which Sully's eyes were drawn after mere seconds of study. No charm or wittiness coloured the features, marked most notably by a wide inhuman grin. Also unsettling were the half-lidded eyes, the slightest hint of blue peeking from between them. At a glance, they reminded Sully of a dead body. But a longer study gave him a different impression. It felt as if the dummy was giving the false impression of deep slumber, enabling it to watch passersby without their ever becoming aware of it.

Seeing Mr. Grin up close drew goosebumps across his skin.

"No offence," Dez said. "But how in the world did anyone find him fun to watch? Creeps the hell out of me just standing here."

Bob stood with arms crossed, and he gave his biceps a rub before answering. "I'll admit to having the same thought. When you see film from the time, back when Warren Malcolm and Mr. Grin were performing for crowds, you begin to understand. In the right hands, a houseplant can be entertaining, and Mr. Malcolm was a very funny man. He had the crowds rolling. It's why they sought him out to perform for the troops. He was reportedly even being courted by Hollywood. Just think, Mr. Grin nearly became a movie star."

"Why didn't it happen?" Dez asked.

"The break-in," Evelyn said. "Malcolm died within days of it. But for that, there's no telling what heights he might have reached."

Sully had kept his eyes mainly fixed on Mr. Grin throughout the conversation, wondering if he'd see the kind of movement mentioned by their clients. Since entering the display area, he'd been on high alert, watching for signs of a ghost nearby. He didn't like forming opinions before entering a situation, worried it might blind him to other possibilities. Having heard about what had befallen Warren Malcolm, he couldn't help but wonder whether the murdered ventriloquist had remained attached to his puppet since his death.

But standing here now with no ghost in sight, Sully had begun to doubt his working theory. In truth, the culprit could be anyone: Warren; someone who'd possessed the dummy over the past century; even a Mr. Grin fan. Certainly many, many soldiers had been killed during the First World War. If one of them had taken a shine to the puppet, it was possible he'd found him after his death.

Anything was possible—and that was the problem. Determining they were dealing with a haunting was the easy part. The hard part would be figuring out who was responsible and getting them what they needed to cross over.

It would be easier if Sully could see the ghost.

So fixated was he on Mr. Grin, it took him a moment to clue

in that he was being watched by more than a ghost. He lifted his gaze and found Dez, Evelyn and Bob all focused on him expectantly.

"Anything?" Bob asked. He had yet to stop rubbing his arms.

Sully frowned. "I do feel something, but so far, I'm not seeing it."

"When you say 'something,' do you mean what I think you mean?"

Sully gave a small nod. "I'm picking up a spirit, yeah. Like I said, though, I don't see it."

Bob's forehead creased. "What does that mean, exactly?"

"Homicide victims are the only ones visible to me, though they can keep themselves hidden if they don't want to be seen." Sully considered how honest to be before deciding he owed their clients a full answer. While he didn't think they were in danger, if the ghost could move a dummy at will, it might also be able to move more threatening objects. He'd hate to withhold his observations only to learn later someone had been hurt because they hadn't had the chance to take proper precautions. "I've got to tell you, whoever this is, they're not happy. I'm definitely picking up on anger connected with this thing."

Bob stopped moving. "Anger? At *us*?"

"I don't know yet. Lots of times, ghosts aren't so much angry at the people around them as they are at their own situation. Sometimes they react when they're looking for justice or answers or have become trapped here. Sometimes they get frustrated at an inability to communicate. And sometimes they even get mad because I show up, and they think I'm going to make them do something they don't want to do. It all amounts to the same thing. Anger among ghosts is like anger among humans. It's natural and it happens for all kinds of reasons. And it doesn't always mean someone's going to lash out."

"But sometimes they do," Bob said. His gaze swung to Mr.

Grin. "Should we be doing something? Putting him back in storage maybe? I would be sick if someone got hurt."

"I wouldn't jump to the conclusion someone will get hurt," Sully said. He chewed at the inside of his lower lip as he considered his options. "If it's okay with you, I wouldn't mind spending part of the night here. I'd like to keep an eye on Mr. Grin, see if anything more happens. I'm hoping I can at least narrow down who I'm sensing and what they want."

Evelyn and Bob exchanged a look.

"We don't typically allow members of the public to stay here after hours, unsupervised," she said.

"We're not exactly members of the public in this instance," Dez said. "And if it's a security issue you're worried about, Sully and I have both need to maintain clean criminal records to keep our licences. And we're both bonded as well."

Bob held up a palm and waved it back and forth. "Of course, we trust you. That's not the issue. It's simply a security policy we have here. No one besides our own staff is allowed to stay unsupervised on the premises after hours."

Sully crossed his arms. "No offence, but that won't help any of us here. You want this solved, and I need to spend some time around here when there aren't a lot of staff or members of the public around. I'm sure you can appreciate what I do isn't easy while under a microscope."

"I can certainly understand what you're saying," Bob said. He trained a purposeful gaze on Evelyn, raising one brow.

"I'm sorry," she said. "I'm just not comfortable." She held Bob's eye, the plea obvious. "It's not only *our* policy, Bob. We have the board to answer to if something happens."

Sully considered asking what she thought was going to happen but decided against it. If they ended up in a discussion about it, he and Dez couldn't exactly go on the record promising nothing untoward or risky would occur. With their history, such a statement would be a full-on lie.

It didn't solve the problem, of course. Without time alone with Mr. Grin, solving the first, necessary part of this mystery would be next to impossible.

Perhaps Evelyn saw it too, because she frowned. "I suppose I could stay a little longer on site. I could stay in my office or in the security suite. The policy states a member of staff needs to be *at* the museum with after-hours visitors, not physically at their side. Would that work for you?"

"That would work," Sully said. "Sorry. I know it's not ideal, but it's what I need."

"Understood," she said. "But if I can make one request, I'm hoping you'll check the place out for more than paranormal explanations. If this is the work of a prankster or an intruder, I want to know."

"Of course," Dez said. "We'll cover all the bases."

"I can wait around too," Bob offered.

Evelyn shook her head. "Not necessary. You go home. I don't mind staying. It will give me a chance to start on that report for the board."

"All right," Bob said. "But if another night like this is required, I'll take it."

Evelyn nodded with a smile, then turned her attention back to Sully and Dez. "Do you need anything else from either of us at the moment?"

"Not yet," Sully said. "Right now, I just need time alone with Mr. Grin."

The speed with which Evelyn and Bob left the room containing the haunted dummy was telling, but he kept the observation to himself. Anyone who'd experienced what they had would be eager to be out of the puppet's presence.

Once they were alone, Dez cleared his throat. "You said you

wanted some time on your own with him. Should I find somewhere else to be too?"

While his eyes never left the eerie face of the dummy behind the glass, Sully managed to grasp a handful of Dez's coat. "Not on your life. Leave me alone with this thing, I'll kick your ass."

"Your foot wouldn't reach that far," Dez deadpanned. But he stayed, hovering nearby as Sully kept the bulk of his focus on Mr. Grin.

With Evelyn and Bob gone, Sully gave the room another visual sweep. Sometimes, ghosts shied away from people. Given recent activity involving the dummy, he didn't think that was the issue, but he couldn't afford to rule out anything yet.

"Do you see anything?" Dez asked.

Sully gave his head a shake. "Nothing. I still sense something though."

"Any idea where?"

Sully tilted his head to the side as he considered this. "It feels close. Really close. Right near the dummy."

Dez's arm brushed up against Sully's as he stepped closer. "Uh, it's not going to make it move right *now*, is it? I swear to God, man, if that thing stands up or blinks or something, I'm going to fall down dead right here."

Sully managed a chuckle. "I don't know. Unless I can figure out who's behind this, I can't get at the motive. And if I can't sort out the reason for this, I can't tell you when or how it might happen again."

Dez frowned. "Great. Just great, man." His gaze moved around the room before ending on Sully. "Well, if you're not getting anything useful from the dummy at the moment, maybe this is a good time for you and me to run a security sweep."

"It's not human-caused, Dez. This is definitely a ghost."

Dez's hand landed on Sully's shoulder. "Hey, I know that and you know that. But like it or not, Evelyn's not on the same page yet, and she wants us to have a look. Let's go and do what she asked for. Afterward, we can come back and spend a little more quality time with Mr. Grim, here."

Sully pinched his lips together as he considered this. "Why do I have the feeling this thing's going to start doing things the moment we're not around?"

Dez smirked. "If it's going to start doing things, I'd actually prefer it if we weren't around."

5

Dez blew out a breath as he slid his cellphone from his pocket and dialled Evelyn's number.

"Sully and I are going to run a security sweep," he told her once she'd picked up. "But we don't want to miss anything should Mr. Grin start moving around again. Would you mind watching your security feed until we return to the exhibit space where you keep him?"

Silence on the other end. Then, "Couldn't one of you stay with Mr. Grin and the other check out the museum for intruders?"

Dez sensed her suggestion wasn't so much based on annoyance as fear. While she wasn't quick to admit to the existence of ghosts, she wasn't particularly keen on witnessing more evidence of it either.

In this case, he couldn't do much to help her. "Sorry, ma'am. In cases where a client suspects an intruder, we run security checks together. For safety reasons."

"Oh, of course," she said. "That makes perfect sense. I hadn't thought."

"Well, it's not your job to think about those things," Dez said, tone kind. "That's what you've hired us for. If you could text me once you're in front of the monitors and can see Mr. Grin, I'd appreciate it. Sully and I will run our check, and you can head back to your office or wherever you're working once you see us return to the exhibit room."

Evelyn agreed. Approximately two minutes later, with no activity from Mr. Grin in the meantime, Dez's phone dinged with a text from Evelyn.

In security suite. Will wait here until you get back.

Dez signalled they'd gotten the go-ahead by giving Sully's shoulder a tap. Then the two of them zipped up their coats and headed out.

HAVING FIRST OBTAINED Evelyn's keys and a map of the building, Dez and Sully did a full check of the exterior, using their flashlights to scan the snow for boot prints that didn't seem to belong. They also searched for other evidence of an attempted break-in, such as scratch or pry marks on or near the doors' locking mechanisms.

While plenty of bootprints existed, Dez read them as being there legitimately, likely left behind by security officers and police doing the same thing Dez and Sully currently were.

Dez put in a call to Evelyn mid-way through the outside check, asking if anything inside held such obvious value as to attract a thief. While many items had considerable historical relevance, Evelyn said nothing much was worth a large sum of money.

Nothing, except perhaps Mr. Grin himself.

"Have you noticed or heard about anyone hanging around the dummy since you've had it on display?" Dez asked. "If someone were interested in getting their hands on it, they'd likely come in as a legitimate visitor and spend some time studying the security setup, both of the museum itself and the case around Mr. Grin."

Evelyn was silent a long moment. "I haven't seen anything myself. And no one's mentioned anyone suspicious either."

It was a long shot, anyway, and not an explanation Dez was truly entertaining. He'd been around Sully long enough to trust his take on things. And his take involved a ghostly, not a human, explanation.

Ending the call, Dez paused to push against one of two large delivery doors, ensuring it didn't shift off the rollers.

Sully's voice sounded over Dez's shoulder. "You and Evelyn talked about the possibility of attempted theft. Are you giving that serious thought?"

Dez gave a dry laugh. "Nope. Just covering bases. I've known plenty of thieves in my life. In this city, people typically steal because they're trying to feed an addiction or get out from under a massive debt. They take things they can easily pawn or sell. We're talking electronics, catalytic converters, copper, stuff like that. I've never heard of someone stealing a puppet—even if it is kind of a big deal as puppets go." He played the beam of his cellphone flashlight along the base of the roll-up door, checking for pry marks. Nothing. "Anyway, I'm well aware this isn't about theft."

Sully shined his light on the delivery man-door. When neither of them spotted signs of a would-be intruder, Sully gave the knob a rattle. Locked. "Okay, so what about the whole prankster theory?"

"Someone moving a ventriloquist's dummy around to scare co-workers and lying about it? I don't know. It's weak, man."

"I know. Like you pointed out, we already know what the deal is. But—"

Dez completed Sully's thought. "Covering bases. I know."

They checked the final door, finding it likewise sealed with no signs of tampering. Exterior deemed secure, they took the search indoors, Dez happy to get back into the warmth.

The outdoor search was easy compared to the museum, crammed as it was with places an unwelcome visitor might hide. Dez sent one more text to Evelyn, asking about motion detection devices. He received one back that the museum hadn't invested in them to this point.

"If someone wanted to sneak around in here, I guess they could get away with it," Dez told Sully.

"Cameras would pick them up though."

"Not if they managed to tamper with the cameras."

"Except that's not what happened." Sully's tone was beginning to sound the slightest bit sour. For a guy with patience like his, it was a bad sign.

"You okay?" Dez asked.

"Fine."

Dez nudged him with his elbow and spoke quietly. He hadn't asked Evelyn if the cameras were audio enabled. Only a few he'd encountered were, but he didn't want to take a chance and risk offending Evelyn with the conversation they were about to have.

Dez leaned nearer to Sully before continuing. "I get why you're annoyed, believe me. It feels like a waste of time to me too, running around an otherwise-empty museum, looking for non-existent intruders. Let's just get it done, all right? Once we do, we can focus on the real issue."

"It gets tiring sometimes, dealing with skeptics," Sully said. "It's not the fact they don't believe in ghosts so much. It's the fact they, by extension, don't believe *me*. It sucks basically being called a liar."

Dez gave Sully's shoulder a solid pat. "She didn't call you a liar. She might think you're slightly delusional ..." He trailed off with a joking smirk.

Sully elbowed him in the gut. "You're a jerk." He rolled his eyes.

They covered what they could of the large museum, checking each of the buildings on Main Street, searching the staff-only areas and storage spaces and checking the insides of every artifact large enough to hide a human being. None of them contained an errant visitor, nor did they reveal evidence one had ever used them as a hiding spot.

In its entirety, the search took well over an hour. At no point did they find anything to back up Evelyn's intruder theory.

"Guess that's that," Dez said. He put in another call to Evelyn.

"Anything?" she asked upon answering.

"Nothing. No signs of intruders or anyone else doing something they shouldn't. Guess it puts us back to our other theory."

"I don't know. What about staff? Might you be able to speak with some of them? If it was a prank, maybe they'd admit it to you, once they realize how seriously we're treating this."

Dez gritted his teeth, making a point not to look at Sully. He hadn't put Evelyn on speaker for exactly this reason, not wanting his brother more frustrated than he already was.

"Let's see how things shake out," Dez said. "We're here now, and we've got some time alone with the dummy. If this path doesn't lead us anywhere, we'll explore another avenue. Did you have a chance to watch the cameras?"

"Yes, and I didn't see anything unusual."

"All right. Sully and I are on our way back to the toy exhibit now. As soon as you see us there, you're okay to head back to your office if you want. Once we've done what we need to do on our end, I'll give you a call."

"Sounds good to me," Evelyn said. "Thank you."

Dez disconnected, then turned to find Sully studying him.

"Still doesn't believe it, huh?" Sully asked.

Dez shrugged. "She'll probably take some convincing, but we've dealt with skeptics before. Given time and more evidence, she'll come around."

Sully gave a shrug of his own. "Unless Mr. Grin's done all he's ever going to do."

Dez raised a brow. "You believe that?"

"No," Sully said. "But I live in hope."

6

Nothing about Mr. Grin had changed by the time Sully and Dez arrived back in front of the glass display cabinet. Neither the face nor the position was any different.

Even the general feeling of anger and hate remained unaltered. The dummy hadn't moved, but neither, it seemed, had the ghost haunting it.

"Anything?" Dez asked, his voice a hoarse whisper.

Sully guessed it wasn't just Evelyn Dez was worried about at this point. He shook his head. "Nothing besides what I felt earlier."

"So the ghost is still around, then?"

"Yeah. Same thing."

"Any idea where?"

Sully gave it a moment. He lowered his head, dropping his gaze from the dummy to focus inward. When using his psychic sight, it sometimes helped to temporarily limit his other senses.

In this case, he quickly discovered, it didn't help much. He lifted his gaze to Dez's face. "I can't pinpoint it. It's a general feeling. I'm not picking up anything specific."

Sully gave it a one more try, walking the area around the case in a search for cold spots or the tingling sensation of electricity ghosts sometimes gave off. Nothing.

"It's weird," he said upon returning to the front of the case and Dez. "The energy the ghost is giving off, I would think I'd be able to home in on it better. But I can't." He chewed at the inside of his lower lip as he considered it further. "Could be, I guess, it used up a lot of its energy moving Mr. Grin around. If so, maybe the ghost's power has kind of dissipated for the time being."

Dez frowned. "So when it regains its energy, something else could happen. That's what you're saying?"

Sully rubbed at the back of his neck. Unfocused as the ghost seemed to be, it had nonetheless succeeded in creating a heap of tension in Sully. "Yeah. Possibly, anyway. But short of setting up a twenty-four-hour watch on this thing, I don't know how we're going to catch it."

"So how do you want to play this?"

Sully sighed. "I don't know. I hate jobs like this, where I show up and there's nothing I can see. It complicates things. I'm not sure where to go from here."

Dez crossed his arms, eyes narrowing. "Okay," he said a moment later. "Let's break it down. If we're dealing with a ghost, let's start with the obvious: Warren Malcolm. There's got to be a police file somewhere, right? Let's see if we can get ahold of it. I'm sure Lachlan can help with that part. If Malcolm's killer was never caught, could be Malcolm's hanging around, looking for justice."

Sully exhaled, a little of the tension leaving alongside the breath. Sometimes Sully felt like he lost himself a little to the pressures of what he did. In those moments, it was a huge relief having Dez nearby to offer perspective. "Good plan. We need to consider something else though. Evelyn and Bob mentioned the man who most recently owned Mr. Grin died not long ago. They said he collected other dark stuff. There's a possibility the ghost

I'm sensing is either him or something connected with another of his objects."

"Can ghosts do that? Jump from one object to another?"

"I don't really know for sure. All I know is I've seen some weird stuff in my life. I'm not ruling anything out."

"So maybe we'll need to try to get our hands on a list of this guy's collected objects," Dez said. "Let's focus on the Malcolm homicide first, all right? Eliminate one theory at a time so we're not spread too thin."

It suited Sully fine. Right now, any concrete investigative path was a good thing since he wasn't getting anywhere with the ghost.

"Do you want to call Lachlan?" Sully asked Dez. "See if he can get us a line on that file?"

"Sure. I'm on it. What are you going to do?"

Sully stared at the dummy, at those dead-looking, half-closed eyes and the eerie grimace. "I need to spend a few minutes alone with Mr. Grin."

Dez tilted his head, studying Sully. "You sure?"

"No. But I should do it, anyway."

Dez's lips pressed together as his brow furrowed. "Okay. I won't go far though. Just through the door onto Main Street, all right? You need me, yell."

Sully forced a smile. "Believe me, if this thing springs into action, you can bet I'll take you up on the yelling thing."

SULLY HAD FACED skepticism as far back as he could remember, so Evelyn's response to him was nothing new. In fact, several foster families prior to the Braddocks had forced him to see child psychiatrists in an attempt to "fix" his so-called mental illness.

The Braddocks were the first people who'd truly believed in him.

Sully had come a long way since those early years, and most of their clients these days sought him out specifically because of his abilities. But others weren't—and would never be—convinced of the reality Sully faced each day. Something about Evelyn's skepticism, and the resulting insinuation he was either dishonest or delusional, rankled him.

Then again, his irritation might have to do with something more than a doubting client.

He felt it as he sat here, cross-legged on the floor in front of Mr. Grin. The anger he'd felt from the ghost as he walked in here hadn't dissipated despite the fact the spirit didn't seem to be wholly focused at the moment. The feeling was everywhere, all around him. Without his being fully aware of it, it had moved inside him, turning what might have been a slight sense of annoyance into the sort of irritability likely to cause him to snap at someone.

He stared one more long moment into those half-lidded eyes before closing his own and drawing in a long, deep breath. Holding it, he refocused his energy and reminded himself of who he was—and who he wasn't. He was patient, he was understanding and he was empathetic. This bundle of frustration and simmering anger the spirit had been instilling wasn't him. He could control it—*had to* control it. As he'd done before with other spirits, he'd do it again now, whether or not he could physically see the problematic ghost in front of him.

One more breath. Calm flooded him, pushing away negative emotion. He pictured it leaving his body and soul like sweat during a challenging workout. He ended by envisioning an aura around himself, focused on closing off any weak spots or gaps until he felt his own strength return in full.

His frustration faded. Evelyn wasn't trying to be difficult. She was anxious and trying to cope with it the only way she knew how. Sully understood, and he could handle it without being a jerk. And he could handle the ghost without letting it rule his mind or emotions.

Back in control, the negative spirit locked safely away from him, Sully opened his eyes.

Mr. Grin's eyelids had lifted.

Sully jumped, one hand coming down to press him up to his knees. His other hand shot to his chest as his eyes widened to near the same size as Mr. Grin's.

"What the hell?" he muttered as he stared, watching for further movement.

There was no question in his mind as he fixated on the flash of painted blue surrounding the dummy's pupils. Mr. Grin was watching him.

Then the mouth moved.

At first, the shift of the lips was so small, Sully thought he might have imagined it. But as he continued to eye the dummy, the mouth parted farther, teeth separating to reveal a black maw in between.

Sully's heart thudded against his ribs as he stared, waiting. He still didn't see anyone, no spirit standing over the dummy controlling it. Yet he knew without the need to see. Mr. Grin wasn't done. He was only getting started.

The lips parted until an inch or two showed between the teeth. Then, faster than they'd separated, they chomped back together. It repeated the action, the mouth opening and closing, opening and closing. Once, twice, three times.

As if Mr. Grin were talking.

Or was it Warren Malcolm attempting to speak through him, the way he'd once done?

"If you're trying to say something, I can't hear you," Sully said. "I can see spirits, but I can't hear them. If you're Warren

Malcolm, I need you to try to show yourself to me. Can you do that? While using the dummy might get other people's attention, it won't let *me* help you."

The mouth moved twice more. The widened eyes bored into Sully's. Then the mouth fell back into its former grimace and the lids drooped.

"Sully?"

For the second time in as many minutes, Sully's nerves leapt. He spun in place to find Dez standing a few feet away, cellphone in hand alongside his hip.

"Something happen?" Dez asked.

Sully glanced from him back to the dummy. The face remained in its former eerie resting state, no indication of further movement nor of additional activity about to happen.

"Yeah, something happened," Sully replied. He provided Dez with an explanation, by the end of which Dez's eyes had taken on the wide-eyed shape Mr. Grin's had a moment ago.

"You're serious?" Dez asked. "You're not screwing with me?"

"Nope. Definitely not screwing with you. Something's going on here. I just can't think what. Whatever's controlling this thing, I can't see it. And since I can't hear it either, that puts me in pretty much the same position as anyone else dealing with it."

Dez hugged at his arms, rubbing his palms over them as if to ward off a chill. "Okay. Oh man. Okay. So you're thinking it was trying to communicate with you?"

"I don't know. I think so. Or maybe it was trying to scare me off, same as it seems to be doing to others. Lots of the ghosts we've dealt with want things like justice or to help a loved one or something. Some just want to scare people or be left alone. Maybe whoever's haunting Mr. Grin is one of those. If it's Warren Malcolm, maybe he views this as the ultimate performance. Unless he blames his fame for what happened to him, in which case he might want people to stay away from him and his dummy altogether."

Dez tilted his head, regarding Mr. Grin. "If that's the case, can't help matters having this thing on display."

Sully shook his head. "No, it definitely wouldn't."

Dez's leaned the other direction, his lips pursing as he studied Mr. Grin. "Hey, Sull? You said you can't see the ghost controlling this thing, right? What if it's because you're not looking in the right place?"

Sully guessed where Dez was headed but allowed him to voice his conclusion anyway.

"What if the ghost is *inside* Mr. Grin?"

Despite the thought having occurred to Sully as well, it nonetheless sent a shudder through him to hear it said aloud. He turned, kneeling once more in front of Mr. Grin, battling mounting dread as he stared deep into the dummy's eyes. He searched for it there, a flash of something—anything to prove a spirit was indeed trapped inside this mass of wood, cloth and sawdust.

If there was, it didn't reveal itself.

"Anything?" Dez asked.

Sully shook his head. "Not saying you're wrong, though. Could be it's just not showing itself, same as if it were a regular spirit." He rubbed his jaw. "I could try touching it, I guess. Usually gets results."

It was true. Sometimes when Sully touched an object associated with a ghost, he'd get a vision, a glimpse of memory not his own. He preferred other means of communication, however. There was never any telling what a spirit might show him. With the ghost of someone who'd been murdered, Sully was often exposed firsthand to the horrors of violent death. If there was one major downside to what he could do, that was it. Sure, he got answers, but it meant experiencing some of the worst sorts of trauma as if it were happening to him personally.

Not an ideal situation by any means.

Dez was well aware of this and appeared about as anxious about the possibilities as Sully was.

"Why don't we leave that option for the time being?" Dez said. "Let's do a little research into Mr. Grin and Warren Malcolm first, see where it gets us."

"If you're right about the dummy being possessed, I'm going to have to deal with it sooner or later," Sully said.

Dez formed a tight and humourless smile. "I know. But for my part, I'm just as happy to make it later."

7

Dez gave a silent sigh of relief when Sully didn't press the issue.

"Hey, did you reach Lachlan?" Sully asked without turning from Mr. Grin.

"Oh. Yeah. I forgot." Dez cast one more look at the dummy before deciding he'd seen plenty. He redirected his gaze at Sully before answering further. "Once I mentioned the name of the dummy, he got pretty excited. He said he thought he had a file on the case in his storage container. Said he'd meet us there."

Sully met his eye. "So we're leaving?"

"That work for you?"

A corner of Sully's lips quirked up. "Yeah, I think I've seen enough of this thing for one night."

Dez waited while Sully regarded the case. "Mr. Malcolm? If this is you, my brother and I are heading somewhere to read up on the police file into your death. You're welcome to join us there if you like. Otherwise, I'd really appreciate it if you'd cut the staff here a break and stop moving the dummy around. If it's help you're looking for, Dez and I are the ones who can provide it. There's nothing anyone else here can do for you."

"Think that'll do the trick?" Dez whispered to Sully as the two of them made their way through the exhibits area toward Main Street, and from there to the office area where Evelyn presumably still was.

"No idea," Sully said. "Best I can do under the circumstances."

Back at the door leading to the offices, Dez led the way through and down the hall. They found Evelyn in her office, working on her computer. Upon spotting them, she looked up and smiled.

"How'd it go?" she asked.

"Have a minute to look at some video?" Sully asked.

The smile slipped. "Why? Did something happen?"

"The dummy moved. I'm curious to see whether it was caught this time on surveillance."

Evelyn stood a little slowly, then brought them back down the hall to the security suite. There, she logged back into the computer and found the data pertaining to the date and the camera in question. Less than a minute later, the three of them were watching the image of Mr. Grin inside his display case.

"What am I looking for?" she asked.

"Mind if I try to find the spot?" Sully asked.

Evelyn shifted aside, allowing him to fast-forward through the recording. From his spot, standing over Sully's right shoulder, Dez watched for the tell-tale body language suggesting the on-screen Sully had seen something unusual. Dez saw it as Sully, on the screen, shot from sitting to kneeling. Having arrived at that spot on the recording, Sully rewound a few frames.

"There it is," he uttered softly.

Evelyn leaned in next to him. Although Dez was mainly focused on the screen, he had enough of a view of Evelyn's profile to catch the widening of her eyes, coinciding with a catch in her breath.

The reason for it was obvious. Despite the fact the image wasn't fully zoomed in, it was easy to see it as Mr. Grin's eyes flashed open and held there, wide and staring. A full three seconds passed before the on-screen Sully noticed the change and jumped. Another few seconds. Then the mouth began to move.

Although Sully had explained what had happened to Dez, seeing it in person caused a ripple of fear to run through him.

"Oh God," Evelyn whispered. "How? How is it doing this?" Once the movement had stopped and the dummy's face had returned to its former position, Evelyn faced Sully. "Did you check for cables or magnets? Anything that might cause this type of movement? Malcolm used mechanisms inside the head to operate the eyes and mouth. Maybe something's malfunctioning in there."

She was grasping again. Dez scanned Sully's face for signs of insult but found none. Only the usual patience.

"We can check," Sully said. "For my part, I'm convinced the reason for this is something you'd rather not hear, but we'll definitely cover the bases you mentioned. I'd rather leave it for another time, though." He didn't mention the fact inspecting the dummy for the sort of things she'd mentioned would involve his touching it—and might therefore lead to an unwanted vision. If she wouldn't accept the existence of a ghost, she definitely wouldn't be keen to hear about psychic visions.

Dez wasn't any more eager to have Sully handling the puppet—not until they'd exhausted other options, anyway. Nor was Dez all that excited about touching the clearly haunted object himself.

Thankfully, they had another avenue.

"We've got a line on some information about Warren Malcolm's death," he told Evelyn. "We'd like to head off and review it tonight. It might contain some additional information about Mr. Grin that could help us out."

He was certain the expression he saw settle on Evelyn's face was relief.

"Of course," she said. "Sounds like a good idea. So you're finished here for the night?"

"Yeah. We'll walk you to your car before heading over to review the info. If you or someone else could check the video feed tomorrow for anything else unusual, that would be great. If Mr. Grin starts performing a circus routine at three in the morning, we'd like to hear about it."

"If he starts performing a circus routine in the middle of the night, I won't be available to speak with you tomorrow," Evelyn said. "I'll be too busy handing in my resignation."

LACHLAN FIELDS RENTED a large storage container in the northeast corner of the city, thankfully on the same side of the river as the museum. It cut back on the driving time, which meant, with luck, Dez could get back home to Eva and Kayleigh and into his bed before too long.

Then again, whenever Lachlan became involved in a case, any amount of overtime was possible.

By the time Dez and Sully made it past the outer security gate and up to the storage container, Lachlan's car was already there. Having used the pin pad on the man door to code their way inside, Dez and Sully found Lachlan seated in an easy chair he'd carted inside years back to give him someplace comfortable to sit while he worked. In his lap, a file folder sat open, its contents appearing worn even from where Dez stood.

"I can't believe the cases the two of you bring me," he said, not bothering to look up at them. "Warren Malcolm. Do you have any idea what a feather in my cap it would be to solve his murder?"

Dez exchanged a glance with Sully before returning his gaze to Lachlan. "*Who* would be solving the murder?"

Lachlan glanced up, finally, fixing Dez and Sully with a raised brow and a smirk. "Hey, we're all in this together, boys. Sullivan might be the third eye of this operation, but he's still a member of *my* operation."

Dez rolled his eyes, succeeding only in drawing a laugh from his boss.

Lachlan pointed at the floor next to his chair, covered by a massive area rug. "Pull up a spot on the carpet. We've got some reading to do."

Dez drew nearer, allowing him to cast an eye over the file and its contents. The pages inside had clearly been photocopied at some point in the distant past. "I hate to think how many nights you spent at the police department before your retirement, copying all of these files. If the KRPD had any idea you have these, your ass would be in a real bind."

"What they don't know won't hurt them," Lachlan said. "Anyway, I don't have copies of *every* case. Just the ones I worked or the ones I pulled out to review during my time in Major Crimes and Cold Case. And, hey, given the number of unsolveds we've sorted out for them, the KRPD should be praising us to the skies."

"Something tells me most police investigators aren't quite as pleased about us interfering in their files as you might think," Dez said.

Lachlan shrugged. "Well, Forbes Raynor hasn't been complaining recently, has he?"

Sergeant Forbes Raynor with Major Crimes—also Sully's

half-brother. No, he hadn't been complaining, but then, he also hadn't been providing details to his commanding officers as to how he was wrapping up some of the cases he'd been closing. Easier to credit a confidential informant than it was to tell them his psychic brother had been communicating with the ghosts of homicide victims.

Sully had already dropped onto a spot on the rug next to Lachlan, who had immediately passed him a few papers from the file he'd ostensibly already reviewed. Dez lowered himself next to Sully, gritting his teeth at the chill seeping through the carpet from the cement pad below. Dez decided he wouldn't be down here for long, but for now, he resolved to suck it up and read over Sully's shoulder.

The top page was a copy of an incident report from July thirteenth, nineteen seventeen, providing details of the initial call reporting the break-in.

Report of a break-and-entry to a residence at 24 Packham Lane. Mrs. Elizabeth Eldridge, housekeeper, arrived at 0647 hours to discover front door locked. Homeowner Mr. Warren Malcolm in habit of unlocking before Eldridge's arrival. When no answer, Eldridge to rear door. Discovered it open and damaged. Entered kitchen, found Malcolm on floor, wounded, unresponsive.

A detailed statement followed the incident report. According to the housekeeper, after the discovery of her wounded employer, she ran from the house and its grounds. Having been dropped off minutes earlier by her husband, who'd unfortunately already driven off, Elizabeth ran to the nearest neighbour's home for help. They let her use their phone to call police.

According to Elizabeth, her husband had picked her up after her shift ended at seven the previous evening. At the time she left, Warren had been fine and in good spirits. He'd been alone as he most often was. He rarely had company, she said, and the list of those who'd recently visited was limited to two: Warren's brother, Lawrence, and his sister, Edith. The housekeeper told police she hadn't seen either of them, nor anyone inside or near the house, nor on the grounds, when she left. The weather had been pleasant when her husband had driven her home that evening, and the sun had not yet set.

Investigators spoke to several others during the earliest stages of the investigation, focusing most of their attention on the siblings. Neither professed to knowing anything more than Elizabeth, and neither claimed to have been at or near the house at the time in question.

Fingerprint technology had been relatively new in KR in those days, but attempts were nonetheless made to obtain prints —particularly when, after a couple of days, it became clear to investigators Warren wouldn't recover. The only prints clearly identifiable belonged to Warren, his housekeeper and his siblings. While a partial print was identified on the doorjamb, it wasn't sufficient for evidence purposes.

Nowadays, forensic investigators could do more with partial prints given available technology, Dez knew. Additionally, oil left behind by a suspect's fingers might prove sufficient to extract DNA.

A lot had happened in the world of forensic science over the past century, but none of those advances helped those struggling to solve the crime back then. Dez often wondered how police managed to function prior to modern forensics. While forensic science didn't necessarily solve cases, it did help to point investigators in the right direction. A well-placed print or DNA sample could be the difference between a suspect who avoided detection and one who found himself in a police interview room facing a murder charge. Legwork remained a necessary part of every investigation, but police back then had a lot more of it to do in many instances in order to make charges stick.

Dez didn't envy them.

It couldn't have been any easier with a case like Warren's. Unsolved homicides were never easy for cops to stomach. Add in the fame element—the fact the world had to have been watching and eagerly awaiting a result—and it must have been like working inside a pressure cooker.

The file contained additional statements—dozens of them, in fact—proving police had tried hard to get to the bottom of what happened to the ventriloquist. According to notes on the file by the initial lead investigator, they had no clear suspects.

"Hmm," Lachlan said from his chair as Dez completed his read of the lead investigator's notes.

"What?" Dez asked.

Lachlan glanced up from the file. "Housekeeper mentioned finding a woman's undergarment in Malcolm's bedclothes while she was cleaning. She added she'd never seen any woman around the place nor heard her employer mention one."

"That sort of thing would have been frowned upon back then, wouldn't it?" Sully asked.

"Yep. They hadn't moved into the Roaring Twenties yet. Enjoying the pleasures of the flesh outside of wedlock was generally frowned upon within respectable society."

Dez smirked. "Pleasures of the flesh?"

"Shut up. You get my point. Sex was for married couples. Someone as famous as Malcolm, it would have been a pretty big deal if he'd been found out."

"They ever find out who the woman was?" Sully asked.

Lachlan frowned deeply as he flipped through the remaining pages. "Nothing here. Whoever she was, he took the secret to his grave."

"So it's possible she's a suspect," Dez said.

Lachlan met his eye. "You think a woman's good for this significant an assault?"

Dez resisted rolling his eyes. "Hey, I've met more than a few women who are plenty capable of serious assault." Rasslin' Rosie Dalton sprang immediately to mind, though he avoided bringing her up. Lachlan didn't like being reminded of the wrestler who'd once choked him out.

Lachlan considered Dez's statement only a short time before giving a slow nod. "Yeah, guess you're right."

"How about Warren?" Sully asked. "How big a guy was he? What kind of physical condition was he in? Any notes on that?"

Lachlan scanned the file. "According to what I'm seeing here, he was a fairly tall and muscular man in good health. Anyone, man or woman, would have faced a significant challenge committing an assault as serious as this one against him."

"Have you come across a pathologist's report yet?" Dez asked. "It might clear up some stuff."

Lachlan dug through the papers still on his lap before extracting a small paperclipped stack. "One of the police reports referred to a significant head injury. The pathologist noted the same thing. Skull fracture, along with brain swelling and bleeding were noted. Those were on top of a range of other serious injuries to the rest of him, including three broken ribs, bruised and lacerated internal organs—I see several listed here—and more external bruises and lacerations than the pathologist bothered to count. We're talking a very brutal assault."

Lachlan tapped on the file. "What's interesting is the lack of defensive wounds or marks to indicate he'd been restrained in any way. The pathologist made a point of noting the absence of any such injuries to the body, which suggested to him—and I concur—that Malcolm was unconscious throughout the bulk of the attack. More than likely, he suffered the head injury first. If he was immediately rendered unconscious, he would have been in no position to fight back throughout the remainder of the assault."

Dez scratched at the stubble along his jawline. "Tells us more than that. We're talking about a massive number of injuries inflicted on an already unconscious man. This was about more than a break-in and theft. It was personal."

8

According to the file, police had pinned many of their hopes to locating Mr. Grin. Find Mr. Grin, and they'd find the killer. Even if the person who'd attacked Malcolm and stolen the dummy hadn't kept it, much might well be gained from either the person who'd ended up with it or the location where it had been placed or dumped.

Unfortunately for police, the search had come to nothing. For decades, no clues to Mr. Grin's whereabouts could be found—not until it turned up during renovations at the old Kimotan Rapids train station.

"Why the train station?" Dez wondered aloud. Recalling his grandmother's oft-repeated childhood warnings about sitting too long on the cold ground, he pushed himself to his feet, moving next to one of Lachlan's filing cabinets. Here, he was able to review a report on the dummy's discovery while leaning his elbows against the cabinet's surface.

Lachlan barely lifted his head from the file he continued to study in his lap. "Huh?"

"The train station," Dez said. "Where they found Mr. Grin. Why would it have ended up there?"

Lachlan at last looked up from the folder, focusing his gaze on Dez's face. "You tell me."

Dez shrugged but answered anyway. "Lots of people would have been bringing trunks in and out of there. Maybe the thief set it down and mixed it up with another one. By the time he or she realized the error, they couldn't go back for it without arousing suspicion. Or maybe they thought someone might have already discovered it. Wasn't like they had any immediate way of finding out about things back then. Not like today, where twelve people would have slapped a video up on social media as soon as someone spotted the dummy."

"Or maybe it was something else," Sully said.

Dez eyed Sully, still seated on the rug, relying on his longer coat to keep his butt from freezing. Sully hadn't said much since they'd come in here, which wasn't unusual for him. It meant when he did say something, it was worth paying attention.

"Such as?" Lachlan asked.

"Maybe the person who had Mr. Grin at that point wanted rid of him."

Dez raised his brows. "You're thinking maybe the dummy was already haunted?"

"Maybe. If it is Warren Malcolm haunting it—and I'm really leaning that way—he could have latched onto it shortly after his death. I'm not sure how he would have found it exactly, given he died a couple days after the attack, but it's a possibility. Could be his spirit was drawn to it somehow."

"Maybe he found it so quickly because he knew his assailant." Dez nodded. "Yeah, it's a decent theory under the circumstances. Killer figured on making a buck or two off Mr. Grin, except selling it wasn't an option right away—too much heat. So he held onto it, waiting for the situation to die down a little. Only, somewhere in the middle, Mr. Grin starts pulling what he's been doing at the museum—moving around of his own accord. If I were the killer, and my victim's most important possession suddenly started coming to life, I'd sure as hell want rid of it."

"Something doesn't make sense to me, though," Sully said. "If the purpose was to steal the dummy to try to make some money, why kill Warren? I mean, it might be he was the best person to extort—make him pay ransom to get it back. But if the purpose was to kill him, why take Mr. Grin?"

Lachlan drummed his fingers on the chair's armrest. "If the latter, the theft might have been a crime of opportunity. Assailant breaks in and does the deed, then spots the dummy and figures on making a little dough. Didn't realize until afterward it wouldn't be as easy as they thought to sell the thing. If the former, it might be Malcolm just got in the way. We're thinking this was a personal thing, so we might need to consider an alternate reason for the theft. Maybe it wasn't about money at all. Maybe it was a way for someone to get at Malcolm by taking from him the source of his livelihood. Only he ended up interrupting and all hell broke loose."

"Good theories," Dez said. "One major problem, though: every one of our suspects will be long dead. Even if we come up with the correct solution, where does it get us? And how will we know we've got it right in the first place without anyone to confirm it?"

Sully chewed at his lower lip. "Seems to me Mr. Grin might still have something to say about it. If we're looking for confirmation, maybe he'll be the one able to provide it."

DEZ ARRIVED home to find Eva still awake and waiting for him in bed.

"Everything all right?" she asked. "How's the job look?"

Dez groaned as he sat on the edge of the bed. "About par for the course where Sully and I are concerned."

"So another Sully job?" Code for cases involving ghosts.

Dez dropped his head into a hand. "Yeah. Another Sully job."

Eva's hand settled on his back, fingers kneading into muscles stiff with tension. "Sorry to hear that. I get the impression you've been pulling in a lot of those."

He gave a dry chuckle. "It's our lot in life, it seems." He shifted as Eva's hand found a particularly tight spot, then sighed as she accurately read his body language and dug in harder, working away at the knot.

Despite the anxiety he felt over the current job, he smiled. He had friends who bemoaned their marriages, grumbling about arguments or frustrations they had with their partners. Dez often felt exceedingly fortunate in having found Eva. Evenings like this served as an unnecessary reminder.

"In case I don't tell you often enough, you're kind of awesome," he said.

She laughed. "Thanks, Snowman. I guess you're kind of awesome too."

Dez allowed himself a couple more minutes of back-rubbing before heading to the master bathroom to get ready for bed. When he returned to the bedroom, Eva was lying down with her bedside lamp on, her eyes not on a book but on him. Usually, that meant something good was about to happen.

Crawling under the covers, he beamed as he took in what were most definitely her bedroom eyes.

"Kayleigh asleep?" he asked.

Eva nodded. "Checked on her before you got home. Out like a light with Pax lying on the bed next to her, playing guard dog."

Dez's grin grew. "Nice."

Eva smiled back. "I was watching Sully and Sarah earlier tonight, the way they look at each other. I was remembering back to our first year together, how all over each other we were."

"That's how Kayleigh happened," Dez recalled. They'd been young, just about to complete police college together, when they'd learned Eva was pregnant. It hadn't been planned or expected, and Eva had worried how it would impact her very new career. But they'd also viewed it as a sign they were meant to be together. Already living together, they got married. Despite the surprise pregnancy, they quickly settled into the excitement of becoming parents, and they'd welcomed their little girl into the world with the same joy they would have felt had they planned for her all along.

It was a whirlwind year, and Dez had never been happier.

"A lot happened that year," Eva said, proving all over again the two of them remained on the same wavelength. She blinked at him through half-lidded eyes. "It seems like such a long time ago. Sometimes I feel like I'm a different person. Do you feel that way?"

God, Dez thought, she's so damn gorgeous. "You're the same person I fell head over heels for. And you've never been more beautiful, more caring and more incredible than you are right now."

She flashed a sexy grin at him. "I meant to ask if you ever felt like you're a different person, but I'll accept your response."

She moved in with a kiss. For a time, Mr. Grin became a very distant memory.

SULLY ARRIVED home to an empty apartment, a small bachelor suite above a pawn shop located in a questionable part of town.

He'd walked in this door countless times just like this. Having spent a couple of years living in an abandoned, rundown mansion in a highly dangerous area of Kimotan Rapids, this apartment had once felt like a godsend. It had provided him with a roof that didn't leak, warmth that didn't rely on how well he maintained a fire and electricity allowing him to store and cook real food rather than limiting him to something from a tin.

It wasn't much—it *really* wasn't much—but it was his. And to him, it meant a lot.

Only now, as he stood here staring into shadows and silence, it felt empty. Like something was missing. And he knew what it was.

Sarah.

Whenever she was here, she filled the place with laughter and light and passion. It felt different when she was around. *He* felt different. While he liked the person he was, she made him a better version of that person. They'd been together close to a year—not long by any means, yet more than enough to convince him of a certain truth.

He didn't want to imagine a life without her in it.

Sully had yet to leave his spot just inside the door, and he jumped as a knock sounded behind him. When he answered it, he found his elderly across-the-hall neighbour, Emily Crichton, peering up at him through her large, thick glasses.

"Hey," he said. "It's late. Everything all right?"

"I was going to ask you the same. I haven't seen much of you lately, and I wanted to see how you were doing."

Sully ushered her inside and to his table, making sure to pull out the best of the old chairs for her. The place had come furnished when Dez first rented it during a difficult time in his life, and the furnishings had never been replaced despite needing it badly. Sully had thought about it more than once, had even gone so far as to poke around online for different styles and prices. He'd never gone so far as to buy, and he was starting to realize why.

This place had been a sort of way station for a lot of people, a place to live until something better came along. It had certainly been that for Dez. Sully had never thought of it the same way for himself, not until lately. The lately part, that had changed everything.

The best part of this place, once Dez moved back in with Eva and Kayleigh a few years back, was always Emily. Sully had discovered a long history with her, one dating back to his infancy. She'd been protector, friend and guide to him. She was always there with a kind ear, a piece of sage advice and a slice of coffee cake.

And now, here he was, contemplating leaving her behind.

"Something's on your mind," she observed.

He debated what to say and how to say it before settling on something easier. "Want something to drink?"

She shook her head. "As you said, it's late. If I have anything to drink now, I'll be back and forth to the bathroom for half the night."

Sully smiled. "Fair point."

"So what's going on? You have a difficult case you're working on?"

Also an easier topic under the circumstances. "Yeah, that's part of it. Another ghost job, one involving a skeptic."

"You usually tolerate skeptics quite well."

"Yeah, and I don't feel any different about this one, except when I'm around the object we're investigating. It's this dummy called Mr. Grin."

Emily's eyes widened. "Oh, really? I remember him." She leaned forward and tapped his wrist. "Not directly, mind you. I'm not nearly old enough to have seen him and Warren Malcolm perform in person. They were much like Edgar Bergen and Charlie McCarthy—very well-known at the time, even after I came along. I also remember the story from the news. It was quite the spectacle when they found Mr. Grin." Her eyes flashed. "You're saying Mr. Grin is haunted?"

"Oh yeah," Sully said. "Very haunted. Problem is figuring out the details. So far, whoever the ghost is, he hasn't come forward to communicate."

"Well, it's bound to be Warren Malcolm. Who else would it be?"

Sully shrugged. "Probably, but I can't rule anything out until I get some solid answers."

"And your skeptical client is troubling you?"

"Not personally, no. It's more to do with whatever's causing the haunting. It's carrying a lot of anger, and I have to work extra hard to keep it from poisoning me. I catch myself getting angry when I have no cause to be."

"Must get frustrating though, having people more or less say you're making up what you can see and do."

"It does. But I'm usually good with it. I'm a patient guy. Give skeptical clients a few days, maybe a week or two for the stubborn ones, and they come around to the truth. In this case, it's the ghost with the anger management issues. I'll just need to be more careful around the dummy until I get this sorted out."

Emily eyed him. Her thick lenses magnified her eyes, which made it extra hard not to squirm when she studied him like this.

"Something else is bothering you, though, isn't it?" she said after a long pause.

With no way to hide from her, he still hedged. "Not bothering exactly."

"What is it?"

He considered again how best to answer. "I know we haven't had as many of our visits as usual, and I'm sorry about that. I've been spending a lot of time with Sarah."

Emily cast him a large grin. "Oh, yes, the lovely Sarah. How is she?"

"Good. Um, the thing is ..."

Emily gave his arm another pat. "You want to move in with her."

He raised his brows at her. Emily wasn't a psychic, but she sure could pass for one sometimes.

"How do you do that?" he asked.

She tapped the side of her head. "There's a little psychic in all of us, Sullivan Gray." Her playful smile softened. "I've been on this planet a while, and I've known you for some time now. Plus, I pay attention. All fine reasons why I can see the way the wind's blowing."

"Okay, yeah," he said. "I've been thinking about asking her. Only, I can't really ask her to move in here. Not that there's anything wrong with this place."

Emily chuckled. "Sully, sweetie, please. It's a dump. I know it as well as you do."

"You ever think of moving too?"

"Nope. Because it may be a dump, but it's *my* dump. I've made a home here, and for some strange reason, I like it." She tilted her head as she regarded him. "You're worried about leaving me here."

He supposed his expression must have answered for him because she continued without awaiting his verbal reply. "Don't be. While I'm not young anymore and not able to do all the things I used to do, I'm perfectly capable of looking after myself. And I know you'll still come and see me, like you do now. Maybe not quite so often, but then our visits have been a little more sporadic lately, anyway."

He smiled sheepishly. "I'm sorry. I guess I've been kind of sidetracked."

"Not sidetracked. You're on the *right* track, the one you're meant to be on. It's only right she should be your priority. And you won't be abandoning me. I don't see it that way, so I hope you don't either."

He dropped his head. "I kind of do. It's been the worst part of trying to decide this. I really like being here for you. I mean, you were there for me at a time in my life when I really needed you. And not just when I was a baby. You've been there through so much more. You've saved my life and Dez's. You've talked me through some really hard stuff. I don't like the idea of not being close by when you need me."

Emily gave another light laugh. "Oh, Sully, it's not like you're moving overseas. You'll be in the same city, for Pete's sake. Stop being so protective of me. You sound like your brother. Go and ask that lovely girl to move in. If you don't, you'll have so many more regrets than what you're worrying about now."

The weight from his shoulders lifted, and he grinned to prove it. "You're pretty awesome, you know that?"

She met his smile. "I'm well aware."

"I've been thinking of asking Bulldog to take my apartment. You know Bulldog, right? Billy Bird?"

"I do, and he seems like a very good person. If it's all the same to you, though, I might ask my niece. She's had some struggles lately between a job loss and a marital breakdown. This apartment might be what she needs at the moment."

Sully raised his brows. "I didn't know you had a niece."

"Great niece, really. My sister's granddaughter. And, no, I haven't spoken about them. My sister and I were never close, so I was never in much contact with her family. Both my sister and her daughter have since passed away, so I took it upon myself to reach out to my great niece. We've kept in touch."

"Sounds like a great solution," Sully said. Another weight lifted. "I'll make sure to keep you posted on what Sarah and I decide."

Emily leaned forward a little. "Are you nervous about asking her?"

Sully dropped his head. "A little. Maybe even a lot. There's kind of a lot riding on what she says."

"Well, you're not asking her to marry you. And I'd be shocked if she said no. I've seen the way she looks at you. I don't think you have anything to worry about."

Emily used a hand on the table to hoist herself to standing. Unsure about the reliability of the table, Sully jumped to his feet in case he needed to make a quick grab. The table held, and Emily shuffled to the door.

Once there, she turned and wrapped her arms around Sully's middle. "Lucky would have been proud of the man her son grew up to be."

Sully had intended to seek Emily's wisdom on his concerns for Sarah's safety should she become a full-time presence in his life. Emily's words made him temporarily forget, the sentiment and the hug causing tears to well in his eyes. Despite fighting back the emotion, his voice came out choked when he answered Emily. "That really means a lot to me. Thank you."

Emily gave him a final squeeze before leaving the apartment.

9

When it came to homicide investigations, retracing a victim's steps was essential. But since they still hadn't positively identified the ghost, the worst thing they could do as investigators was to commit to a theory at the expense of all other possibilities.

As Dez got up the following morning, he considered the best move might be to check out the locations where the dummy had last been—most recently, the home of the last owner.

With this plan in mind, he headed downstairs, made a quick breakfast and saw Kayleigh off to school. He'd already said goodbye to Eva earlier this morning as she left for her shift with the Kimotan Rapids Police Department's commercial crimes unit.

Dez checked his watch, decided it was still a little early to call the museum and opted to get a run in. He took Pax along, the large black hound easily keeping pace with his long legs and threatening repeatedly to tow him along at an even faster clip. Once he returned, Dez refilled Pax's water dish and left the dog happily lapping away while Dez hopped into the downstairs shower.

By the time he'd towelled off and dressed, the clock on his

cellphone told him he was now within the museum's opening hours. He put in a call to Evelyn's desk phone first, but when he was unable to reach her that way, tried her cellphone. This time she answered.

"It's Dez Braddock," he said. "Sully, Lachlan and I dug through some information last night about the Warren Malcolm homicide and the Mr. Grin theft. I was thinking it might be a good idea to check into the dummy's more recent history, from the time it was located to when it was donated to the museum. What can you tell me about the most recent owner?"

"James Holmes. Listen, while I understand your wish to check into Mr. Grin's most recent whereabouts, I was really hoping you'd have a word with some of our staff members. Perhaps someone's behind the activity at the museum or might know of someone coming in and doing it."

Clearly, Evelyn hadn't given up on finding a non-paranormal explanation.

Dez held back a sigh. "We can ask. But we do need to pursue other avenues as well—even ones you might not place much stock in."

"I don't mean to offend," she said. "Please, don't take it the wrong way. You have to understand, I grew up in a family that questioned everything. My parents didn't believe in God or spirits or anything else they couldn't see with their own eyes. They were extremely scientific about everything, to a fault really. It was actually embarrassing for me in school, especially when Christmas came around. We didn't even celebrate the holiday, not in the same way others did. So for me to now be asked to consider the existence of ghosts, it's a big stretch. I really am trying."

"I'm not offended, and neither is Sully," Dez said. "But if you're talking about belief in things you can see with your own eyes, maybe you need to consider you actually have seen some stuff. If we don't find the sort of explanation you're counting on, you'll be left with what Sully and I already know to be true. I'm not asking you to believe. I'm just asking you to be open-minded about the job we do. Let us do what you're paying us for, and I promise you, we'll fix this so you don't have to worry about moving dummies again."

"For which I would be eternally grateful. Let me know what you need in the meantime, and I'll do my best to get it for you. And I'll also do my best to be more openminded while I'm at it."

Dez couldn't ask for more. "Thanks. First thing I need is the address where this James Holmes lived. Given he kept all kinds of dark stuff, it's something we should check into."

"Sure. He had a manor house outside of the city, this side of Rocky Creek. Place is well over a century old. Beautiful place, but comes with its share of unpleasantness."

Dez had been silently gauging the travel time to the Rocky Creek-area house. Now he stopped to raise a brow. "How do you mean?"

"Well, I don't think I mentioned Mr. Holmes also willed to us a number of other items besides Mr. Grin—some of which we refused simply because we didn't want them here. Thumb screws, a rope said to have been used to hang people at the old prison, the car in which the Kelso brothers were fatally shot by police after the series of robberies they committed—those types of things. We discussed it in great detail, certainly. I mean, we could attract a number of people to the museum if we put items like those on display. But in the end, we're a place for families, for children. Showing things like that would have taken us too far from our mandate."

Dez nodded though Evelyn wasn't there to see. "Gotcha. Makes total sense. So Mr. Grin—he's different?"

"Before he was associated with a notorious crime, he was

famous for bringing smiles around the globe. We would have been crazy to refuse the offer to give him a new home here."

Dez scratched at his jaw. "Did you take anything else from Holmes's collection? I mean, you mentioned the Model Ts and some clothes and things. But anything you'd consider dark?"

"Ultimately, no."

"So those other creepy items—"

"Remained with the house, as far as I know."

"Okay," Dez said. "We'll want to access the house. Do you happen to have contact information for his lawyer or executor—whoever's handling his estate?"

"Certainly, but if you have the Warren Malcolm murder file, you should already have information on the whereabouts of Mr. Holmes's residence."

Dez, hand poised over a notepad in the hopes of an address or land location, stalled. "Why's that?"

"Well, one could argue it was Mr. Holmes's most macabre purchase of all. The house where he lived and died was the one where Warren Malcolm suffered his fatal attack."

10

DEZ DIALLED both Sully and Lachlan as soon as he got off the phone with Evelyn, connecting the three of them through a conference call.

"You serious?" Sully asked once Dez finished sharing what he'd learned.

"Yep. Wish I wasn't."

"Who'd want to live in a place like that?"

"You'd be surprised," Lachlan said. "Plenty of people find crime fascinating. Remember the Podnicki murder? Bit before your time, but he was the politician who took an axe to his wife and her mother."

"I know the Podnicki thing," Dez grumbled. Everyone knew it. Sometimes Lachlan acted like Dez and Sully were missing brain cells because they'd been born decades after he had.

"Don't get your panties in a twist, Braddock. Anyway, guy who bought the place was obsessed with the crime. Even had a room in the house devoted to the case. Ex-cop. Kind of lost his marbles after a shooting incident in which he nearly died."

Dez thought they were straying from the point. "Okay,

anyway, I was thinking we might want to get ourselves into the house. What do you think, Sull?"

"If whatever's moving the dummy was present in the house, it could still be connected to it somehow. If it is—and if I'm lucky—maybe I can draw it out there. If it is Warren, the results might be different there than at the museum. The amount of energy and emotion tied into homicide scenes can be pretty significant."

"You'll need to get access to the house," Lachlan said. "You mentioned the client provided contact info for the lawyer. You handle that yet, Braddock?"

"Not yet. Wanted to touch base with you guys first, make sure we were on the same page. I'll call right away."

"Leave it to me," Lachlan said. "Lawyers love me. Just email me the name and contact info."

Based on the amusement colouring the tone, Dez was pretty sure the truth about the Lachlan-lawyer lovefest was the exact opposite. "Lachlan—"

"Relax. I'll be on my best behaviour."

"Which isn't saying much."

Lachlan laughed before getting back down to business. "You mentioned the client still wants us to talk to the staff to be sure this isn't some elaborate prank."

"Sully and I did a full sweep. No evidence of a break-in or detailed prank. We all know what the real issue is here. So does Bob Lindberg, the curator."

"Sure, but Evelyn's the one we're ultimately reporting to. She'll be the one ensuring we're appropriately paid for our services. She wants a line of questioning followed, we'll follow it—even if we know it won't lead anywhere. Question is, who's going to do it?"

"If we can get permission to enter the house today, I want to get on it," Sully said. "The sooner, the better. The amount of anger attached to this thing and the way this spirit interacts with the physical world, I can't guarantee people will be safe. At the very least, it might end with some people quitting their jobs out of fear. That's the exact opposite of what Evelyn and Bob want."

"Good point. If I can get you into the house today, I'm assuming you'll want Dez with you."

"Not a question of want. I *need* him with me."

Lachlan harrumphed. "Guess that leaves me doing the pointless staff interviews."

"Not seeming quite so necessary now, are they?" Dez joked.

"Shut up, Braddock. Sullivan, I'd suggest you get yourself over to your brother's. Rocky Creek is on the east side of the city, nearest Dez and Eva's. If I can get you in immediately—and I fully intend to—I'd like you both ready to go. If I know lawyers, time is money to them. He or she won't be happy to add waiting around for you to show up at the house to their to-do list for today."

Sully arrived at Dez's house within the hour. By then, Lachlan still hadn't called back with news.

Eager to speak about anything not ghost-related until they absolutely had to, Dez turned to a more personal topic. "Talk to Emily yet?"

Sully leaned back into the sofa cushions. His body language, previously just this side of tense, showed immediate signs of relaxation. His shoulders dropped away from his ears and the muscles along his jawline released. "Actually, yeah. Last night."

Dez leaned toward him, elbows on knees and fingers knitted. "And?"

Sully smiled. "All good. She's happy for me. And she thinks

she can get her niece to move in across the hall from her. I guess she's fallen on some hard times."

Dez nodded, answering Sully's grin with his own. "Totally awesome, man. Another problem solved. So what's your next move?"

"I guess—I hope—a big move. Kind of anxious about it, though."

"She's not going to say no, if that's what you're worried about."

Sully met his eye. "Part of it, but not the big thing. It's what I told you before. What I do—what we do—it's dangerous sometimes."

Dez smirked. "It's dangerous quite a lot. Let's be honest."

"Exactly. And I attract some pretty creepy stuff."

"I'll second that. But you told me Sarah does well with creepy. If that's what you're worried about, don't be. She's no shrinking violet."

"I know. You're right. But God, Dez, I feel bad enough when stuff happens to *you* because of me. I don't know what I'd do if something happened to Sarah."

Dez grasped a handful of Sully's hoodie and hauled him toward him. "Hey. Bad stuff hasn't happened to me because of you, you hear me? Bad things happen because they happen. Hell, most of the stuff that's happened to me is because of the job we're in. It's dangerous, end of story. If you want to get into it, I'm only here because you've saved my life about a zillion times. It's not like ghosts wouldn't exist just because you weren't there to see them, right?"

"You're just trying to make me feel better."

"Is it working?"

Sully patted Dez's hand. "Maybe. Let me get back to you on that."

Dez released him as his phone rang. Lachlan's number popped up on the call display.

As usual, Lachlan didn't beat around the bush once Dez hit the talk button. "Got ahold of the lawyer. She tells me the reason Holmes bequeathed so much to the museum was because he had no family beneficiaries. He was childless, and he wasn't a fan of his niece and nephew. And apparently, he wasn't one for socializing, so few, if any, friends. He frequented auctions and the like, and he seems to have intended for the bulk of his property to be dealt with via auction. His way of giving back to those like himself who enjoy such things, I suppose."

"But not Mr. Grin," Dez said.

"Or other rather macabre items he attempted unsuccessfully to leave to the museum," Lachlan said. "Might be a reason for it, though his lawyer wasn't able to share the details with me as she had a quick telephone appearance to make on a court matter. She did agree to meet you at the house today—provided you can make it over there by noon. I'd suggest you get moving."

Dez checked the clock on his phone and mentally calculated the amount of time it would take them to get to Rocky Creek. He exchanged a look with Sully. "Guess we'd better. What's her name?"

"Jill Mann. Know how to get there?"

"No, but you've got the file on you. I'm sure you'll text me with directions." The remark had been tongue-in-cheek.

"Watch it, you big buffoon," Lachlan replied before proceeding to provide a set of directions to an estate approximately ten minutes this side of Rocky Creek.

"You're going to go talk to the museum staff, I presume?" Dez asked once he'd finished tapping the directions into his phone's notes app.

"Guess so. Not the most enjoyable task, but a necessary one

under the circumstances. Just you keep me in the loop, you hear me? First sign of anything spooky around there, you can catch me on my cellphone."

"First sign of anything spooky around there, you'll have to catch me first," Dez said.

11

As he steered the SUV toward Holmes's estate, Dez eyed the passing countryside.

Rocky Creek had been aptly named long ago for the waterway winding through the area, an offshoot of the much larger Kimotan River.

The town itself was built on a flat piece of ground through which the creek cut. Farther upstream, the water rushed more violently over and through rock, countless years having carved out small rapids which attracted kayakers wanting a rush without the danger of the much larger ones for which Kimotan Rapids had been named.

It was next to a section of the rapids near Rocky Creek that Warren Malcolm had made his home over a century ago. A large wrought-iron gate stood sentry at the entrance to a short, tree-lined drive. The trees had been left to grow wild, their lower-most branches well placed to scratch any vehicle taller than the average half-ton truck. Despite this, Dez could see well enough down the lane to make out the main entrance of a two-storey brick house boasting a set of once-white columns, large windows and an A-frame section of attic overlooking the drive.

A callbox was situated this side of the gate, but despite Dez's persistent pressing of the button, nothing happened.

"Maybe she's not here yet," Sully suggested.

Dez drummed the fingers of his right hand on the steering wheel. "Guess not. Or it's not working." His gaze drifted out the windshield in the direction of the house. "Place is creepy as all hell, isn't it? I can't believe this Holmes guy died just this year. Seems like no one's lived here for at least a decade."

Sully shrugged. "Guess he didn't bother much with upkeep. We don't know how old he was when he died. Maybe his health wasn't great for a while. And it does sound like he was kind of a recluse. Could be he wasn't any happier having people coming to his home than he was going to theirs."

"Maybe." Dez shuddered. "Jeez. Can you imagine being all alone in a place like this with Mr. Grin hanging around? Never mind all the other stuff he had."

"I can't imagine. Or at least, I don't want to."

Having a psychic brother, Dez had learned quite a bit about the paranormal. One thing Sully had told him was that while not all items connected with violent events were haunted, plenty contained energy nonetheless—like a sort of psychic fingerprint left behind through time and use. When the item was connected with murder or another kind of violent death, the sort of energy it contained—and even gave off—was highly negative. Having surrounded himself with it, James Holmes must have felt something unpleasant from time to time, whether or not he had any psychic sensitivity.

"What should we do?" Dez asked. "Want to try scaling the wall? I could boost you and you could try to open this sucker from the other side."

"Like go by myself to the house to dig around for a buzzer for the gate? Not on your life."

Not on Dez's life either. The only thing worse than entering this eerie-looking property with Sully was being forced to go in alone because Sully had inexplicably vanished once inside. "Uh, nope, not what I was getting at. I meant—"

Dez was interrupted by the arrival of a small car pulling up behind them from the main road. An attractive blonde woman, supermodel-thin and well-attired in a knee-length dress, fitted jacket and heels, stepped from the car and approached the SUV's passenger side. Dez put down the front, passenger-side window before Sully could hit the button.

The woman stuck a well-manicured, ringless hand through the window. "I'm Jill. You're obviously Desmond and Sullivan."

Neither Dez nor Sully corrected her with the names they more commonly went by before Dez returned her handshake. "Thanks for coming. We appreciate it. I know you're busy, so we'll make this as quick as possible."

Jill shook her head and produced a set of keys. "Don't worry about it. I'm not going in. You're free to have a look around yourselves. You can return these to Lachlan once you're done; he can get them back to me."

Dez resisted a glance at Sully. Rarely were lawyers this free with their clients' personal property, whether or not they were dead.

Maybe Jill read something in his expression because she quickly added, "Really. Don't worry. Lachlan trusts you, and I trust Lachlan. He's one of my dad's best friends."

Lachlan boasted a wide swath of friends in interesting and helpful places. It seemed somewhere along the way, he'd managed to find another.

"Judge Mann, by chance?" Dez asked.

Jill's face broke into a grin. "You know him?"

"I had to testify in his court a few times back when I was still in policing. He seemed like a nice guy. Didn't let the lawyers get too bitchy with me." He grimaced. "Uh, no offence."

Jill laughed. "None taken. I'm not a criminal lawyer, anyway. Mainly business-related matters and loads of wills and estates." Her smile fell away as her gaze tracked back toward the gate and beyond, her muscles tensing along the jaw and brow. Slowly, almost imperceptibly at first, her brows lowered.

"Everything all right?" Dez asked.

Her eyes snapped back to his. For a moment, it was as if she'd forgotten where she was and who she was with.

"Fine," she said. She pressed the keys forward as far as the window, holding them there by forefinger and thumb as if handling a dead rodent. "Just let Lachlan know when you're finished with them."

Sully took the keys and Jill spun back toward her car.

Sully jumped out of the SUV, causing Dez to rush to do the same.

"Wait," Sully called out.

Having reached the driver's side door of her car, Jill turned to face him, expression reading impatient. If she were a cartoon, she'd be tapping her foot.

"Something's wrong," Sully said. "What is it?"

Again, her gaze shifted toward the gate. This time, it didn't linger before she returned her attention to Dez and Sully. She crossed her arms, the movement reading protective rather than defensive or annoyed.

"I feel silly saying it," she said.

Dez tried for a soothing smile. "Don't. Not sure what Lachlan filled you in on, but we've pretty much heard everything."

Her eyes drifted from Dez to Sully and back again as if feeling them out, weighing what she should and shouldn't say. Her fingertips dug slightly into her lean arms.

"Please don't tell anyone I said this," she said. "But something about this house creeps the hell out of me. Not just its history or the collection of unusual items accrued by Mr.

Holmes. It's the place itself. I feel stupid saying this. It doesn't even make sense to think it, let alone utter the words out loud, but it's almost like the house is alive. Like when I'm inside, it's watching. Does that make any sense?"

As she spoke, the sleekly styled, businesslike Jill Mann fell away, leaving in her place a woman both confused and frightened by something disassociated from the world she'd so carefully constructed for herself. Dez felt bad for her.

"It makes complete sense," Sully said. "I know it's no consolation, but houses are like an extension of the people who live inside them. Lots of times, you can walk into a place and feel whether the memories it holds are mainly good or mainly bad. Places like this, with all the horrific stuff they hold, become poisoned in a way."

"I thought it must be my imagination getting the best of me. I mean, all the things he owned, all those terrible histories, I told myself it was getting to me thinking about it." She tilted her head. "You're saying there's something more to it."

Sully nodded. "Unfortunately, yeah. At least, there probably is. That's really why we're here—to find out for sure."

Jill cast another dark glance down the lane. "Oh God. I have to come back here at some point to help sort through this stuff. So far, no one's expressed interest in buying the property, so I've been granted a little leeway timewise, but someone's going to need to finish putting his affairs in order. Since I was his lawyer, I'm stuck with it. Not like anyone else would want the job."

"I thought he had a niece and nephew," Dez said.

Jill gave an indelicate snort which seemed out of place on her. "Please. I don't represent them, so I feel fine telling you this provided it goes no further. While they want whatever money they can get their grubby hands on, neither wants to put in any work sorting through this property. Which is fine since my client didn't include either of them in his will. There's a lot to work through in court yet, but I don't foresee things going in their favour. My client was clear in his instructions. Unfortunately, it leaves me with sorting everything out as we move forward."

Sully cast a glance over his shoulder at the gate before returning his gaze to Jill. "Whenever you need to come back here, give Lachlan a call, all right? Or you can call me directly. Either way, I can come with you. You shouldn't be here alone if you're uncomfortable."

Dez knew what Sully left unsaid. Emotions like fear not only attracted negative spirits, but they also empowered them. Last thing either would want was for Jill to become the victim of a ghostly attack because she'd been forced to come back here alone while afraid.

"We'll both come with you," Dez added.

Her responding smile seemed built on tremendous relief. "Thank you so much. You have no idea."

Sully gave a dry laugh. "Unfortunately, I do."

"Yeah," Jill said. "I guess you do. I looked you up. I kind of half-hoped at the time the stories in the paper were exaggerating what you claimed you could do. But let me tell you, half an hour alone in that house made me rethink my opinion on the supernatural."

Dez chuckled. "Yeah, we've been in a few houses like this. If Sully hadn't made me a solid convert years ago, I would have changed my mind very quickly while visiting some of those places. Listen, before you go, can you tell us a bit about your client? How old was he? What was he like? Why'd he move here? Anything you can provide would be helpful."

Jill's lips pressed together, her eyes tracking upward and to the side. "I don't know how much I can tell you really. I barely knew him. He was in his late eighties when he passed. And I'd imagine you'll ask, so I'll just tell you now, he died as the result of a fall at home. He had a home care aide who came in once a day, and she found him at the base of the main staircase, dead. The coroner and the police investigated, and they concluded there was no evidence of anything untoward. It appeared he simply tripped."

"Any idea on what?" Sully asked.

"That's the super-creepy part," Jill said. "They couldn't say for sure, but I was told they found one of his collected items at the top of the stairs."

Dez didn't want to know. Unfortunately, he didn't get a choice. Jill finished the story without further prodding. The words had Dez wanting to turn tail, shove Jill and Sully into their respective vehicles and get the hell out of here.

Jill shivered as she spoke the words. "I was told it was a ventriloquist's dummy."

12

Dez was unable to catch the shudder that ran through him.

"You're kidding," he said.

Jill frowned. "I wish. Awful, isn't it? As I understand it, the home care aide was so freaked out, she wouldn't even go back in to get her supplies. She said she'd have someone come in and get them rather than stepping foot inside this house again."

"Would you be able to find us a name and contact number for her?" Dez asked. "Might be a good idea to talk to her."

"I'm sure I can, although I'd prefer to talk to her first to make sure she's all right with it."

Dez imagined how that conversation would go. Anyone as scared as she'd been by her experience wouldn't likely welcome the idea of reliving it through questions from private investigators. Depending on her existing beliefs about the paranormal, she might even believe she'd be opening herself to something worse by talking about it.

"If you could try to persuade her, we'd appreciate it," he said. "Given she spent time in the place, she might have some insights which would help us out."

"Certainly, I'll try." Jill tilted her head to the side as she regarded them. "I've got to say, you're different from some PIs I've dealt with. Kinder, more considerate. I appreciate it. It speaks well of you."

"Sully sees only the ghosts of homicide victims," Dez explained. "Most of the people we help—both living and dead—have been through enough without having to deal with a pair of jerks besides."

Jill smiled. "In that case, I'm glad they've got the two of you to turn to. Anything else you need before I go?"

"One thing," Sully said. "The stuff Mr. Holmes collected—how much of it is still in the house?"

Jill peered again down the lane as she chewed briefly on her lower lip. "Honestly? Almost everything. At some point, I expect an auction will be held as per his wishes, but I need to catalog everything first." She returned her gaze to Sully and Dez. "If your offer still stands to come with me at that point, I'd be grateful."

"Just let us know," Dez said. "We'll make it happen."

With a nod and smile, Jill extended her hand once again to both of them, then returned to her car.

Dez waited until she'd pulled onto the main road before eyeing Sully. "I'm really not looking forward to going in there now."

Sully stuffed his hands into the pockets of his coat. "Yeah. Me neither."

"Guess the sooner we start, the sooner we can leave." Dez shifted his gaze to the gate and the lane beyond. A light wind had come up and was blowing the trees around, branches on the untrimmed trees appearing to reach toward the road like fingers, waiting to grab at anything attempting to enter. "Tell you one thing. I'm glad we came early. Being here after sunset seems like a bad idea."

Sully nodded but said nothing as he made his way with the

keys to the gate. Dez moved to the driver's side of the SUV, watching as Sully twisted the key in a large iron-enclosed lock at the gate's centre. Sully struggled with it briefly, and Dez caught himself half-hoping it wouldn't work. But a moment later, Sully's efforts were rewarded with a loud click.

Sully met Dez's eye, lifting his brows in question. Dez easily read the expression.

Ready?

Dez shrugged but gave a tight nod. Then he slid back in behind the wheel, listening through the still-open passenger-side window as Sully walked the gate open. It swung jerkily, announcing them with a piercing screech. The sound reminded Dez of a horror movie.

Reluctantly, he drove through, waiting on the other side until Sully had resealed and relocked the gate from this side. Dez used the button on his side to put the opposite window back up. A moment later, Sully jumped inside, tugging the car door closed behind him.

"Gate needs oiled," he muttered. "If there's anything waiting for us in that house, we won't be taking it by surprise."

Dez frowned. "You had to say it."

"Sorry."

"You're not sorry. At all." He heaved a sigh. "I hate this."

Sully slouched low in his seat. "I'm not crazy about it either. Like you said, at least we're here now and not at night, right?"

Remembering his own point about getting this over with, Dez put the SUV back into drive and crawled up the lane, veering a few times to avoid particularly low-hanging branches. "Can you imagine being the home care lady? Hell, can you imagine being James Holmes? Living alone in a place like this would have been bad enough, but to be here with all those creepy things?"

"Except he had those creepy things with him by choice,"

Sully reminded him. "Maybe he didn't believe in the paranormal. If so, he wouldn't have seen the things he owned as anything other than interesting historical artifacts. And he clearly had interest in dark stuff anyway if he was collecting these things. Some people don't get creeped out easily."

"You don't get creeped out easily. Doesn't mean you'd purposely surround yourself with that crap."

Sully folded his arms over his chest and squeezed at his biceps. "No way in hell. Some people gather this stuff on purpose—gives them a thrill or something. Others probably think they're doing the world a favour by keeping items with bad energy out of circulation. Either way, I think most people who pick up these types of things don't have a clue what they're dealing with. I understand this stuff, and that's exactly why I wouldn't touch it. Not without a very good reason, anyway."

Unfortunately, they had such a reason now—one they couldn't back away from. Not when they were being paid to be here.

"This sucks," Dez said.

Sully huffed out a breath. "Tell me about it."

Dez kept his speed low as he continued toward the house, telling himself he was avoiding branches and potholes. In reality, he dreaded the idea of reaching the place. As they drew nearer, he could see many of the windows on the ground floor and some on the second storey were boarded up, telling him the house's interior would be excessively dark.

He hadn't thought to ask Jill if the electricity had been kept on in the house now that winter was pretty much over. Ordinarily, the cold temperatures in this part of the country meant power needed to be kept on or restored in the winter to retain any hope of selling it down the road. Lack of power meant no heat, and lack of heat during a freezing winter meant cracked water pipes, ruined foundations and various other damage. Good luck getting a decent price on a home if that happened.

Dez couldn't imagine anyone in their right mind wanting to buy a house with a history as shady as this one had—and the jury was out as to whether James Holmes had been in his right mind. Still, the house had one of those classically elegant façades, and it stood near enough to Kimotan Rapids to make it potentially attractive to the right wealthy buyer—one willing to overlook the creepy factor.

Whatever there'd once been of a driveway was largely covered in weeds and puddles left behind by melting snow, so Dez stopped a short distance back and pushed the stick into park. Neither he nor Sully moved, each fixated on the house through the windshield.

"Guess we should get this over with," Sully said.

"Yep," Dez replied.

Still neither moved.

Finally, they exchanged a glance.

"What are you thinking?" Dez asked, although he was far from sure he wanted an answer.

Sully shrugged one shoulder, indicating the house. "I'm not sure how this place will affect me. Maybe the stuff he owned doesn't carry much energy. If that's the case, it won't be a big deal. But if it does …" He trailed off.

Dez knew where Sully had been going with it. It served as a reminder he didn't need. While Sully was the one with the psychic ability, Dez had a crucial purpose all his own. "If I see it's hitting you hard, I'll get you out of there."

Sully managed a slight smile. Then he faced front once again, drew in a long breath and shut his eyes. Dez gave him the time to centre himself, taking comfort in the fact Sully had learned over time how to better guard himself from negative spirits. And when Sully couldn't, Dez could.

Yeah, this sucked, but they could do it. Together.

"Good?" Dez asked once Sully's eyes cracked open.

"Good," came the reply.

It served as Dez's cue to step from the vehicle. Sully, keys to the property in hand, followed.

They made their way past the puddles to the house's front entrance.

13

SULLY GRITTED his teeth as the front door creaked open with the same horror-movie quality noise as had the gate.

A remark plucked at the tip of his tongue as to the dire need for maintenance, but it died there as his eyes adjusted to the dim light inside. As predicted, the home's interior was deeply bathed in shadow due to the boarded-up windows, but the light from the opened front door had created a break in the darkness within the entry hall. There, straight ahead—in the manner of many a classically constructed manor house—lay a grand staircase.

And there, at its base, lay the wretched figure of an elderly man.

The body of James Holmes had been removed long ago. It left Sully in no doubt as to the nature of what he was seeing.

Dead as the result of another's homicidal actions, James had remained behind as a ghost.

"What is it?" Dez asked.

Sully indicated the spot with a jut of his chin. "I see him."

Dez pressed closer, his arm brushing against Sully. "The dummy?" Dez's voice squeaked a little at the end.

Save for what Sully was currently looking at, the sound

would have brought on a grin. As things stood, all Sully could do was shake his head and offer a verbal correction. "James Holmes."

Dez shifted even nearer, arm now fully pressing against Sully's. "Where? The stairs?"

Sully nodded. "At the bottom. He's not moving."

"What's that mean?"

Sully merely shook his head in response. He had no idea. From here, the building's most recent owner appeared very much like a dead body, the way he must have looked when he was discovered by the home care aide.

Sully took a few steps forward, resisting the urge to fumble for a light switch. Sometimes, the slightest change in a building's atmosphere could cause a ghost to vanish—or to react in some other, and not always pleasant, way. At this stage, Sully decided he first needed a closer look.

He took another couple of steps, setting his feet down carefully and quietly as he moved.

"Sully?" Dez's voice was hushed, nervous.

Sully put an arm back toward Dez, fingers splayed. "Hang on."

Another couple of steps. Sully's heart thudded against his ribs as he neared the dead man. James's face was turned slightly away, his neck bent so horrifically as to leave no question as to the manner of his death. One arm lay twisted beneath him, one leg out and resting on the stairs. His eyes, once Sully was near enough to observe them, were open, fixed in a death stare at something toward the top of the stairs. As death had fully taken hold of the man, the eyes had clouded over, the sheen leaving their surfaces. But he had no doubt about the emotion locked on the face.

Terror.

The same terror Sully now felt crawling up his body, as if through tendrils winding up his legs through the floor.

He kept his eyes open, not daring to lose sight of the ghost for even a moment. He attempted instead to divide his focus, the visual portion locked on the ghost while, internally, he worked on separating himself from what he was seeing. He was anxious, yes, but this fear wasn't his. It belonged almost entirely to James.

"Sully?" came Dez's voice. "What's going on?"

Sully didn't get a chance to answer. He felt it before he saw it. A hand locking around his ankle.

The vision started without further warning.

He was shuffling down a semi-darkened hallway, thinking about making his way downstairs to the kitchen for a glass of warm milk before bedtime. Deep wood panelling soaked up what light was emitted by a row of mounted sconces. His gaze drifted over the sconces, providing a reminder he'd soon forget about the need to replace a few burned-out bulbs. Phoebe would be in in the morning; he'd ask her about it then. Given how shaky his balance was lately, she'd have an easier time stepping onto a chair or step stool to change out the bulbs than he would.

As quickly as he thought about the lightbulbs, he became distracted by the shadows along his route. They seemed heavier some nights, seemingly capable of hiding all manner of evil things. He'd never feared the dark, neither the nighttime sort nor the kind resulting from tainted human souls. Truth be told, he'd thrilled in it, surrounding himself by it. Since his youth, he'd found it fascinating, the dark side of humankind, the terrible things people did to each other. He'd never been the sort himself to harm others, so he didn't understand it. Not fully, anyway. And it was in his lack of understanding that he found the fascination.

So too with supposedly cursed and haunted objects. He'd never been sure such things were real, had sought out anything that might solve this greatest of all mysteries. But while he'd had so-called psychics come through here, purporting to feel the presence of evil, James himself had never sensed it. Certainly, he'd never experienced it.

Not until the damned puppet.

Not long after acquiring Mr. Grin, the inexplicable became a constant. Doors opening and shutting were the least of it. The damned pile of wood and Bakelite. Moving from room to room, watching him. Waiting. No matter what he did, he couldn't keep it restrained. Not even chains and locks.

Prickles ran down his spine in a steady flow. He'd never feared the dark. Not until now.

The dark had come alive, and for James—tired and frail and very, very alone—it was terrifying.

And so when, at the opening to the main staircase, he spotted movement out of the corner of his eye, he supposed he should have anticipated it. Perhaps, too, he should have anticipated the feel of something small yet solid catching his ankle.

He didn't. And so he tripped, tumbling hard and fast down the stairs before landing with a sickening thud on the floor at their base.

Somewhere, in that fleeting moment between life and death, he had occasion to glance up into the darkness.

Straight into the gloating, ghoulish face of Mr. Grin.

14

Awareness returned as suddenly as it left.

Sully found he was no longer standing—not fully, anyway. Rather, he'd ended up leaning back against Dez, upper body in his older brother's grasp as he was dragged backward, away from the stairs and toward the light from outside.

He tried to get out a verbal assurance that he was okay, but the words got caught in a mumble. He'd left the vision behind with the now-invisible spirit of James Holmes, but part of it remained with him nonetheless. It was like dying himself, experiencing these kinds of visions, and they always drained him.

Dez hefted him up as they reached the front door, causing Sully's feet to come completely off the floor. He hung there in Dez's arms, limp, mentally searching out physical sensation in his limbs. With horror, Sully realized he had gone completely numb.

His heart didn't share in this sudden inability to move, pounding out a mad rhythm in his chest as Dez lugged him farther from the house. He'd never fully gotten used to visions from ghosts, doubted he ever would. But this was different. He was paralyzed, as if he'd come away from the vision with the snapped neck suffered by the ghost whose experience he'd been forced to share.

Through mounting panic, he became aware of Dez alternating between grunting from physical exertion and uttering words meant to calm. "It's okay, Sull. Hang on. It's okay. I've got you."

Sully did his best to focus on the words rather than the incredible dread. It wasn't until he was lying on a patch of grass, Dez's worried face peering down into his, that the panic began to ebb. With Dez on the verge of panic himself, Sully needed to find his way back. It wouldn't work to have both of them flipping out at the same time.

Sully locked his eyes onto Dez's and focused on forcing his lungs to take in longer and deeper breaths. He managed two and was rewarded by a tingling in his hands and feet. His voice came next.

He managed a few words, although they came out sounding a little weird given Dez's shaking hands were currently squeezing the sides of his head and face. "Relax, Dez. I'm okay."

Dez released Sully's head, dropping his hands—one to lie flat against Sully's collarbone while the other balled up the material of his hoodie. "What happened?"

"Give me a minute."

Dez's eyes left Sully's, travelling over the length of his body. "You went totally limp in there. I thought you passed out, but you hadn't. What's going on?"

"I can't feel much from the neck down."

Dez jerked, full attention back on Sully, who was quick to add, "But it's coming back. I'll be okay. Just take a breath and try to stay calm."

Dez ran his hand down his jawline. "You're telling me you're basically paralyzed, and you want me to calm down?" He sucked in a breath. "Are you actually hurt? Like physically?"

"No. This is coming from the vision. It'll pass."

Dez glanced from Sully toward the SUV and back again. He levered Sully's upper body off the ground and bent toward him.

With returning feeling, Sully tapped Dez on the back before he could lift him into a fireman's carry. "Hang on. We can't leave."

"Damn straight, we can leave. And that's exactly what we're doing."

"We can't. Come on, Dez. We're here for a reason."

Dez released him but remained where he was, hovering over him. Sully was relieved to find he was able to stay seated upright without help. His sensation was nearly fully back, flesh prickling the same way it did when a limb fell asleep. He gritted his teeth against the sharp discomfort as it encompassed the majority of his body.

Dez heaved an exasperated sigh as he sat back fully. He didn't appear any happier about the situation, but he didn't make any further attempt to take the two of them out of here.

"How'd you end up paralyzed, exactly?" Dez asked.

Sully described the ghost he'd seen and the vision it had given him. "He ended up at the base of the stairs, staring upward. I don't know if he was alive or already dead and seeing things as a spirit, but he remembered Mr. Grin sitting on one of the upper stairs, watching him. I had the impression James broke his neck during the fall. If he'd lived, he would have been paralyzed."

Dez's eyes narrowed. "So the dummy *tripped* him? Intentionally? That's what he showed you?"

Sully shrugged. "Guess so. He felt something on his leg. Something small but strong. When he looked, Mr. Grin was sitting up there. James was scared of him. He made that pretty clear."

Dez shook his head. "So you're telling me this thing isn't just moving around on its own. It's actually homicidal?"

"Well, whatever's haunting it is homicidal."

Dez raised a brow. "What reason would Warren Malcolm have to go around killing people? Why kill this Holmes guy, for instance?"

Sully frowned. "If it *is* Malcolm. I don't know. It doesn't make sense to me either. Maybe he's confused and sees everyone as a threat. I mean, a century stuck inside an otherwise inanimate object, most of which was spent locked inside an abandoned trunk—that's got to mess with someone's mind, dead or not."

"Fair point," Dez said.

Sully, feeling a bit chilled and damp now, attempted to stand but wasn't quite ready to manage it on his own. Dez helped him the rest of the way.

"You know," Dez said, "we really don't know much about this Warren Malcolm, do we? I mean, we know what he did, that he was an entertainer and everything, and we know he was a private person—which isn't surprising given the work he did. But we don't know what he was like. Maybe the fact he was alone so much was because no one could stand him. How do we know he wasn't a lunatic or something?"

Sully finished brushing off the back of his jeans and straightened. "We don't. Not yet, anyway. Until I can manage a conversation with whoever's haunting the dummy, we're kind of flying blind."

Dez's gaze returned to the SUV. "You sure you don't want to bail on this thing? I've got a pretty good sense of why Jill doesn't want to go back in there alone, and let me tell you, I fully share her views on the subject."

Sully forced a smile, one he hoped would both calm Dez and make himself feel better. "We have to. At some point, someone's going to have to go back in there, Dez, whether it's Jill or a real estate agent or a potential buyer. We can't leave it the way it is, not if there's any risk to anyone."

"What about Mr. Grin? If that thing's going around plotting people's deaths, we can't leave it where it can hurt anyone. Right now, it's sitting in a display case at a museum filled with people."

"I know. I was thinking about that."

Dez shoved his hands into the pockets of his coat. "Any idea what we should do? I mean, we can't exactly take the thing home with us, can we?"

Sully scratched his head. "Honestly, I have no idea. Not yet. I'll have to give it more thought."

"Could you pull the ghost out of there and send it on its way?"

"It might come to that. I like to give them a chance to cross over the nice way, but I'm not willing to risk anyone's life to help a spirit—especially one who's already apparently killed someone." He turned from Dez back to the house. "For now, though, it's James I'm worried about. I don't want to leave him here like this."

Dez shuddered as he, too, faced the house. "You think he just lies there like that? All the time?"

"I don't know. It's possible. If he's locked into that moment, he might."

Dez grimaced. "That would suck. Okay, let's go see if we can deal with it."

Sully led the way back inside the house, although he took his time as he crossed the threshold. Inside, he pushed the wide front door all the way open, giving himself and Dez as much light as they could get.

A shape remained at the base of the stairs, although it now appeared to him as no more than a shadow. Likely, James had used up a lot of energy grabbing Sully and implanting the vision. It made Sully feel even worse for him. Sure, he hadn't used the best judgment in collecting the items he had over the course of his life, but he certainly didn't deserve what had happened to him.

Sully approached the shadow, stopping before getting close enough to touch. He didn't want to risk either another vision or, worse, the awful paralysis.

"Mr. Holmes," he said, "my name is Sullivan Gray. I can see you, but I can't hear you. I know you're probably tired right now, but I'm hoping you can find the strength to show yourself to me. There are things I want to ask about, and you should be able to nod or shake your head to respond."

Behind Sully, Dez cleared his throat.

Sully took the hint. "Oh, and if you can avoid touching me again, I'd appreciate it. I want to help you, but I'll need you to help me too. All right?"

A flicker of movement from the shadow, sort of like a shudder, suggested James was trying to do as requested. Ordinarily, Sully might have offered himself up to the ghost, advising him he could use some of Sully's energy to supplement his own. Sully had discovered early on in life he—along with his run of ill-fated electronic devices—acted as something of a battery for ghosts. But Sully wasn't eager to put himself out there for more after what he just went through.

More shivering from the shadow. Then, finally, Sully saw the beginnings of an outline form. A very human outline.

"Anything?" Dez asked.

Sully held up a hand as a call to wait. Another long moment passed before Sully found he could again make out the details of the man lying at the base of the stairs. Wide, helpless and frightened eyes stared up at Sully, a desperate plea contained in their depths. Sully didn't feel he lost any information with his inability to hear the ghosts. What they felt, what they needed, was often written all over them. And what he couldn't see, he could sense—often as keenly as if it were happening to him directly.

"It's okay," Sully said. "I'm going to help you. I promise."

He knelt where he was, still keeping his distance. Though he didn't get the impression James wanted to harm him, desperation and fear made people do things they wouldn't ordinarily do.

"I know what happened to you," Sully said. "And I understand why you're afraid. But you don't have to be. Mr. Grin is gone. He can't hurt you anymore."

The terror in James's eyes seemed to dwindle a little, without fully fading.

"I think the reason you're paralyzed is you're feeling trapped within the moment of your death," Sully told him. "It can happen because of the fear you felt at the time. Once you let go of it, I think you'll find you can move again. Mr. Grin is gone. You donated him to the museum. That's where he is. He's not here. Not anymore. You're safe now, Mr. Holmes. You can cross into the light. I can help you."

Sully allowed himself to open a little further, moving closer when he felt James's dread fade even more. His fingers twitched out a rhythm, palm lifting off the floor by the wrist. One arm, then the other, shifted then came fully off the floor. Next, James tested out his legs.

The remaining shadow clinging to him faded, drawing back like a curtain holding back the daylight. Light filled the spirit, energy flooding him as a doorway invisible to Sully opened to allow James in.

Sully rose to his feet as James did. This time, when James came toward him, Sully didn't flinch.

A hand reached out to touch Sully's cheek. A flash of thought came from James, but this time, it didn't feel like an invasion. The spirit, while ready to cross over, was not leaving without worries. Mr. Grin was still at the forefront of his mind. That and the museum to which he'd bequeathed the dummy.

"Don't worry," Sully said. "I won't let it hurt anyone else."

James turned, gaze penetrating the shadows of the main floor before lifting overhead. More worries.

"I'll check the house," Sully said. "If anything else here is a threat, I'll take care of it. It's not your responsibility anymore."

A nudge from behind drew Sully's attention back to Dez. "Maybe he knows something about Warren Malcolm or whoever might be inside the dummy. Something that might help us."

Sully smiled. Dez, freaked as he got about ghosts, nonetheless had a way of finding opportunities Sully sometimes missed.

Sully focused on James. A new worry had formed on the spirit's face, one Sully grasped as James's eyes drifted to a spot to his right, toward something invisible to Sully.

The doorway.

"You won't get stuck here," Sully assured him. "I promise. If this one closes, I can open another one."

The answer seemed to alleviate James's concern. He drifted to the left and down a hallway, the dull light he emitted all Sully could make out in the blackness ahead. James paused for a moment before vanishing into what Sully supposed was a room.

"Is there working electricity in here?" Sully asked Dez.

Dez took a couple steps to the side and flipped a switch on the wall. Nothing happened.

"Of course not," Dez muttered. "Why would we be so lucky?"

"They probably cut it once the weather started to improve," Sully said. "No need for it now that winter's pretty much over."

"Fine for everyone else. Not so good for those of us who need to be in some creepy-ass place."

Sully smirked. "Relax. We'll be fine."

He dug out his cellphone. He'd charged it fully this morning, but as often happened, his battery had drained and now showed fifteen percent.

"Got your phone?" he asked Dez.

Dez growled his annoyance as he pulled out his own phone and tapped the screen for the flashlight. He handed it to Sully.

Sully shined the beam ahead to where he'd last seen James. Then he plucked at Dez's sleeve with his free hand as indication to follow.

Sully led the way down the hall until he spotted a doorway. As he drew near enough to see inside, he spotted the dull light emanating from James. Sully stepped into the room, casting the light around the space, illuminating as much of it as possible.

They were standing inside an office—the one from the vision. A desk stood in the centre near a boarded-up window. Bookshelves and display cabinets lined the walls. Along one wall, a glass cabinet stood empty, its door partway open. A thin chain trailed down one side, a lock hanging open from one of the links.

Mr. Grin had been in there once. No longer.

But it wasn't to the cabinet that James gravitated. He'd made his way toward the opposite wall and now stood facing Sully, eyes locked on him with purpose.

Sully reached back, finding Dez's reassuring presence immediately behind him.

"What's going on?" Dez asked.

"He wants to show me something. Stay close."

"You got it."

Sully drew nearer to James, taking comfort in the sound of Dez moving with him. James didn't shift from his spot, waiting there until Sully was near enough to see him better.

"What do you want to show me?" Sully asked.

James lifted the arm nearest the wall, extended his index finger and pointed downward. Sully angled the cellphone flashlight in the same direction, finding nothing at the end of the beam but a block of panelling lining the lower wall.

Sully tilted his head as he regarded it. It took him a moment to clue in.

He lifted his gaze back up to meet James's. "Is there something behind it?"

James gave a slow nod.

"Some sort of hidden compartment?" Dez asked.

"Guess so," Sully said. He took another couple of steps, closing the rest of the short distance. He crouched in front of the indicated panel and rapped on the wood beneath the shelf. Sure enough, he was met with a hollow sound. He next placed his palm flat against the wood's surface and pressed, shifting gently in one direction. Nothing happened, but when he moved it the other way, the panel start to give. The sound of wood scraping wood filled the room as he slid it open far enough to see inside.

There, in the shadows within, lay a large wooden box, one with a locking mechanism. The locks, Sully noted, were open.

He lifted his head to again meet James's eye. "You kept Mr. Grin in here at the end, didn't you?"

A nod.

A locked box sealed behind a hard-to-shift panel. Even that hadn't been enough to hold the haunted dummy.

So why had it remained for so long inside a trunk at the train station? Had the spirit controlling it been more or less hibernating all that time, or had it been somehow trapped? If the latter, how was it Mr. Grin was once again powerful enough to evade all attempts to keep him locked up?

Clearly questions to which James didn't have the answer. After all, if he did, he'd probably still be alive.

Sully was still puzzling over this when James's finger again pointed toward the box. While Sully had no way to hear what James wanted to tell him, the message seemed clear.

Get the box.

Sully would need to pry the panel quite a bit farther to the side to slide the box out. He tried, finding it stuck.

Dez batted at Sully's shoulder. "Let me."

While Sully was plenty strong, there was no question Dez was by far the stronger of the two. Sully straightened and stepped back, giving Dez room to work.

"It's stuck," Dez said between grunts as he heaved on the panel. "How the hell did anything crawl out of here? For that matter, how did James put it in here in the first place?" Another hard pull, then Dez paused. "Hang on. I think the panel board is out of its groove a little. Give me some light."

Sully stood at Dez's shoulder, aiming the flashlight at the base of the panel. Sure enough, the board had slipped from the groove.

Sully met James's eye. "Did you do this on purpose, to make it harder for Mr. Grin to escape?"

James gave a nod.

"I can't move it around much because the box is in the way," Dez said. He peered up at Sully. "Might have to break the board."

James nodded again.

"Do it," Sully told Dez.

For some reason, this made Dez grin. He stood, facing the panel. "Stand back," he told Sully, before unleashing on the board. His kicks first splintered and then fully cracked the panel.

"You're like a twelve-year-old," Sully said.

Dez chuckled as he pried the broken wood free.

The item inside now lay exposed, revealing itself as an old despatch box. Dez drew it out, hefting it onto the desk. Sully played the light over its surface and was surprised to find it wasn't James Holmes's name etched into a steel plate on the surface.

"Warren Malcolm," Sully said. He caught Dez's eye. "This was his."

Dez lifted a brow. "What do you think is inside?"

Sully shrugged, fingering one of the locking mechanisms on the front. "Only one way to find out."

15

With Sully working at one latch, Dez took the other. It involved less work than Dez had expected, both locks snapping open easily.

He exchanged one more glance with Sully. Then he lifted the lid.

What initially appeared as a large, empty space greeted them. At first glance, it didn't seem big enough to hold Mr. Grin, but Dez supposed it would probably be plenty if the dummy was folded over. While Dez hadn't yet touched Mr. Grin, he expected its body and limbs—excepting the head, hands and feet—were made of some sort of cloth material and filled with light stuffing.

For not the first time, Dez wondered at this. How an inanimate object had been able to escape from seemingly impossible locations was beyond him. Unfortunately, the situation had become even worse now that Sully had learned the puppet was used to kill a man.

How the hell did they get these cases?

Dez didn't have much time to think about it, which was just as well. Sully was already digging through the despatch box, having discovered a variety of newspaper cuttings lining the bottom, dating from the early part of the twentieth century.

Sully removed one about Warren Malcolm and Mr. Grin entertaining troops in France. "If it weren't for what we're investigating, this would be pretty cool."

"Yeah, if it weren't for the fact Mr. Grin is more a sadistic, homicidal maniac than an entertainer, I'd agree with you."

Dez removed the rest of the papers from the base of the box and thumbed through them. More newspaper reports, a few programs from various performances and some publicity shots. Nothing overly useful as far as he could tell.

Sully seemed to think otherwise as he settled into the desk chair with the clippings, taking the cellphone flashlight with him.

"Maybe we could take this stuff with us, huh?" Dez asked. "I'd like to get out of here sooner rather than later."

Sully smirked. "Nervous?"

"Damn right, I'm nervous."

"I still need to help James cross over."

"So maybe you could do that now?"

Sully laughed, leaving Dez battling the desire to smack him. Sometimes Sully could be really annoying.

Dez distracted himself by returning his attention to the box. The base was thick—unusually thick, actually. While the interior was roomy enough, it seemed there should be another two or three inches of space at the bottom.

A probable reason popped into Dez's brain.

Hidden compartment.

He reached back inside, running his hands along the base and the edges. He felt the sides too, searching out a button or a switch—anything that might act as a release. Nothing.

He gave his attention to the exterior, checking first the sides, then lifting it enough to feel underneath. Still nothing.

"What are you doing?" Sully asked. Apparently, he'd found something to interest him besides newspaper articles.

"Searching for a catch."

Sully leaned forward so fast, the back legs of his chair lifted and dropped with a thud. "You think there's a false bottom?"

"Just a hunch." Dez plunked the upraised side of the box back onto the desk's surface with a huff. "Maybe I should go kung fu on this box too."

Sully put out a hand, grasping Dez's wrist. "Hang on a sec there, Jet Li. Let's check with James first."

Dez crossed his arms and waited while Sully did his psychic thing. Sully's gaze drifted from something to his side and up—James's face, Dez guessed—and back to the box. Then he stood, leaning over the box and shining the light inside. Another few seconds passed. When Sully reached in with one hand and pressed on a spot near the inner back of the box, approximately where wall met base, there came a scrape of wood. Whatever James had showed Sully had worked.

Sully pressed a little harder. More scraping and the front side of the base lifted toward them. Dez located a letter opener on the desktop, using the sharp end to lever the base upward. Despite wanting the hell out of this house, Dez's heart gave an excited thud as the cellphone beam revealed further papers within.

With the false bottom lifted off, Dez stared down at a variety of letters and photos.

Sully turned his head toward what, to Dez, was an empty spot next to him. "This is what you wanted us to see?" He paused, then nodded. "You feel like you're ready to go?"

Dez stalled in his search of the box's interior, watching Sully as he did what he did. Moments like this, Dez sometimes found he wished he could see what Sully did. Sure, he hated the idea of seeing ghosts, but he had to admit it would be cool to actually observe these moments when Sully was able to grant spirits this final, lasting peace—an escape from their painful, frightening world to a better one.

A smile played over Sully's lips, lighting his whole face as his eyes fixed on something in front of him. After a few moments passed, he turned his gaze back to Dez, making no attempt to conceal the sheen of tears in his eyes.

Dez found himself smiling. "He's gone?"

Sully met the grin and nodded. "Yeah. He's at peace."

"Does this mean Jill will be safe coming back here?"

Sully gave it a moment, ultimately shaking his head. "No. James was never the threat. He ended up becoming a victim of his own collection. There are things here. Dark things. I don't know for sure I can deal with all of it."

"You can't send them over like you've done with others?"

"Human ghosts are one thing. I know I can open a door to the light. But I think whatever's here … I don't know. It doesn't feel human, exactly."

Dez had a pretty good idea where Sully was heading. He didn't want to hear the word out loud, didn't even want to think it. Not until they were out of here, the house growing ever smaller in the rearview mirror.

For now, there was something they could deal with, and that was exploring the contents of the box in front of them.

"Let's leave all the other crappy stuff for now," Dez said. "I don't want to know."

Sully patted Dez's arm. "You don't say."

Dez gave in and smacked him. "Let's take this stuff and go."

Sully held up a hand, palm out, as a call for pause. "Hang on. Just thinking, what if it's connected to Warren Malcolm's murder? We might already be tampering with evidence. If we remove it besides, we could be in some trouble."

Dez frowned. "Sometimes, I want to strangle you." He sighed. "Okay, point taken. Let's figure out why James wanted us to see this stuff so we can get the hell out of here. And the faster the better."

"With you on that."

Dez and Sully worked side by side, pulling the items from the box to study them in better detail. The photos seemed the easiest, so they picked through those first. It didn't take long, given they located only three. One showed Warren standing next to a woman, the photo clearly not a professional job. A second was a portrait of an infant. And a third—also a candid shot—showed the same infant being held by Warren. None of the photos contained any identifying information written on the back.

"Who do you think this is?" Sully asked.

Dez shrugged. "No clue. Maybe the letters will tell us more. I mean, he was unmarried, right? And he wasn't known to be a ladies' man or a social butterfly."

But a read of the first letter started to suggest something very different.

"Huh," Dez said as he scanned the signature on the bottom. "Faye Lomax. Think she's the woman in the photo?"

Sully had already unfolded a second letter. His brows lowered as he squinted at it in the low light. "Yeah, I'd say so. She mentions a baby in here—Paulette."

Dez craned his neck to check out Sully's letter for himself. Having skimmed the bottom half, he tapped on one of the lines. "Look at this. 'Our little girl is an angel.'"

"Huh. So much for Warren being a total recluse. Paulette was their baby. They had a relationship."

Dez lifted the top margin of the paper, allowing him to better see the date Faye had written. "Sully, check this out. The date reads May third, nineteen seventeen. Approximately two months before Warren was killed."

Sully gripped the paper with both hands, his eyes going to the same spot. "Yeah, you're right. What do you think it means?"

Dez wasn't sure, but he was beginning to have some suspicions. "It was nineteen seventeen, Sull. People didn't just go around having babies outside of marriage. It was kind of a big deal."

Dez reached into the box and plucked out another letter while Sully took a different one. Dez checked the date first—July third, nineteen seventeen. Same month the break-in occurred. His gaze snapped to the first line.

Frank knows.

"Frank," Dez muttered aloud.

"What?" Sully asked.

Dez angled the letter toward Sully and pointed to the spot. "'Frank knows.' How much you want to bet Frank was her husband?"

Sully raised a brow. "I wouldn't play the odds against you." He looked up from the letter to meet Dez's eye. "These letters—if police had seen them at the time, they would have been seized as evidence, right?"

"I can't speak for police methods at the time, but I expect they would have. I mean, if Frank found out about the affair or learned he wasn't Paulette's biological father, he would have been some pissed. Quite possibly pissed off enough to commit murder. That would make these letters and photos compelling evidence, at least insofar as making Frank a major suspect."

"Since they're still here, it's unlikely police ever saw them," Sully said. "Which means Warren probably had them hidden at the time of his death, probably in the same place we just found them."

Dez rubbed at the back of his neck. Only a few letters in, and he was already getting a stiff neck. "How'd James figure out they were in there?"

Sully shrugged. "Beats me. Maybe he didn't. Not on his own, anyway. If Mr. Grin is possessed by Warren's ghost, maybe he showed James where they were. Or it could be he was digging through the house for anything Warren left behind. Seems the sort of thing a curious guy like James would do. Probably doesn't matter. And I can't ask him now, anyway."

"True enough." Dez took his phone back from Sully and placed a call to Lachlan.

Lachlan answered just before the call went to voicemail. "You find anything?"

Dez didn't get into the stuff about James's ghost, instead providing the barebones details of the despatch box find.

"Frank," Lachlan said once Dez had finished. "Given the time period and the apparent secrecy involved with the whole Malcolm-Faye relationship, we're probably safe in assuming this Frank was married to Faye."

"That's what we were thinking," Dez said. "I know you're not around the Malcolm file now, but I was wondering if you recall any mention of a Frank or Faye Lomax."

"Nope, which makes plenty of sense given the fact this evidence was apparently concealed all this time. Bloody hell, Braddock, we might just crack this case." The excitement in Lachlan's voice was impossible to miss.

Dez realized he'd need to break Lachlan's bubble. "The Malcolm homicide is about as cold a case as you're likely to get in the KRPD, but it's still an open police case. We're obligated to inform them about this."

Lachlan harrumphed. "You're a real spoilsport, you know that?"

"Better spoil your sport now than face an obstruction charge later."

"Good point. All right, here's what I want you to do. I'm in the middle of the most damned boring witness interviews ever with these staff members. I swear, one more person tells me about their hinky feelings regarding this dummy, I'm going to lose it. Anyway, you two grab some photos of the items in that box. Document everything you can. Then email everything to me and I'll get it printed out. After—and only after—get Sully to call Forbes Raynor. If we can get him in there to take charge of the investigation, great. Leastwise that way, we won't get shut out of this thing."

It was about as much compromise as their boss was likely to offer. "On it," Dez said. "Nothing else useful from staff there?"

"Nope, nothing, and I'd be shocked if there were. On this occasion, you two got the plum assignment. Don't ever tell me I don't do you any favours."

Dez rolled his eyes. He had a feeling Lachlan wasn't likely to let them forget it—ever. "I'll give you a call once we send the stuff and talk to Forbes. Quick question: Jill mentioned a home care aide who found Holmes. We had intended to get an interview, but with what we've turned up, it might not be necessary."

"Yeah, I'd rather focus on your current find before we lose control of it. Eyes on the prize."

They disconnected, leaving Dez to explain the plan to Sully. Once he'd been caught up, Sully nodded.

"Shouldn't take us long to photograph all of this," Sully said. "I can give Forbes a call right now, see if he can come out."

"They'll probably have to send an Ident unit," Dez told him. "They'll want to take photos of their own of the spot we found the box, and they'll be the ones taking charge of any evidence. Count on it, the KRPD will want this handled very carefully. It's likely to make international headlines, a story this unusual."

Sully grimaced. "Great. Just what I need. More headlines."

Dez gave him a sympathetic smile. "Sorry, buddy. I know. If it helps, we could try to skim over the ghost stuff."

A corner of Sully's mouth quirked up in a humourless half-smile. "So how are we going to explain the hole you kicked in the wall?"

Dez frowned. "Bad mood?"

Sully shook his head. "Yeah, that's you all over."

Sully's head tweaked to the side, his eyes flashing open at the same time. Dez didn't need to see whatever it was Sully had to feel his own nerves jump in response.

"What?" Dez demanded.

"Ssh."

"Don't shush me," Dez hissed.

"Ssh!"

And just like that, Dez was back where he so often found himself—part of him wishing to see what Sully did so he could better perceive the threat while the other part of him was grateful as hell for his psychic blindness. Ignorance could be bliss.

Except, just because you couldn't see a raging bull charging you didn't mean you weren't about to be gored.

Dez leaned in to whisper."Gonna need you to talk to me here, Sull."

"I saw something."

"I figured as much, thanks. I was hoping for something more specific."

"Thought you didn't want to know."

And there it was.

"Okay," Dez said. "Just don't say the d-word out loud."

"I don't know for sure it's a demon. I—"

Dez cut him off with a smack. "I said, don't say it out loud! Hell, just because you can't hear them doesn't mean they can't hear *you*."

"Thanks for the breakdown, Dez. I didn't know that."

Dez rolled his eyes. Not two seconds later, a pair of loud bangs sounded on the wall near the door to the hall.

The door that, thanks to the boards covering the windows, was their sole escape.

"Sully?"

Sully stared at the doorway another long moment. Then he spun back toward Dez. "Forget leaving these things in here. Put them back in the box. We need to take it and go."

Sully didn't scare easily. If he was seriously spooked, Dez figured he himself had good cause to be downright terrified. He picked up the letters and photos from the desk's surface and stuffed them back into the despatch box, not worrying at this point about bending or tearing anything. As far as he was concerned, given the choice between taking hell from Lachlan or the police over slight damage to evidence or sustaining damage himself from a demonic entity, Dez would take the former any day.

Dez handed his phone back to Sully and lifted the box. "Go. I'll be right behind."

Aiming the flashlight on their escape route, Sully dashed ahead, toward the doorway. Dez followed, staying as close to him as possible without risking tripping them up.

Dez made it to the opening to the grand staircase when a solid impact to his chest shoved him back. He fell hard, the despatch box whacking into the bottom of his chin as he landed on the floor.

His name on Sully's lips had him looking up. Sully was a silhouette against the still-open front door, his rigid posture suggesting he was as shocked as Dez. Sully moved, but whatever had nailed Dez moved faster.

He felt a grip on his ankle, hard and ice cold. One second, he was lying in the hall; the next, he was being hauled with impossible speed back into the study.

Sully's shout was the last thing Dez heard before the door slammed shut, sealing him inside.

16

SULLY DREW up short at the slammed door, eyes wide and heart racing.

The despatch box containing the letters and photos lay forgotten on the hallway floor, Sully's thoughts focused solely on his brother and whatever it was that had attacked him.

He allowed himself only a few seconds of shock. It was more than either of them could afford.

This wasn't an ordinary spirit. Not even close. It was like Pineview Prison all over again, like the entity in the death row cell, comprised of so many dark and troubled spirits.

Not a demon, not really. But damn close.

And it had Dez.

Sully rushed forward and grasped the doorknob. Though the knob twisted easily in his hand, the door refused to budge.

Sully slammed his palm against the wood. "Dez! Dez, can you hear me?"

"Sully!"

The terror in Dez's voice turned Sully's blood cold. He stopped pounding the door and put his shoulder then his boot to it instead.

Still, it refused to budge.

Panic seized at him with as much force as the dark entity used to dragged Dez inside the room. Sully tugged at his hair, inadvertently pulling strands loose from the tie at the base of his skull.

Stop.

The word sounded in his brain, his own voice, free of fear.

Calm down. You know what to do.

His head snapped up. Yeah, he did know what to do. But before he could control whatever this thing was, he'd need to get ahold of himself.

"Sully!"

"It's okay, Dez! I'm coming!"

He took a deep breath, centring himself, gathering his power. If it had come after him, that would have been one thing. Instead, it had gone after Dez.

It was about to regret its choice.

Sully reached out psychically, seeking out the energy inside the study, locating first its core and then its edges. It wasn't like a regular spirit—this one a churning mass of energies, a ghostly tornado glued together by rage and hate—but it was a spirit nonetheless. And spirits he could control.

He had to.

Having locked onto the entity, Sully stretched out his consciousness, closing his eyes to better focus. He sensed it the moment he grabbed hold of it, felt the surprise and the indignation as he hauled it backward in his psychic grip. For a moment, it was as if he could see through its eyes as it was dragged off Dez, leaving him curled on the floor, gasping for air.

Sully didn't allow himself to refocus on Dez. The entity required his full attention, and he gave it, forcing it back farther, through the door and back into the hall.

As he dragged it nearer, its indignation flipped to rage. This was a thing unused to being manhandled. Like the worst violent criminal, it had grown used to being the thing feared. Not this. Not being helpless to a single living man.

The entity's thoughts and emotions coursed through Sully. He let them, just as quickly letting them go. He continued to haul it backward until he felt sure another foot would bring it within his own aura. He could complete what he called a reverse possession—bringing with it a frightening and intoxicating level of power—but he knew better. He needed to send this thing packing. Only then would this house be safe.

He saw only shadow as the thing writhed in front of him, the same shadow he'd seen in the hall while he and Dez had been inside the study minutes ago. It had caught his attention then; now it commanded it.

Or it had—past tense. Dez, head bloodied, back bowed as he slumped from the now-open study door, snapped Sully's attention from the entity.

It proved a costly mistake. One quick yet brutal impact and Sully's feet left the ground. He was flung backward, a rag doll for the spirit to discard. He hit something and felt it give way within the same moment, the force of it both shocking and painful. Another fraction of a second, and Sully hit something else equally hard. This time, the barrier—a wall, he suspected —held.

He slid down the wood panel, sagging against it, backside coming to rest partially on what felt like a stair. His eyes had instinctively sealed shut while he flew through the air, and now he forced them open. The shattered wood of the stairway's railing was the first thing he saw. Beyond that, the shape of Dez below, poker straight with tension, mouth and eyes wide with shock.

Sully shoved away from the wall, intending to push himself

to his feet. A shadow flitting past gave him something else with which to occupy himself.

"Sully, no!" Dez shouted. "Leave it! We need to get out of here, right now!"

The words came out strained with movement and from changing direction, telling Sully Dez was running toward him. Sully didn't look, too busy visually seeking out the shadow spirit. He couldn't make it out, not now. Didn't mean it wouldn't be back.

A few seconds passed. Then Dez's hands were on him, heaving him to his feet.

"Come on," Dez said, voice tight. "Move it. Now!"

Dez continued to tug until Sully gave in and moved with him.

"The box," Sully reminded him as they reached the base of the stairs. He started to pull to the side, toward where he'd last seen the despatch box.

Dez's fingers wrapping tight around his upper arm formed an unbreakable barrier. "Don't. I've got it. Move!"

Sully moved.

Another couple of seconds put them outside.

Sully reached inside long enough to locate the doorknob and pull, slamming it behind them. Now free of the house, Sully felt normal return. Here on the front step, layers of wood, glass and brick created a fortress, sealing the bad stuff inside.

Dez, despatch box held in shaking hands, had gone one better, taking himself not only away from the door but right off the front steps. "Sully, come on. Vehicle. Now."

Blood eked from a cut near Dez's hairline, and he had returned to a hunched position as if guarding a yet-unseen injury. The desire to confront and send the entity on its way took a backseat in Sully's brain, concern for Dez now at the forefront.

Sully came off the front steps, trailing behind Dez until they reached the SUV. Dez opened the rear door and placed the despatch box on the seat. By the time he slammed the door, Sully was at his side.

"You okay?"

Dez batted away Sully's hand as he moved to touch at his head. "I'm fine. How about you?"

Sully tried again, reaching for the gash in Dez's forehead. "Looks like it hurts."

"It doesn't tickle."

"You hurt anywhere else?"

"Just my ego," Dez growled. As if to prove his point, he straightened a little. "Took what felt like a couple of kicks to the gut. Drove the wind out of me and hurt like a bitch, but it feels better already. What about you? You took out the railing like it was made of toothpicks. Probably dented the wall besides."

Sully mentally scanned himself for injuries. "Might need someone to pull out a few slivers; otherwise I think I'm okay."

Dez turned him and lifted his jacket and shirt at the back. Sully felt first one sharp twinge in the middle of his back, then a second lower down.

"Yep, a few bits of wood in here. Good you were wearing a couple layers of clothing, or you'd have made a pretty effective pincushion."

Sully waited until Dez had yanked out the splinters he could get to before sliding his clothing back in place. Situated, he moved for the driver's side of the SUV, holding his hand out, palm up, for the keys.

"What are you doing?" Dez asked.

"Driving."

"Hell you are."

"You've got a head injury. Keys."

Dez grumbled out an indecipherable complaint but did as

told before circling the vehicle and sliding into the front passenger-side seat.

Sully dropped in behind the wheel. He'd just started the vehicle when Dez interrupted with, "What the hell was that thing?"

"You didn't want to know, remember?

"Shut up. What was it?"

"Not a demon, if it helps any. I'd say it's a conglomeration of everything James Holmes collected over the years. Basically, all that dark energy kind of found each other and got combined into one big, bad entity. It's what gives it the kind of power it has."

Dez glanced back at the house, then to the steering wheel and Sully. "Can you explain and drive at the same time, maybe? The sooner we're away from this place, the better."

Sully complied. In all honesty, he felt pretty much the same.

"Are you saying it's like the thing we tangled with at Pineview Prison a while back?" Dez asked.

Sully nodded. "Yeah. Same sort of deal."

Dez grimaced. "Damn. That thing was a bitch to handle. Think we'll need to get Jack, Dad and Aiden involved?"

Flynn and Aiden Braddock, both the victims of homicide but keen upholders of all things justice-related, had found new life after death as reapers. "Tracker" Jack Winter—a murdered lawman from back when Kimotan Rapids and its surrounding communities were nothing more than frontier towns—was, for all intents and purposes, their boss. Sully and Dez had called on them a number of times in the past, usually when they were involved in a case involving major evil. They made for some awesome backup. Plus, they could deal with demonic entities, sending them over to the other side where Sully couldn't reach.

The fact Sully's abilities didn't extend to being able to open portals to hell struck him as a welcome limitation.

While backup was never a bad thing, Sully didn't want to go there. Not yet.

"I'll give it one more try." Catching Dez's expression, he added, "When we're back up to par. Now that I know what we're dealing with, I think I can handle it."

"You think? Sorry, Sull. I'm not letting you go back in there unless you can change your 'I think' into 'I know.'"

"Okay, I *know* I can handle it." At the closed gate, Sully eyed Dez. "I don't want to go running to Dad, Aiden and Jack every time the going gets tough. They've got enough on their plate. The only reason it got the better of me this time was because I let myself get distracted. It won't happen again."

"You really think this is the moment to prove yourself?" Dez shook his head with a bleak smile. "You're not fourteen anymore. This isn't about showing you can stand on your own two feet."

What Dez had said should have been true—true enough Sully had to stop to consider it while Dez got out to open the gate. By the time Sully had driven through and Dez had gotten back in, gate closed and locked behind them, Sully had figured out why it was so important he do this himself.

"I want to move in with Sarah," he said. "With what we do—you and me—sometimes, I end up bringing negative energy—bad ghosts—home with me. If I can't handle things like this, I can't risk exposing her to them. You see what I'm saying?"

Dez pressed his lips together. Another truth had dawned, one Dez was no happier about acknowledging. "It's not fair for you to go without the things that make life worth living."

"If you knew the things you'd be dealing with might tail you home, wouldn't you have thought twice before marrying Eva and having Kayleigh? Wouldn't you have thought about it before bringing them into your world? I need to know I can handle this, Dez. Not just for me and you and our family, but for

Sarah. I love her. If anything happened to her because I failed to protect her, I wouldn't be able to live with it."

Sully watched the thoughts play out across Dez's face. He wasn't happy about this, any of it. Sully knew it because he knew his brother better than almost anyone. Dez wanted the best for him, which included the same sort of happy family life Dez had forged for himself.

But Sully wasn't Dez. While they lived and worked in the same world, Sully's world included elements Dez's didn't. Not fully, anyway. Sully's gift meant he attracted the spirit world like moths to a flame. Most of the time, those moths were harmless—dead people in need of help. But sometimes, those moths brought flames of their own, and Sully knew far too well how easily he could get burned.

He'd die before he let Sarah burn alongside him.

"I get what you're saying," Dez said. "But it's not all your responsibility. You can't stop every bad thing, Sull."

"If that's true, I can't be with Sarah."

Dez heaved a sigh and faced the windshield. For a long moment, he didn't speak. "Okay. If you need to do this, we'll do this. But you're not tackling it alone. You've got people you need to protect, but so do I. Tell me when, and I'll come with you."

There were moments in life when words were nowhere near good enough. Sucking back emotion, Sully reached out an arm and gently grasped a handful of Dez's jacket, giving his ribcage an affectionate knuckle-rub before releasing him.

"Thank you," Sully said. The words came out deeper than normal, choked with emotion.

Dez gave him an answering pat. "Don't mention it."

Sully shot him a smile. Then he put the SUV into gear and turned onto the main road, heading back toward the city.

17

By the time Sully arrived back at his own vehicle parked outside Dez and Eva's house, he'd had plenty of time to think. And as sometimes happened, too much thinking brought with it too many dark thoughts.

Dez was about to climb out when he paused, passenger-side door partially open. "You okay?"

This time, it was clear he wasn't asking after the state of Sully's physical health.

"Yeah," Sully said. He'd never been good at lying to Dez, and this proved no exception.

"Sull—"

"I'll be okay."

Dez closed his door, the movement a precursor to further conversation Sully wasn't sure he was up to participating in. "Why don't you go to Sarah's this evening?" Dez suggested. "I think you should talk to her."

Sully was way ahead of Dez on this one. "Because I know what she'll say. She'll tell me I'm being paranoid. But you know I'm not. Hell, after what just happened, you know damn well I'm not."

Dez frowned, positioning himself so he was more fully facing Sully. "You remember a few years back, when we first started getting heavy into investigating the ghost-related stuff? Remember what I was like—how overprotective I was of you?"

Sully chuckled dryly. "You say that like you're not now."

"Come on. I'm nowhere near as bad."

"Okay, yeah. You've gotten better. What's your point?"

Dez crossed his arms—as well as a man with tree trunks for arms could cross them in a confined space. "Point is, I realized you were a grown man capable of taking care of himself. And I came to that realization because I forced myself to take a step back and let you out from under me. It wasn't easy. Hell, still isn't sometimes. My instinct is always going to be to protect the people I love. But you've also got to have some faith in those people, Sully. I mean, you worry about *me*. I know you do. But you don't shut me out of stuff because of it. Not now, anyway. Why?"

There were moments when Dez—largely a big, warm, emotional, protective goofball—truly impressed Sully with his brand of unexpected wisdom.

"You sound like Dad," Sully told him.

Dez raised a brow. "I'll take that as a compliment."

Sully smiled. "You should."

Dez beamed back at him before returning to his earlier point. "You didn't answer my question."

"I know. You asked why I don't shut you out when things get dangerous. It's because I trust you. More than that, I rely on you."

"Essentially what every solid partnership is based on. I worry about Eva all the time—admittedly less so now that she's not working patrol anymore, but still, you get my point. Thing is, I know she's a strong, independent, intelligent woman who's fully capable of taking care of herself. Hell, she's probably better at looking after herself than I am."

Sully smirked. "And she could kick your ass."

Dez mirrored Sully's expression. "And she could kick my ass. Listen, I know the risks you're talking about are different from the sort of stuff most people are exposed to, but my point remains the same. If you want things to work out between you and Sarah, you need to stop thinking of her as someone you need to endlessly protect and start thinking of her as your partner. You can and should protect your partner, but you also know they're there to protect you. Same way you and I work."

Sully tilted his head and quirked a brow. "Uh, not quite the same thing, Dez."

Dez chuckled. "I take your point." His gaze travelled to the backseat, to the despatch box lying there. "Tell you what. Why don't you take the box tonight, go through it with her? She's a smart cookie. Might be she can help you work through things."

Sully laughed. "Sounds to me like you want the evening off."

Dez uncrossed his arms and shrugged. "Hey, if the opportunity's there, why not? I'd love some family time if we can swing it."

"We can swing it." Sully grinned. "You're a good brother, you know that?"

"Damn straight, and don't you forget it."

Dez started to open the door again but paused to flip the visor down and prod at his forehead. "Maybe I should clean this up a bit before I see Kayleigh."

"Good plan. Think you can sneak past her?"

Dez pressed his lips together before shaking his head. "Forget it. My kid's seen me in far worse states than this. Speaking of tough women, my little girl's turning into one."

"And she could also kick your ass."

Dez laughed and got out of the SUV.

Sully called Sarah via Bluetooth while en route toward the downtown core. As her voice came through his vehicle's speaker system—"Sarah Leffler, KR Tribune newsroom"—he couldn't help but smile.

Damn, he thought to himself, I have it bad.

Bad, of course, being good in this instance. "Hey."

"Hey, you," she said. "Whatcha up to?"

"Was going to ask you the same thing. Have some time to meet up this evening over at your place?"

"Well, I was going to wash my hair …"

Sully waited for the laugh and grinned once he heard it.

"Of course, you can come over. What time?"

"Now too soon?"

"I'm still at work. Got stuck with a little OT. Late interview." Her tone was the sound of an eye roll. Sarah was a reporter for the city's main newspaper, and overtime was an all-too-frequent part of the job.

"No problem," Sully said. "Let me know when you're done and I'll meet you."

"Better idea. Why don't you swing by my office? I love showing off my gorgeous boyfriend." She laughed.

Heat rose on Sully's cheeks, and he was relieved no one was there to see. Especially Dez. "I'll be there in a few minutes. Is there somewhere I can do a little work while I wait? I've got some stuff to read through related to a case we're working."

"Sure thing, love. I'll set you up in the library. Unless you want to sit with me and watch me work."

While Sully loved the idea of sitting with her and watching her work, he knew damn well he'd get nothing done if he went that route.

Downtown, Sully parked at a meter as close as he could get

to the large building housing the paper's offices. Days were growing longer as winter came to an end, but the height of the glass and steel towers surrounding him meant the sun disappeared much sooner in this part of the city. The street leading to the Tribune felt cold and dim as a result, and Sully found his mind travelling back to James Holmes's house and the shadowy rooms and halls containing such evil.

He wished he'd kept his thoughts in check when he discovered Sarah waiting for him in the lobby. Immediately, her face fell.

"What's wrong?" she asked.

Burdened by the despatch box, he met Sarah with a one-armed hug and a quick kiss. "Nothing anymore. How's your day been?"

"Long and annoying. How about you?"

"Don't ask," he said.

"What's in the box?" she asked. She'd asked it in a funny voice, and Sully suspected she was referencing a movie. He felt like an idiot asking which one so kept the question to himself while honouring her attempted joke with a laugh.

"Long story," he said. "I'll tell you all about it later if you want."

She grinned.

He walked beside her as she returned to the newsroom, his lips turning up into a natural smile as she prattled on about what she'd done throughout the day. As she talked, he felt his blood pressure ease and some of the weight lift from his shoulders.

This is what Dez was talking about, he thought.

As they entered the newsroom, Sully gave a wave to the day's remaining reporters, trying to ignore the obvious grins on the faces of a couple of the women. Once he and Sarah were safely inside the library, she laughed.

"Oh my God, you're like the world's sexiest man around

here," she said. She gave his butt a squeeze. "And you're all mine."

Sully quirked his lips and leaned in for a kiss.

Sarah pulled back a moment later, motioning to a long table and a set of chairs. "This work for you?"

He nodded. "Perfect. Thanks."

She left him to it. Sully pulled out one of the chairs and sat, tugging it in with a scrape against the scuffed and cracked tile floor. Plenty of buildings in the downtown core were new, but some—such as this one—had been here quite a while. Buildings this old had stories. Probably had a ghost or two besides.

Difference was, the ghosts in the Tribune offices wouldn't likely try to kill anyone.

Sully buckled down, turning his attention to doing what Lachlan had asked him to do—photographing and documenting everything in the box. Lachlan was probably right: given the nature of the case, the police would be very eager to get their hands on the box as soon as they learned about it.

Admittedly, he wasn't eager to tuck back into its contents. As he'd observed numerous times in the past, any object could be latched onto by spirits, and there was plenty of reason something might have connected itself to this box or its contents. Of course, following recent events, Sully's anxiety regarding this case was running high, making it difficult to know whether what he felt about the item in front of him was coming from the spirit world or himself.

He took a breath and another, then focused as he once again placed his hands on the box. No visions or weird sensations. Good. Last thing he wanted was to end up on the floor with Sarah's colleagues around to see.

Deciding the box wasn't overly problematic in and of itself, Sully flipped it open and removed the contents previously contained within the hidden compartment. He laid the photos out first, placing them where he could see them. Using his cellphone, he photographed each separately, emailing those to Lachlan when finished. He did the same with each of the letters in turn, photographing both sides of the envelope as well as the contents of each. He didn't bother reading them yet, focusing first on this part of the task. Each letter and its corresponding envelope got its own email, ensuring they'd be easier to sort through later. Only once he finished his emails to Lachlan did he begin reading the contents of the letters themselves.

Frank knows.

The letter—one of the last, he noted upon scanning postmarks—jumped out at him right away.

Sully's phone pinged with an incoming text from Lachlan.

Got tit.

Sully smirked. Lachlan.

Dots indicated he was trying again. Then, *Go tit.*

At least Lachlan was trying to text.

Sully sent back a thumbs-up emoticon and went back to his work, deciding to leave the later stuff and start at the beginning. Better to try to get some perspective as to the path the relationship had taken.

He had two years' worth of letters to go through, although he noted they were few and far between in spots. The reason became apparent the more Sully read.

He glanced up at the sound of someone approaching and smiled a greeting at Sarah.

"How's it going?" she asked as she slid into the open chair next to him.

"Okay. Just reading through these now. How about you?"

"Filed my story. I can leave anytime." Her gaze moved over the collection of papers atop the table. "Although I'm thinking it might make more sense to finish this here. Looks like you're right in the middle of it."

Sully smiled apologetically. "I am, I guess. Is that okay?"

"We can stay as long as you need. Want a hand?"

"Love one." He started by filling her in on what he, Dez and Lachlan were working on. One of the great things about Sarah was how well she did with Sully's brand of weird. She didn't balk, laugh or attempt to offer up any well-meant but incorrect alternative explanations. She simply listened, chin propped on a hand, as he took her through what they'd learned so far and what their working theories were.

When he came to the part about the attack on him and Dez at the Holmes estate, her eyes widened and her mouth dropped open, but she didn't freak out or demand Sully find another line of work.

"That must have been so scary," she said. "Are you guys okay?"

"Fine," he said. "Although I might need you to do what Dez started and pull a few more slivers out of my back. It still feels like there's some stuff poking around in there."

"Does this sort of thing happen a lot?"

Sully shrugged. "More often than either of us would like. Part of the job, I guess."

She nodded as she frowned. "Okay."

He wanted to pursue it, to find out what she was thinking, but he wasn't certain what question to ask.

She solved the problem for him. "What you and Dez do, it's a pretty big deal. I can't think of anyone else who does what you do."

"I guess that's true. I haven't met anyone else who communicates directly with homicide victims. Doesn't always make it easy though—not for me and not for the people I care about."

She laid warm fingers over his. "No, it's not easy, and I'm sure as hell going to worry whenever you're on one of these jobs.

But I'm also really proud of you. What you do, bringing people peace the way you do, it's pretty incredible."

He couldn't think of anything to say in response. No combination of words seemed good enough to explain how much her support meant to him. He held her eye as he turned his hand, catching her fingers in his and rubbing her knuckles with a thumb. If he couldn't tell her, hopefully he could show her.

Her answering smile and soft gaze told him he'd managed it.

She ended the contact first, using her free hand to pat his. A raised brow and an inhale told him a question was coming. "This shadow thing that went after you—it sounds pretty powerful."

"It was. Is."

"Powerful enough to control the ventriloquist's dummy? I mean, could it be it's not the dummy at all doing this stuff but this spirit you encountered?"

Sully considered this. "The shadow entity struck me as being grounded within the house. If it's connected to the stuff James collected, it's unlikely it can just up and leave."

"Except it might also be connected to Mr. Grin. The way the dummy tripped this Holmes guy on the stairs, it makes me think it was tapping into some strong mojo. I mean, it seems to be possessed by energy all its own, but maybe this shadow entity acted like a supercharged battery or something—if that makes any sense."

Sully pinched at his lower lip as he considered Sarah's theory. "It does, actually. Thing is, though, it's still managing to move around on its own even though it's not actually inside the house."

"Didn't you tell me once spirits can move between locations? I know some are kind of trapped in places, but you said others can travel around."

"They can."

"So why couldn't the one possessing Mr. Grin? Maybe it hides inside the dummy when it's at the museum, but it travels between the museum and the house otherwise. Could it be it gets charged up doing that? Like recharging an electrical device?"

Sully hadn't thought about the possibility. Most spirits he encountered were kind of solitary, locked within their own torment and memories, not often interacting with other spirits or even living people. Entities like the one at the Holmes estate or Pineview Prison were an exception. Admittedly, Sully didn't understand much about them. As such, he couldn't deny Sarah might be correct.

"I guess Dez was right again," Sully said.

"About what?"

"You. He said you might have a theory or two of your own. What you're saying makes sense. Thing is, if you're right—if this spirit has found a way to boost its power—we might have a problem."

Sarah frowned. "Which is?"

"If the spirit haunting Mr. Grin decides to attack anyone else, it's fully capable of getting the job done—and it can do it anywhere and anytime it wants."

18

Not a whole lot else came out of the letters, which Sully passed along to Lachlan when he called him shortly after.

"We know Malcolm was having an affair with a married woman," Lachlan said. "And we know the hubby, Frank, appears to have found out shortly before the homicide."

Sully leaned back in the chair inside the newsroom library. "We know one other thing. A few of the letters mention Frank was a member of the Army and was fighting overseas when the affair was going on. The stuff he must have seen and experienced over there might have left him with some significant trauma. Bad enough dealing with that, but to arrive home and find out your wife was involved with someone else while you've been serving your country—that must have stung."

"Had the letter in question been sent right at the same time or after the break-in, I'd feel better about the theory. Most people, when they learn something like that, they're going to act on it right away if they're going to act on it at all. They don't sit and stew for a couple of weeks and then suddenly explode in a fit of anger."

"Unless he had PTSD. Might make it more possible he'd have blown up later on."

Lachlan made a humming noise. "Maybe. I won't rule it out. Not until we know more about it. We'll need to do some digging into Frank and Faye, see what we can find out. Check obits, find out if they've got any descendants who are still alive and willing to talk."

"Already on it," Sully said. "Sarah's at her desk, running some newspaper archive searches for me."

"Oh." Lachlan's tone read amusement. "You're putting your lovely lady to work for us now, are you?"

"She's helping out," Sully said. "She finds the whole thing pretty interesting."

"Long as she doesn't get any ideas about putting it in the paper."

Sully rolled his eyes. "She's not like that. I mean, I'm sure she'd appreciate an exclusive at the end of all of this, but she won't jump the gun."

"You know her best."

Sully stared up at the ceiling, studying the tiles and searching for patience to deal with Lachlan's cynicism. "Yeah, I do."

"Okay," Lachlan said. "But I'd rather she not go along on interviews."

"Won't be happening. Relax. She's checking some names for me. After that, I'll call Forbes."

Lachlan grunted. "Ugh. Raynor. Right, I'd forgotten."

"No choice, Lachlan. We've probably left it too long already. He's going to be pissed."

"I know, and I don't care. Whatever you do, don't let him talk you out of continuing this investigation. We don't have to quit what we're doing; we're just not allowed to hinder what they're doing."

"I get it, thanks." There were still plenty of times Lachlan seemed to forget Sully had been at this longer than five minutes. While he usually rolled with the punches, sometimes his patience for Lachlan's know-it-all ways wore a little thin.

"Won't surprise you to learn none of the employees at the museum had anything useful for us," Lachlan said.

"I gathered as much after we spoke earlier today. How's Evelyn taking it?"

"Not well. Seemed pretty antsy about the whole thing when I left. For what it's worth, she isn't talking about getting a second opinion from a separate PI firm though I don't think she's overly happy with our results so far either. She was hoping we'd find a rational explanation."

Sully rubbed at his temples. Too much on the go today meant he'd developed a slight headache, the sort which would worsen if he didn't get his hands on some painkillers soon. "Ghosts are a rational explanation. Just because some people don't believe in them doesn't mean they don't exist as a perfectly accurate reason for things happening."

"Hey, you don't need to convince me. You converted me quite some time ago. And for what it's worth, I think Ms. Harlow is coming around too. We've been thorough, and we've poked holes in her initial theories. What's left, as improbable as it might seem to her, has to be the truth."

Sully paused in massaging his forehead to smirk. "Sherlock Holmes said something like that, didn't he?"

"And you don't mess with Sherlock. Once you get those names, see if you can line up whatever interviews you think will be helpful to us. With the passage of time, it might be a long shot, but you never know. More than one person has been known to make deathbed confessions."

"On it," Sully said. "I'll keep you posted."

He disconnected with Lachlan a moment later, then dialled Forbes's number. Forbes didn't answer, so Sully left a vague message on his cellphone's voicemail, asking for a callback. Sully thought he should check on Sarah's progress, but the library was blissfully dim, free of the fluorescent lights crisscrossing the newsroom ceiling. He was giving the bridge of his nose a rub when Forbes returned his call.

"Right in the middle of about twelve things," Forbes grumbled. "This better be good."

"Would you count fresh evidence in a century-old cold case good?"

"Depends on the cold case." Judging by the slight rise in Forbes's tone, there wasn't much "depends" about it. Forbes had known Sully long enough to realize information he brought forward tended to be solid. That, and the kind of info police wouldn't likely get anywhere else thanks to the sources involved.

Sully fed out a little more line, anyway. "How about the murder of Warren Malcolm?"

"Refresh my memory."

"The ventriloquist who died following a home invasion in nineteen seventeen? Mr. Grin?"

"The dummy they found in the old railway station? You serious? You got it cracked?"

"Not cracked, not yet. But we've found some info you'll want to check out." Sully gave Forbes a rundown of what they'd found and how, adding that he had it with him now. "You interested?"

"Damn right, I'm interested. Putting a case like that to bed would make international headlines. Where are you? How soon can you come in?"

"I'd rather stay at arm's length if possible. We're planning on working the case from our end."

"I'd rather you didn't."

"I know, but we're still doing it. There are things I can do and people I can communicate with you can't."

Forbes groaned. "You really know how to make my life a misery, don't you, kid? All right, listen, I really am in the middle of a bunch of stuff right now, but first thing tomorrow, we need to arrange to meet. And you need to hand over everything you have to me, savvy?"

"Got it. First thing."

They disconnected and Sully stuffed the letters and photos back into the despatch box. He tucked it under his arm and headed back into the newsroom to check on Sarah's progress.

She was, by now, one of only two reporters left. Across the room, a couple of editors were busy giving the day's copy one final read and laying out the pages headed to the presses. One television had been left on above their heads, with the audio down to near-mute, meaning Sully and Sarah would need to keep their conversation quiet if they wanted to avoid anything being overheard.

Sully pulled up the wheelie chair belonging to Sarah's absent desk mate. "How's it going?"

"Pretty well," she said. She ripped a piece of paper from her notebook and presented it to Sully. "I found an obit for Warren Malcolm as well as a write-up on his death in which the reporter interviewed his brother, Lawrence. Between the two, I managed to find enough info to piece together a bit of a family tree. After that, I was able to locate some likely addresses and phone numbers for Lawrence Malcolm's descendants. I printed off everything I mentioned to you, but I jotted down the phone numbers and addresses on this paper to make it easier for you."

"How about Frank and Faye?"

"That too." Sarah paused, tearing off a second sheet of paper. This one, she placed on the desk next to Sully, slapping the flat of her hand atop it before he could take it. "This is weird, though. You mentioned something about a baby named Paulette, right?"

"Yeah. The letters suggest she was Warren's child, born while Frank was serving overseas."

"Right. Well, here's the thing. There's no mention of a Paulette anywhere—not in any of the obits I found. Not for Faye, not for Warren, not for Frank, not for their other three kids. It's like she dropped off the face of the earth."

Sully frowned. This was unexpected. "Huh." A new possibility popped into his head, one so horrible, he didn't want to voice it aloud. He did anyway. "God, if Frank was the one who assaulted Warren, what if he did the same to Paulette? She was the offspring of an affair. Maybe he hurt her too."

Sarah grimaced. "That would be horrible, but I think you should consider another possibility. Maybe they simply put Paulette up for adoption. Or changed her name. Paulette could have been a Malcolm family name, and Frank wanted something else to make him think of her more as his. According to their obits, the other kids were older or younger than Paulette would be though I wouldn't rule out the possibility Frank and Faye hid the actual birthdate and substituted one that fit better with Frank's return from the war. The youngest daughter was said to have been born in nineteen eighteen. Frank returned in 'seventeen apparently, so a nineteen eighteen birthdate might work in that scenario."

Sully grinned. "Want a new job?"

Sarah laughed. "I don't know. I'm still kind of partial to my current one. Just promise me we can get an exclusive at the end of this."

"You bet." Sully scanned the information on the paper, then took the printed stories and obits Sarah had located. He'd snap photos later and send them to Lachlan and Dez.

For now, all he wanted was to head home. Or, to be more

accurate, what he hoped would be his future home if he could lay his reservations to rest.

"Got room for me tonight?" he asked.

Her smile made him tingle. "Damn right," she said.

Sully had just picked up the despatch box when his cellphone rang. He expected Lachlan. What he got was Dez.

"What's up?" he asked.

"Nothing good." Dez's tone, a combination of disgusted and anxious, backed up the words. "I had a call from Evelyn. She got home and found something pretty disturbing."

Sully held back a groan. There went his relaxing evening. Dez's too, no doubt. "Do I want to hear this?"

"Nope," Dez said. "She walked into her kitchen to start supper. Mr. Grin was sitting on the counter."

19

THE PHONE CONVERSATION with Evelyn made Dez shudder whenever he thought about it. Her voice—cracking with barely suppressed terror—had done nothing to quell his own mounting dread.

He'd set out as soon as they disconnected, Evelyn begging him and Sully to come and take the dummy. In the meantime, she told him she'd be locked inside her car in the driveway, waiting and chain-smoking cigarettes.

She'd spoken in a nervous babble, sounding nothing like the poised and confident woman Dez had gotten to know. It made him even more anxious about the job. He was still nursing a headache from the ghostly attack at the Holmes estate. Now, he and Sully would have to safely remove a possessed and homicidal puppet.

Good God, he thought for not the first time. How had his life come to this? In his policing days, danger meant attending alcohol-fuelled domestic disputes or calls involving suspects discharging firearms. Never did he picture job hazards including wrangling a murderous ventriloquist dummy.

Sully called as Dez was en route to Evelyn's house in the

north end of the city. He answered via Bluetooth using his vehicle's speaker system.

"Where are you?" Dez asked.

"On my way. What else did she tell you?"

"Nothing helpful. She was too freaked out. I couldn't make much sense of it, frankly."

"Okay. We'll talk to her when we're both there. Don't go inside until I get there."

Dez gave a dry laugh. "No problem here."

Operating on a bit of a head start, Dez reached Evelyn's home first and pulled into the empty spot in her driveway. He glanced to the side and ducked his head, meeting her eye through the car window. She gave a shaky smile, one suggesting she was trying for brave but was coming up short. He met it with a smile of his own, going for both kind and confident. He wasn't certain he managed to convey the latter with any conviction.

He shut off his SUV, pocketed his keyring and stepped out. Only once he turned toward Evelyn's car did he hear her locks click open. He pulled open the front passenger-side door and folded himself into the small space. The moment he was inside, the locks snapped back into place, sealing them inside.

"How you doing?" he asked.

Her laugh sounded both a little high-pitched and wild. "Oh, you know   not so good." Her eyes grew shiny with tears, but she sucked them back with a noisy, deep breath. "This can't be happening. This seriously can't be happening."

"I know it's a lot to take in," he said.

"Mr. Fields was out today to interview staff. They all made it clear to him they weren't involved in any of this. I've been trying to get my head around it, but I just … How do you do it? How do you make sense of it?"

Dez shrugged. "Honestly? Sometimes you can't. If it was just me investigating these things, I'd probably do the same as you. I'd search for explanations, something logical based on the world I can see and hear and feel with my own senses. But I've got Sully. If he comes up with something else, I know to take it as gospel. I trust him. I've had to accept this stuff only makes sense if I believe in a world I can't fully experience myself."

Her gaze had been fixed on her garage door through the windshield. Finally, she faced to Dez. "Can he fix this? Can he stop whatever's happening?"

To this question, at least, Dez had a solid answer. "He won't quit until he does. Neither of us will."

Evelyn nodded. This time, when she smiled, it didn't waver.

"Will you wait here with me until Sully arrives?"

"Of course." Dez considered leaving it there; ordinarily clients didn't want to know the PI they'd hired was afraid. But he had a feeling in Evelyn's case, she could do with knowing she wasn't alone in her fear. He offered her a smile and a raised brow before responding. "No way in hell I'm stepping foot in there alone with that thing."

The comment did the trick. A real laugh burst from her, and her posture relaxed.

He followed up by changing the subject. For most people, family was an easier topic than the paranormal, so he tried leading Evelyn in that direction. She'd gone as far as to tell him her family had been in the area for several generations, although she admittedly didn't know much about her father's side. It was as far as they got before Sully's vehicle pulled up on the street, but the conversation had the desired effect. Evelyn seemed much calmer now. She'd even seemed cheery as she chatted about her family situation.

Dez's own family situation was now walking up the drive, so he climbed out of the car to greet Sully.

Sully tweaked his head toward the car, a silent question as to

Evelyn's current state. Dez replied with a nod and a thumbs up, and Sully's attention cut to the front of the house.

"Guess we should go in," he said.

Dez wasn't so keen on the reluctance in Sully's tone. "You don't sound excited."

"Uh, no, can't say I am. Are you?"

"Shut up, Sully."

Sully led the way to the front door, giving Evelyn a wave through the car window as he walked past. Dez caught his arm before Sully could grab the doorknob.

"Hang on. So we remove this dummy. Then what? We take it back to the museum? It'll just leave. It already did. Somehow or other, it managed to materialize here."

"I thought of that," Sully said. "I called Lachlan en route and asked him to check into something for me. I couldn't figure out how Mr. Grin has managed to get out of every box that's held him—except one."

"The train station," Dez said. "You're right. How didn't he get out of there all those years?"

"It wasn't just a regular trunk. It was lined with iron. I've heard this before, that ghosts can't cross iron. I don't get why, except maybe it's too hard and dense. I guess it doesn't really matter why; what matters is it worked."

Dez squinted at him. "Hang on. What about Pineview Prison —all those ghosts wandering outside their cells? How'd they get past the iron bars?"

"Plenty of space between the bars; no gaps in the trunk holding Mr. Grin. Anyway, only the cell doors had iron bars. The walls were concrete or stone. Far as I know, those aren't an issue for ghosts. Anyway, back to Mr. Grin—I think whatever's haunting him either couldn't get to him while he was locked inside that trunk—"

Dez completed the thought. "Or the ghost was trapped inside

with the dummy. God, if that's what happened, no wonder it's so miserable. Hell, if it's pissed off about being trapped inside for all this time, it might explain why it killed its last owner and why it's going around terrorizing people at the museum. It wants revenge."

"The ghost does, you mean, not the dummy." Sully pinched at the bridge of his nose.

"Headache?" Dez asked.

"Yeah."

"I know the feeling."

Meeting Dez's eye, Sully said, "Right, yeah. How you doing? You okay to head inside?"

Dez clenched his jaw. "Let's get it over with. Maybe we can find an iron box somewhere. Doubt the police will hand over the original trunk."

Sully patted the pocket of his coat. Dez heard something metallic rattle in response. "Iron chain," Sully said. "Best I could come up with on short notice. Hopefully, we can find something better later on, but this might hold the dummy for now, at least."

"Might," Dez repeated. "I hate that word."

"Me too, but right now, it's the best we've got."

Hand on the knob, Sully gave Dez one more look, then opened the door.

Sully heaved a breath and led the way inside.

20

By the time Sully arrived in the kitchen, Dez hard on his heels, the dummy was no longer on the counter.

"Maybe it went back to the museum." Dez's voice was a whisper in Sully's ear, his face near enough for his breath to tickle. "How the hell's that work, anyway?"

"Teleportation, I guess." Sully had kept his own voice low, although he suspected the ghost already knew they were here, whether or not they were quiet. He could feel the crawling sensation he got when near a spirit—particularly those of darker dispositions.

This one was nothing if not dark.

"Teleportation works for physical objects?" Dez asked. "I thought only ghosts could do that."

Sully was busy scanning the room for any sign of Mr. Grin. "They're the cause of it. I don't understand how it can happen either, but it does. You ever put something down somewhere but can't find it again only to have it reappear somewhere else, or even in the same spot you previously searched? That's them. Usually, I think it's a way for them to let us know they're around or to have some fun with us, though obviously it works for less benign reasons too."

Dez frowned. "Great. That's great, Sully. Just when I think I've heard the last bad thing about this paranormal crap, you come up with something new."

"Sorry." Sully finished his visual sweep of the kitchen and connected dining room before turning back to Dez. "We'll need to search the place until we find it. It's here somewhere. I can feel it. Just don't mention—" Sully patted his pocket meaningfully.

"Wouldn't dream of it," Dez replied. "I hope you're not going to suggest we split up. Because no."

Sully smirked. "Wouldn't dream of it."

They made their way slowly and methodically through the split-level house, checking beneath furniture, in drawers and cupboards and behind large objects. They started at the lowest level and worked their way up. Throughout the search, Sully felt the unnerving sensation something was watching or listening.

When they reached the midway point on the stairs leading to the uppermost floor, Sully felt it: a wall of energy, almost like a forcefield had been thrown up to keep him away.

Mr. Grin was here, and he wasn't happy to see them.

Sully put out an arm, drawing Dez to a halt behind him.

"What?" Dez asked.

Sully shook his head as indication he couldn't answer yet. His attention was elsewhere, fully focused on the energy in front of him. It felt heavy, although not nearly as heavy as the entity at the Holmes manor. By now, he believed he could accurately guess at the reason. If whatever was possessing Mr. Grin had started at the Holmes estate, it was like dealing with an appendage lopped off the entity's body. Dangerous, yes, but not as devastating as it would be were it back at the estate.

Whether it was because of the dummy's connection to the Warren Malcolm homicide or simply because it was one of numerous items with a dark past lying under that roof, Sully couldn't be sure. For now, it didn't matter. Keep Mr. Grin locked up and away from the estate, and hopefully it wouldn't be capable of hurting anyone else.

Hopefully.

With Dez maintaining his silence, Sully reached out to get a better idea for where Mr. Grin was hiding. The feeling seemed strongest across the hall, from a doorway slightly to the left. Sully headed there, pushing through energy as thick as fog until he stood fully inside a bedroom.

The master bedroom.

Great. How the hell was he going to break it to Evelyn the thing had been inside her bedroom?

He moved past the bed, past a dresser, homing in on the closet. He didn't pause, didn't hesitate, just grabbed the handle and yanked the door open.

The negative energy was so thick, he could have chewed it. It was here.

Somewhere.

He felt its anger, but this time, he gave into it, letting it feed his own. He was sick of it, tired of this thing terrorizing people this way. No more. Not again.

As he stood in the middle of the walk-in, Dez a solid and reassuring presence behind him, Sully whipped his head to the right. His eyes snapped, without his directing them, to a spot along the lower wall.

Laundry hassock.

Bingo.

Again, Sully didn't hesitate. He grasped the lid, yanked it up.

Mr. Grin stared up at him, eyes wide, mouth open in its maniacal grin.

Dez gasped, but Sully didn't give in to what should have been shock. No room for that now.

He grabbed the dummy and lifted it.

The vision hit him hard, invading his brain without warning.

The kitchen at the Holmes estate, only not. It was earlier, far earlier.

Nineteen seventeen.

He had the impression of a gramophone playing somewhere inside the house, but as usual, Sully couldn't hear it. He couldn't hear anything.

Warren Malcolm stood before him, his face twisted in a combination of anger and fear. He was shouting. Sully—or whoever's consciousness he'd been forced into—was shouting.

Warren jabbed an index finger at something behind Sully. A back door.

While Sully couldn't hear, the meaning was clear.

Get out! Get out! Get out!

A black cane adorned with a large fake jewel, raised in the right hand of the man whose vision Sully shared.

Warren's eyes widened. Mouth formed an "O." He took a step back, hands raised, palms out.

No.

The cane swung. Warren caught the first blow on the shoulder. Though silent to Sully, the fact Warren was howling in agony was obvious.

Loathing, rage and power filled the attacker as he stepped forward. A second blow landed, this one on Warren's upper chest, approaching the neck. A third, higher up, on the side of the head.

Warren turned and ran. The attacker pursued, catching him before he made it past the table. A chair toppled as Warren caught it with a hip. He went down with it.

The assailant took advantage, raining down blow after blow. The world was tinted red, the target of the man's fury blurred behind it.

He saw enough to know when Warren stopped moving.

Even then, he didn't stop.

The vision ended as abruptly as it began. Sully's eyes

snapped open to find Dez looming over him, hands grasping the sides of his face.

"Sully? You with me? Talk to me."

It took a moment and a little more glancing around for Sully to fully place himself back within Evelyn's walk-in closet in the present day.

Despite his temporary befuddlement, one thing was immediately and abundantly clear to him. His hands were empty. "Mr. Grin?"

Dez pointed to the side, a few feet away. There sat Mr. Grin, bound in the chain Sully had concealed inside his coat. The dummy's eyes had drooped to half-mast, the mouth in its regular resting shape. What was more, the awful feeling previously rolling off the thing had dropped back significantly. Where it had earlier been a whirlwind, it now felt more like a mild breeze.

Sully sighed. "You did it."

Dez tilted his head as he peered down at him. "Did what?"

"Got it under control."

Dez beamed. "What, serious? You mean, it's done?"

"Not done. Just trapped. We need to find something to lock it in, something iron-lined like the trunk they found it inside at the train station. Just temporarily until I can get it dealt with permanently."

"Can you haul it out and send it to the other side or whatever?"

Sully pushed himself to sitting, Dez helping him get there. He shook his head. "Not that simple. I think this is a part of the larger entity. It's been empowered by it. To really get rid of it, we'll have to deal with the big daddy."

Dez grimaced. "Like the head vampire. Kill the main one and you get rid of the lesser ones it created."

Sully smirked. "Something like that."

He allowed Dez to pull him to his feet, standing there a moment before trying to walk. Part of him still felt trapped within that time and place a century ago. He still saw it, his hand, his cane, delivering what would ultimately become a fatal beating.

"Sure you're okay?" Dez asked.

"Getting there."

"What did you see?"

Sully filled him in on the details of the vision. Putting it into words, repeating it, made him relive it. Yet, as usual, no words could convey the full horror of the moment.

Having concluded, he scrubbed a hand down his face, as if by doing so he could rid himself of the lingering effects of the vision. "God, I just … I don't usually get these. Not like this."

"Like what?"

Sully met Dez's eye. The connection gave him something of a boost, a further and badly needed grounding in the here and now. "I usually see things through the eyes of the victim. I've seen and felt murder from their perspectives so many times, I don't even want to think about it. This—seeing it through the eyes of a killer …" He trailed off with a shudder.

Dez landed a hand on his shoulder. "You'll be okay. Remember, it's not you. It's them."

"I know, but I felt it like it was mine. All that rage." He wrapped his arms across his body and rubbed at his arms, staving off another shiver.

"I don't know how you do what you do. I really don't."

"I don't either." Though Sully cast another glance at Mr. Grin, he didn't allow himself to linger there for long before returning his gaze to Dez. "Thanks for the save. Again."

Dez shrugged and tried for a smile. "I owed you after the whole mess at the Holmes place."

"You'll never owe me anything." Sully heaved a breath,

pushing out more tension as he exhaled. Finally, he turned back to the dummy. "Let's get this thing out of here."

When he took a step toward it, Dez caught his arm. "I've got it. Only thing that scares me more than handling that thing is letting you touch it again."

"Hate to break it to you, but someone's going to have to keep this thing until we solve this in a more permanent way. Under the circumstances, it'll have to be me."

"Sully—"

"You know I'm right. You can't take it home with you." Sully didn't say anything more, not in front of Mr. Grin. He didn't want to say the words "Eva and Kayleigh," didn't want this thing to know about them. It might be trapped, but it was listening. He was sure of it. If it ever managed to get free, the first thing it would want was revenge.

But it wasn't just about protecting Dez and his family anymore, Sully realized. He had Sarah now. And he was supposed to go back to her place tonight.

Not anymore, not so long as he had to babysit this thing. Once again, his so-called gift was forcing him to change his plans.

Dez gnawed on his lower lip as he lifted the dummy. "Maybe we can find somewhere to stash it."

"Can't risk it, not until we can find a safer place to keep it."

In response, Dez set down Mr. Grin and pulled out his phone. He punched something in, and a few seconds later, Lachlan's voice came through the speaker.

"Any chance you can wrangle us up an iron box of some sort?" Dez asked.

"For what?"

Dez's eyes darted to the dummy, then to Sully. Sully shrugged.

"Mr. Grin," Dez said. "We're thinking iron's the only thing

that'll hold it. Thing somehow managed to magically transport itself from the museum to Evelyn's house."

"How the hell?"

"Wish I knew," Dez said. "Guess it's a thing. Doesn't make a whole lot of sense to me."

"Iron, huh? Big enough to stuff that thing inside? Might not be able to get anything for you on short notice like this. A safe would do it, if I can think of someone I trust who has space and the inclination to keep a haunted object inside."

"It has to be something transportable enough we can move it," Sully said. "I can't risk putting this thing inside anyone else's home—especially not now that I've chained it up. It'll be mad as hell and looking to get back at someone once it's free."

"I said I'd find someone I trust. If I tell them not to handle this thing, they won't."

"What about their kids. Significant other? Friends? If I'm not close by to keep an eye on things, I don't know what could happen. It needs to be moveable, Lachlan."

"All right, all right. I'll see what I can do. Since you're on the phone talking about iron, one other thing just occurred to me. The iron-lined trunk they found the dummy inside at the train station—we've been talking like this was one person behind the incident involving Warren Malcolm, but a trunk that heavy would have taken at least two people to move. So maybe even if we can figure out the identity of the second guy, we'll be in a position to figure out who the killer was."

"Sound like a question for tomorrow," Dez said. "I'm tired, and we need to get this thing out of here. Once you get a line on that trunk or safe or whatever, let us know."

They disconnected, and Dez dropped the phone back into his pocket. "Let's get the dummy back to your place. I'll stay with you there tonight."

Sully gave Dez a smile. "I appreciate it, bro, I really do. But it's not necessary. Cart this thing up to my apartment for me, and I'll take it from there. As long as I don't touch it, I'll be fine. Anyway, it's possible the chain will keep the ghost from being able to nail me with a vision even if I do touch it. So don't worry."

"You know me," Dez said. "Worrying is all I do."

21

SULLY SAT on the unmade sofa bed, every light on inside his tiny bachelor apartment as the evening wore on.

He had the television on and was streaming a show he usually enjoyed, but he was struggling to focus. A short distance away, propped on one of the chairs in the kitchen, sat Mr. Grin.

Sully had risked repositioning it twice since Dez had put it down there earlier. Sully had first turned it so it faced away from him, preventing him from seeing its eerie expression. The move made the situation worse though—made it feel like the ghost possessing Mr. Grin could be hatching a plot in secret. So Sully had adjusted it to more or less face him—not full on, which would have been way too creepy. He'd placed it in such a way so he could see the face without feeling like he was being stared at —the best solution he could hope for under the circumstances.

There was a silver lining. Sully hadn't gotten any more visions when he touched Mr. Grin. He couldn't swear as to why, though he hoped it was because he'd succeeded in controlling it through the iron links in the chain. If the visions weren't occurring only because the ghost wasn't sending any at him, that put the ball in the spirit's court—and Sully didn't want the ball anywhere near there.

He didn't know whether he should be relieved or concerned when a knock sounded on the door. Although he'd turned down Dez's offer to stay, he couldn't deny company—living human company—would be welcome right now. On the flip side, having anyone else around the dummy didn't strike him as a good idea either. He was already a target. Last thing he wanted was to allow someone else to become one.

He paused halfway to the door, absolutely not wanting Emily within sight of this thing as long as it was possessed. When a second knock sounded, he knew it wasn't his neighbour.

He knew that knock.

"What are you doing here?" he asked, opening the door to find Sarah on the landing.

She shrugged. "You said you couldn't come over tonight. I wanted to see you."

Sully cast a quick glance over his shoulder. Yep, Mr. Grin was still there. Thanks to Sully's last attempt at positioning the dummy, it now fully faced the door. Not exactly the sight he wanted awaiting his girlfriend. "I love the idea of hanging out. I really do. But—"

She held up a hand to stop him mid-sentence. "But you're babysitting a haunted ventriloquist's dummy. I'm aware. I'm here anyway."

Sully risked pushing partway into the hall, thereby putting Mr. Grin temporarily out of his eyeshot. He needed to have this conversation and to keep it from the ghost as much as he possibly could.

"You can't be here," he told Sarah. "This thing is dangerous."

Sarah crossed her arms. "Exactly—which is why I'm here. I'm not letting you sit up with Slappy alone. That's what you're going to do, right? Sit up with it all night? No way you're risking sleeping until you're sure it's fully under control."

Sully sighed. "Yeah, that's what I'm planning to do. But Sarah—"

"No buts. We're together, right? We're a couple. That means something to me."

"It means something to me too."

"It means you want to protect me," Sarah said. "Newsflash, cowboy. I don't need a protector. I need a partner. You willing to stop being such a macho dork and meet me halfway? Let me help."

His grin came without his expecting it. Never in his life had anyone called him a "macho dork," and he found it amusing. And he was pretty sure he'd never been more in love with Sarah than he was right at this moment.

He forced away the smile. "I don't like it."

"You don't have to," she said.

He studied her another long moment. Her words closely mirrored those uttered by Dez not so long ago, enough it gave him extra food for thought. He wanted no less than before to keep her safe, but maybe he needed to have some faith in her too, the same way Dez did in Eva.

"Okay," he said. "Come on in."

LACHLAN CALLED SHORTLY before eleven that night with the good news he'd found a friend with an unused gun safe.

"Thing's a bitch to move, I'm told, but it's ours first thing if we want it," Lachlan said.

"No chance of getting it tonight, huh?" Sully asked.

"Sadly, no. The buddy in question used to work with me on the police force. His wife was friends with my ex-wife."

"In other words, she hates you," Sully concluded.

"Bingo. I'm not getting anywhere near there until morning. If Patrick tries going anywhere with that thing now, and she asks what's going on, he'll either have to lie or he'll have to deal with the resulting argument. Best we wait until she goes to work in the morning and go grab it then."

Sully wasn't happy about it, but he understood the issue. At least, come morning, he'd have a better means of keeping Mr. Grin and its attached ghost in a place where the risk to others would be alleviated. He disconnected with Lachlan and pocketed his cellphone.

Sarah hadn't moved, eyes still fixed on the dummy.

"It really is creepy looking, isn't it?" she muttered.

"Yep," Sully said. He wrapped an arm around her and pulled her closer to him. "I don't think I said this, but thank you for coming to keep me company. I appreciate it. I appreciate *you*."

"Ditto, cowboy."

It seemed the opportune moment to discuss what had been on his mind lately. "Hey, I know we haven't talked seriously about it, but I've been doing a lot of thinking lately. I don't know yet how it would work, given what I do, but I was wondering if you've given any thought to you and me moving in together."

She turned to him, eyes flashing wide, perfect teeth showing through a beaming grin. "Are you kidding me? Of course, I've thought about it. I think about it all the time. I've wanted to ask you to move in with me a thousand times, but I wasn't sure you'd be up for it. I didn't want to ask in case, you know, you said no. I mean, I know you help Emily out a lot—which I adore you for—and you've got this whole psychic PI thing going you worry will impact me. But, yeah, I'd absolutely *love* to live with you."

A weight fell from Sully's shoulders, one he hadn't realized had been sitting there. All this time, he'd thought his reservations were solely about the possible danger to Sarah or his worry for Emily. Apparently, he'd been afraid of being rejected as well.

He tugged her into a hug, enjoying the warmth of her. "I love you."

"I love you too." Sarah pulled back enough to meet his eye. "So that's it? We're doing this?"

He cast a glance over her shoulder to where Mr. Grin continued to sit, unmoving and silently watching the room through those half-lidded eyes. Sarah grasped Sully's chin, drawing his gaze back to her.

"Don't," she said. She pointed to her own eyes. "Right here. This is about us. You and me. We've got this, cowboy. You get me?"

He smiled. "I get you."

And then he kissed her.

Before he'd been placed on dummy duty, he'd hoped for a different kind of intimacy. But making love with Mr. Grin sitting across the room, watching and listening, was a whole new level of creepy Sully wasn't willing to explore.

Thankfully, Sarah seemed to have drawn the same conclusion without Sully's needing to put it into words. So they simply stretched out together, Sully lying behind her, one arm wrapped around her waist.

They fell asleep with the television on, half-listening to the droning of the program's narrator. The muted noise was comforting, the relaxed tone providing something of a sense of normalcy which put Mr. Grin temporarily on the back burner.

When Sully awoke, the show they'd been watching was over and a new one had started. He clicked off the set and stretched to peer over the pullout's back to where Mr. Grin sat.

Had been sitting.

The chair was empty.

Sully's heart thudded as he sat up, a whispered curse word on his lips. Sarah muttered something unintelligible in her sleep but didn't awaken as Sully crawled over her and scanned the room. No sign of Mr. Grin. Nothing on the chair but the discarded chain.

Sully had pulled the elastic tie from his hair before lying down. Now he ran hands through the loose strands, tugging it back from his face. Somehow, the chain hadn't been enough to restrain the dummy.

Damn it.

His first thought was that Mr. Grin had been teleported somewhere else—God forbid, back to Evelyn's house. His second thought hit hard—the ghost would hate nobody more right now than Sully, the guy who'd put it in this difficult spot to begin with. Even if it wanted to hurt the dummy's new owners at the museum, Sully was the immediate threat, the one who would stand in its way and prevent its following through on whatever plans it might have.

He searched for calm, used it to reach out psychically. Yes, Mr. Grin—and the attached ghost—was still here.

Somewhere.

"Where are you?" he whispered into the space before him. He hadn't expected an answer and didn't receive one. Nothing but silence.

He glanced back at the pullout, ensuring Sarah was still asleep, and more importantly, wasn't being watched by a possessed puppet. All clear on a first glance, so he went one further, getting down on his hands and knees and peering under the pullout.

Nothing.

Nor was there anything behind the furniture in the living

room area or in any of the kitchen cupboards. The front closet also appeared to be dummy-free.

He tried again, reaching out once more with his mind. Still, he sensed the ghost but couldn't pinpoint it. He questioned why before settling on an answer.

He was scared. Scared for Sarah. Harder to calm himself and control his abilities when he was too occupied being controlled by his own worries.

Back to a physical search then. Lucky thing he had a bachelor pad.

Living area cleared, Sully turned his attention to the bathroom. As he entered the small room, he saw nothing—nothing save the tub, across which the shower curtain had been drawn.

Had he pulled it closed himself?

Living in a sketchy area, Sully had taken to keeping a baseball bat in the large storage closet. He debated going to get it before opening the curtain, but the museum probably wouldn't thank him for destroying a valuable historical item.

Then again, given recent events, they might thank him for it.

He gave it another moment's thought before deciding. No. No bat.

He drew a breath, took one large step forward to close the remaining distance and grasped the curtain's edge. Planting one foot forward and one back—fighting stance—he tore open the curtain.

Empty.

What the hell?

A shriek from Sarah had Sully spinning in place and racing from the room. As he reached the space between the short front hall and the living area, he stopped dead.

Mr. Grin stood in the centre of the room.

Stood. No one propping it up.

Sarah had pressed back against the wall, terror-filled eyes

fixed on the dummy. Sully took only a second to visually check on her—seemingly unharmed—before returning his attention to the dummy.

Mr. Grin's eyes were fully open, staring at Sarah.

"Leave her alone," Sully growled.

The storage closet was within reach, more or less. Just a couple of steps away. He remembered where the bat was, could lay his hands on it relatively quickly. Problem was, he wasn't sure how fast Mr. Grin could move.

The chain seemed the best bet, but it was farther away, on the opposite side of the room—and across the room from Sarah.

He'd have to draw Mr. Grin's attention. "Your problem is with me," he said.

Mr. Grin's head spun toward him. Its large eyes pinned him in their stare. Hate and rage rolled off the dummy, poured from its eyes. For a moment, Sully froze. Only for a moment.

Then he dashed for the closet. With a yank, Sully pulled the door open. The bat was there, just within reach.

Before he could grab it, a force strong enough to nearly count as physical hit him like a truck, sending him flying into the closet. He toppled over a pile of recyclables and hit the shelves, falling hard. For a moment, he lay stunned.

It was all the time the spirit needed. The door slammed shut, sealing Sully inside.

He struggled to climb to his feet, but the junk surrounding him made it hard. Sarah called his name but he didn't waste time or breath yelling back, instead focusing on trying to stand.

It was too dark to see whether the dummy was inside the closet with him, but the ghostly energy was definitely here. He felt it now, strong and hate-filled.

And it was here for him.

He heard the scrape of something heavy against a wooden shelf overhead. He got his arms up just in time to protect himself from an array of boxes and other junk as they flew from the shelves and landed on him. One—probably the slow cooker he'd received from his mom last Christmas—made it past his defences and nailed him on the side.

The baseball bat only made things worse.

He was hit from behind, but he knew exactly what it was. He recognized the metallic scraping as it lifted from the floor. He took the first blow to the leg, a second landing nearer his ribs. Instinct had him curling in on himself while scrabbling for anything he could use as a shield.

Another blow fell, then another. Forearm, shoulder.

He located the slow cooker box and shoved it upward, catching a strike meant for his head. Additional hits came with such force, the box slammed against him, pinning him to the floor. Two more shots now, lower down, one to his hip, another to his leg, near where he'd been nailed earlier.

He needed to stand, needed to get out of the closet. But the more he shifted, the more he opened himself up to further assault.

Goddammit.

Gritting his teeth against the pain and the fear, Sully held onto the box, shielding his head as well as he could. Again, he tried to focus, but between the pain and the fear he heard in Sarah's voice beyond the door, focus didn't come.

Eventually, the ghost would run out of energy and the attack would end. Question was what condition he'd be in by the time that happened.

Once more, this time squeezing his eyes shut, he sought focus. He pushed out with his senses and, this time, very nearly grabbed hold of the spirit.

A few more hard blows severed the connection.

Goddammit.

Then, for some reason, it stopped.

Silence fell. Everything went still.

For a moment, he wondered if this was the calm before the final storm, a sign a massive, devastating strike was about to land.

But that, he realized, was his fear talking. No, the danger had passed. He could feel it.

As the door was yanked open, he knew without a doubt he was right.

Sarah stood there, hair mussed, eyes wide and chest heaving with rapid and shallow breaths. But she was nonetheless standing, which was, to Sully, a tremendous win.

"You okay?" she demanded, reaching for his hand.

"The dummy," he got out, breathless himself. He meant the words as a warning, but she only shook her head.

"It's all right," she said. "I handled it."

He took her hand, using her support to stumble to his feet. "How?"

"You mentioned ghosts don't like iron. You had a cast iron frying pan on the stove, so I ran for it and nailed the little bastard with it. Seemed to take the wind out of his sails. After that, I wrapped the chain back around it."

Sully came free of the junk and the closet, scanning the area until his eyes settled on the dummy, lying bound in the middle of the floor, this side of the kitchen table. Sully shook his head, a near-manic laugh leaving him.

"You're amazing, you know that?" he said.

Sarah managed a shaky laugh to answer his. "Told you. Partners."

Sully hugged her hard, pain to his battered body be damned.

"Yeah," he said. "Partners."

22

DEZ'S STOMACH flipped as he touched base with Sully by phone the following morning. "Mr. Grin did what now?"

"Not Mr. Grin, exactly," Sully said. "Technically, it was the ghost haunting it."

"Whatever. You okay?"

"He looks like a piece of abstract art," Sarah said, her voice sounding like she stood next to Sully. "And not one I'd pay money to hang on my wall."

Dez grimaced. "Go to the hospital?"

"Tried to convince him. He said no."

"Sully," Dez growled.

"I'm fine. I've had worse."

Dez didn't doubt it, except worse didn't often come at the hands of a puppet. He opted to let it go for now. He'd see Sully soon enough and would decide at that point whether he should drag him to the hospital himself. Sometimes Sully's high threshold for pain meant he ignored injuries he shouldn't.

"Hate to ask," Dez said, "but did you get any sleep last night?"

"Nope," Sully said. "Stayed up to watch Mr. Grin. I don't

know how he wiggled out of the chain, but he did. He won't have as easy a time with the gun safe."

"You've got it?"

"Lachlan's on the way to pick it up from his buddy now. I'd rather not drive today given I feel like I could drop at a moment's notice. Sarah needs to get to work soon, so would you mind picking me up? I told Lachlan we'd bring Mr. Grin with us. If we're going to be driving around today, talking to people, I want to make sure the dummy's somewhere I can check on it every so often."

"Yeah, sure," Dez said. "I'll come get you. Incidentally, how'd you get the creepy little asshole under control last night?"

"Sarah," Sully said. "She clobbered Mr. Grin with my cast iron frying pan."

A laugh bubbled up from Dez's chest. "Remind me never to mess with you, Leffler."

"Better not," Sarah said, voice playful. "I've got a mean swing."

"Seriously, though," Dez said. "Thank you. I owe you one."

"Nope. No way. We're sharing responsibility for keeping our guy here safe now. All in a night's work."

Dez chuckled. "I'll buy you dinner, anyway." Then to Sully, "I'll leave here in a few. See you soon."

"The sooner the better," Sully said. "Sarah's out the door pretty quick, and I don't mind telling you I'd rather not be alone with this friggin' thing ever again."

WITH KAYLEIGH at school and Eva at police headquarters for the day, Dez started for Sully's apartment as soon as he was off the phone. Pax had been eager for a car ride, but Dez worried about having the large dog near a ventriloquist's dummy which was both dangerous and very chewable. If Mr. Grin didn't try to hurt Pax, Pax might well destroy the dummy. Either outcome was bad.

Instead, Dez had left Pax happily gnawing on a soup bone, the best concession he could come up with.

Dez arrived at Sully's to find Sarah still there but anxious to leave.

"Thanks for coming so quickly," she said as she met Dez's hug at the apartment door. "I'm running late, and I can't come up with a believable excuse."

"Yeah, the fact you were battling a puppet isn't likely to fly," Dez said. "Thanks again, huh?"

She shook her head. "Forget it. Just look after him for me."

Dez grinned at her. "Always."

He entered the apartment, eyes immediately shooting to Mr. Grin, seated on a kitchen chair and wound up in chain. Sully and Sarah exchanged a quick hug and a peck on the lips, and then she was gone.

"Ready to go?" Sully asked. He started toward the dummy without awaiting an answer.

Dez grabbed his arm, holding him back. "I've got it. You've tangled with this thing enough for the time being."

Sully didn't argue, so Dez blew out a quick breath, crossed the room and scooped up Mr. Grin, careful to ensure the chain stayed in place. It was looped around the dummy's neck, shoulders, middle and legs. The head remained free, but they couldn't do much about it. The body was made of cloth with wire framing—not really breakable; the fact it was undamaged by the frying pan said as much. The head was another story. Dez would personally be happy to smash it into smithereens, especially after last night's events, but he was hired to fix the situation for the museum, not cause a new one.

With Sully leading the way downstairs, Dez trailed behind,

lugging Mr. Grin with him. He couldn't wait until they could get this thing stuffed into the gun safe and locked safely away.

At Dez's SUV, the two of them stared at each other over the top of the vehicle.

"What should we do with it until we get to Lachlan's?" Dez asked.

Sully frowned. "Guess I should hold it. We can't risk the chain slipping off with the vehicle bouncing around on the road."

Dez grimaced. "We're going to look like idiots, driving around with that thing in the front seat."

"Would you rather I sit in the back with it and have you look like you're chauffeuring a dummy?"

"Fair point. Get in."

With Sully holding Mr. Grin on his lap in the passenger seat, Dez drove them to Lachlan's home in the North Bank area, not far from their office. Stop lights were annoying, with more than one driver smirking and pointing out the chained dummy to the other occupants of their vehicles. At least one passerby whipped out a phone to record the sight, leaving Dez to wonder which social media app they'd end up on later.

When they arrived at their destination, Lachlan was waiting on his front porch, bundled up in his coat and holding a book in one hand and a steaming cup of what was likely tea in the other. A mid-length, not overly deep lockbox sat on a dry patch of driveway. Judging by the size, it was intended for handguns rather than long guns, but there'd be room enough to stuff the dummy, provided the walls weren't too thick.

Dez didn't think he'd ever been so happy to see an inanimate object in his life.

Lachlan set down his book and tea and made his way to them as they stepped from the vehicle. "Will this work?"

"After all this, it better," Dez said.

Sully was already headed for it, so Dez joined him and flipped open the lid. It was empty with no shelves to get in the way. Sully didn't miss a beat before laying the dummy, chains still attached, inside.

Dez slammed shut the lid before noting the lock. "Have a key?"

Lachlan produced one from his pocket. "Naturally."

Dez took it and locked the box, taking a moment to test the lid. Nope, this thing wasn't moving.

He turned his gaze up to Sully. "What do you think? We safe?"

Sully's eyes, previously fixed on the box top, shifted to Dez. One corner of his lips quirked slightly. "Yeah. We're good."

Lachlan folded his arms. "In that case, we need to discuss the day's plan. I've reached out to the people Sully's lady friend tracked down for us. Two of them have either moved or changed their numbers, but I'm sure I can find them if we need to. I was able to get ahold of one of the Lomax descendants—granddaughter named Amelia Friedmann. I kept the conversation vague. Figured if I told them I had Frank figured for a murder suspect, they wouldn't be overly pleased to meet with you."

Dez raised his brows. "You're not coming?"

"I've got a meet arranged with Warren Malcolm's great-niece, June. My thought was to send you to see Friedmann, Braddock, and to take young Sullivan here with me. June was quite excited about the idea not only of meeting Sully, but to see the dummy. Figured two of you would throw a fit at the idea of me taking off with it unless Sully's there to keep an eye on things."

This was true, though Dez wasn't pleased about the idea of Sully being around the dummy unless Dez was there to lend a hand should things go sideways.

"I'd rather she waited to see it until we've sent whatever is haunting it packing," Dez said. "It's too dangerous." He turned to Sully. "Speaking of, you haven't showed me any of the injuries you ended up with last night."

"And I hadn't planned to. I'm not five."

Dez rolled his eyes but let it go. While Sully had been moving a little stiffly, he didn't seem worse for wear, all things considered.

"Could you at least try to convince her to wait on seeing Mr. Grin?" Dez asked.

"That much, you and I can agree on," Sully said. "I'll see what I can do to get her to hold off."

Sully's phone rang, and he cringed. "Damn it. Forbes. I forgot, I was supposed to arrange to meet with him to hand over the despatch box and the stuff inside."

Lachlan checked his watch. "Can it wait? Time's a-ticking."

Sully frowned. "Considering we're talking about a very well-known, open homicide investigation, I'm not sure he'd be too forgiving."

"Which of us has farther to travel?" Dez asked Lachlan. "Whoever's got less ground to cover could run the stuff to Forbes."

"Police will want more than our physical evidence," Lachlan reminded them. "They'll need interviews, including info on how you came upon the stuff."

"This is Forbes," Sully said. "He'll hold off as long as he can. He's cool."

Dez was pretty sure this was the first time anyone had described Forbes Raynor as "cool," but he kept the thought to himself.

Both interviews ended up being in the city, so the question of who met with Forbes didn't come down to who'd be closer.

Dez wasn't surprised when Lachlan made an executive decision to have Dez make the drop. As much as Dez sometimes found Forbes's personality grating, Lachlan found it unbearable.

Then again, Lachlan found a lot of people unbearable. Unfortunately for him, the feeling was all too often mutual.

Dez called up Forbes once he helped load the lockbox into the trunk of Lachlan's car and saw off Sully and Lachlan. Forbes agreed to meet him on the street in front of police headquarters, so Dez headed over once he got off the phone.

Wanting to keep things short and sweet, Dez redialled Forbes once he was five minutes away. By the time he pulled into the drop-off zone in front of the building, Forbes was emerging through the front doors.

Instead of climbing in, he made a hand signal as an indication for Dez to pull out and meet him farther up the block. Dez obliged, making for the next block where he found a spot in front of an apartment building.

Dez unlocked the doors, allowing Forbes to slide into the passenger seat.

"I'm going to need you and Sully to come in at some point to provide a statement," Forbes said. No hello, then.

"We will," Dez said.

Forbes continued as if Dez hadn't spoken. "Continuity of evidence is going to be a problem. You removed the box from the scene of the incident and went through it already."

Dez resisted an eye roll. "Realize that. But it's not like anyone's going to court on this, right? And we couldn't very well leave it there either. Abandoned houses—especially ones with dark histories—are like magnets for urban explorers and vandals. Anyway, Sully and I were dragged and tossed around like rag dolls by whatever's haunting the place. Didn't want to risk some poor sucker with the Ident unit getting flung through a wall or a window. If you could hold off until we finish what we started, that would be a help."

"I'm taking possession of this now. I can't hold off. We're talking about one of the biggest cases in the city over the last century. I need to move on it."

"If you're not careful, the only moving you'll do is getting thrown across a room by a demonic entity. Trust me, I've been there. You wouldn't enjoy it."

Forbes frowned deeply, causing a network of lines to reveal themselves on either side of his mouth and between his brows. "How close are you?"

"Close. We've got two people to speak with today. And Sully was in temporary communication with whatever's possessing the dummy, so I'm hopeful we're closing in on finding out who it was."

It was a gross exaggeration. Sully's vision, as far as Dez had been told, included no real identifying features. Regardless, the killer was long dead; no charges would ever be laid. As for closing in on a conclusion, Dez still wasn't convinced they'd ever get there. All he really wanted was to keep this thing rolling until they had what they needed to separate the ghost from Mr. Grin and send the thing to whatever afterlife awaited it. Then, hopefully, they could do the same for the Big Bad over at the Holmes estate.

If they could pull it off before anyone else wandered in there and got hurt, all the better.

Forbes regarded Dez through narrowed eyes. "You guys really get off on making my life difficult, don't you?"

"If by difficult, you mean preventing you from going head-to-head with something out of a horror movie, then sure. Hey, by that measure, I'd love it if someone would make my life difficult once in a while."

Forbes gave the eye roll Dez had earlier held back. "Okay,

fine. Here's what I'll do. I'll need to chat with our Cold Case investigator, and I happen to know she's away today. You keep it for now, and I'll make like it's all a big surprise when you call me tomorrow, advising you found this stuff. If I take charge of it today, I'll need to get it to Ident right away, and I guess that's not going to work for the two of you knuckleheads." Forbes shook his head. "If anyone ever found out about the stuff I hold back to help out a PI agency, I'd be flipping burgers down at Chippy's inside of five minutes."

"No one'll find out," Dez said. "Not from us, anyway. Tell you what, give us a bit of time to get the ghost stuff dealt with. Then we'll get the box back to the spot where we found it and call it in to you like we just found it, all right?"

"I'll pretend I didn't hear that." Forbes slid out of the vehicle, pausing at the open passenger-side door and leaning back inside. "How much trouble is this thing going to be?"

Dez formed a straight line with his mouth before answering. "Enough."

"I'd offer to help, but something tells me it wouldn't be much use."

"Wish there was a way to make it work. We could use all the backup we could get."

Forbes gave him a tight smile and shut the door. Dez waited until Forbes started back toward the police station before pulling into traffic and making for the address belonging to Frank and Faye Lomax's granddaughter.

23

Amelia Freidmann lived in a two-storey home in the Riverview area, not far from the old downtown core.

One of the oldest neighbourhoods in Kimotan Rapids, Riverview—named for its prime location next to the Kimotan River—had seen far better days. Once a favourite neighbourhood for young families and those working in the nearby downtown area, it had since seen a severe decline in property prices while suffering an increase in crime and social problems.

While it appeared Amelia took great pride in her property and had kept it up, there were signs she wasn't flush with cash, judging by a range of peeling shingles and missing planks from the picket fence.

Dez contemplated briefly what to do with the despatch box. Initially, he considered tucking it beneath his coat on the backseat floor, but his instincts ran counter to this idea. He knew plenty about continuity of evidence; if it was out of your sight, there existed a possibility someone could interfere with it—or worse, make off with it. People committing smash-and-grabs on vehicles wouldn't waste time examining a box's contents; they'd snatch it up and run. And Dez didn't want to have to call Forbes and tell him he'd lost the evidence.

Mind made up, Dez tucked the box under his arm and carried it from the SUV to the house.

By the time he made it up the steps onto the veranda, a woman in her seventies had opened the door for him.

"You must be Dez Braddock," she said, extending a hand for him to shake. "I'm Amelia. Please, come in. And don't bother about your shoes. Place is a mess."

Dez gave his boots a thorough wipe on a welcome mat outside the door, repeating the process on a second rug inside the front entrance. "Nice house."

Amelia beamed. "Thank you." She gave a sheepish smile before passing a hand over a table in the entryway, leaving a trail in the dust. "Well, it used to be. Place needs a good going over. Can I get you anything to drink? Tea? Coffee? Water?"

"No thanks, ma'am, I'm fine."

"Please, call me Amelia."

Dez followed her from the entry hall into a snug yet comfortable sitting room. The furniture suited the house, as if it had been there since the place had been built.

"How old is the house?" Dez asked.

"Over a century, built nineteen eleven. My parents owned it, and before that, my mom's parents had it. They were the original owners, actually."

Dez raised a brow. "Do you mean Frank and Faye Lomax?"

"I do. You've done some research already, it would seem."

Dez shrugged. "A little. Not much. There's a lot I don't know, which is why I'm here."

"I'll do my best. I certainly learned as much as I could about my family history, though admittedly, there are things even I struggled to uncover. My family on my mom's side were always very private people."

Not words Dez had hoped to hear.

Amelia lowered herself into a chair, leaving a small couch for Dez. He noted what looked to be some dog hair on the cushions, but given he hadn't seen or heard a dog, he wondered whether she'd recently lost a pet. She seemed happy for Dez's company; he hoped she had someone else in her life to fill any void.

Dez was debating how best to get into the topic at hand when Amelia did it for him. Her eyes having first drifted to the box, she lifted her curious gaze to Dez's face. "What's in the box?"

Oh boy, Dez thought. If anything came of this interview, police would want to speak with her eventually as well. And once they found out he'd carted the despatch box in here, the story he and Forbes had agreed on fell apart.

Oh well. Couldn't be helped now.

"It's a box containing some letters and photos we found at a house that used to belong to Warren Malcolm," Dez said. "Are you familiar with him?"

Amelia's eyes lit up. "The ventriloquist! I sure am. It was all over the news when they found the dummy. Mr. Something-or-other."

"Grin," Dez supplied. "That's the one. Anyway, our clients asked us to do some checking into the dummy, and it led us to the house and this box. It's actually kind of the reason I'm here."

"Mr. Fields mentioned over the phone something about a connection between my grandmother and another man. You don't mean to tell me the man he was referring to is Warren Malcolm?"

"Actually, yeah," Dez said. Time to bite the bullet. "Our understanding is your grandmother, Faye Lomax, was romantically involved with Mr. Malcolm."

Amelia's lips formed an O-shape. "You're having me on."

"I know it's a lot to take in, but we found evidence to back this up. I wonder, do you have any photos of Faye? It might help to make it totally clear."

Amelia nodded and stood. Dez watched her as she left the room and again as she returned, checking for signs she was troubled by the way this conversation was going. If she was, she gave no indication. More so, he'd say she was intrigued—excited even—by the possibility of a saucy secret in her family's past. Put a couple of generations between events, and it was interesting how perceptions changed.

Amelia had brought with her a photo album, one which had very clearly seen multiple decades. Dez recalled a similar one at his grandma's house, its cover and black cardboard pages held together by heavy string woven through a series of holes. Amelia placed the album on the coffee table, circling it to sit on the empty spot next to him.

"When my mom passed away, I made sure to keep her old photo albums. You could say she was the family historian. I've basically taken on the same role." She opened the cover and flipped through a couple of pages, pausing once she came upon one showing two side-by-side photos—one a studio portrait of an attractive woman, the other a man dressed in an army uniform.

"My grandparents, Frank and Faye," Amelia said. She turned over another page, revealing a wedding photo of the two. "They made quite the dashing pair, didn't they?"

Dez was more focused on the woman in the photos. Without a doubt, this was the same Faye Lomax he'd seen in the photos from Warren Malcolm's despatch box.

He opened the box, picking through the contents until he located the pictures. He plucked out the one of Faye and Warren together and handed it to Amelia to inspect.

She squinted at it, then tugged her glasses down her nose to peer over the rims at it. "Oh my." She glanced up at Dez. "Are you sure they were involved? I mean, they certainly appear very cozy, but maybe they were just friends. By all accounts, my grandparents were happy together."

Or maybe that was simply the face they chose to show the world, Dez thought. He pictured social media images of couples he knew, all of them suggesting they were very much in love. He could think of at least three of those couples currently in the midst of marital breakup. He couldn't imagine the situation would have been much different a century ago, back when divorce was all but unheard of.

"Do you know who this baby is?" he asked Amelia, passing her the photos in question.

Amelia once again stared over the top of her glasses at the images. "I know people sometimes say babies all look the same, but she doesn't seem to be any of my grandparents' children. I believe she's a she, anyway?" She lifted her gaze to Dez for confirmation.

Dez nodded. "She, yes. Her name was Paulette. We wondered whether it might be she was raised by your grandparents under a different name. If so, they would have had to fudge her actual birthdate as she was conceived and born while your grandfather was overseas—at least according to the correspondence we've seen."

"Would I be able to see this correspondence? I'd be very interested."

"I have to hand it over to the police," Dez said. "I wanted to get your take on it first, though, which is why I'm here. I can let you read over a letter or two, but I can't leave them with you."

He removed the most crucial letters, searching for the postmarks in question before handing them to Amelia for review. She read silently, brows raising on occasion. When she finished, she handed them back.

She shook her head. "There's no way Paulette was raised by

my grandparents under a different name. I have baby photos of my mom and her siblings, and none of them are this baby." She raised her brows. "What do you suppose happened to her?"

Dez returned the photos to the box as Amelia returned them. "No idea. Part of what we're trying to figure out."

Amelia's eyes flashed wide, and she gave a little gasp before tapping Dez on the forearm with an index finger. "You know what's interesting? I started a family tree on an ancestry site, and I did one of those DNA kits in the course of it. Well, the site shows you other people who've done DNA tests if they're found to be close blood relations. Most people showing up on my DNA results page are relatives I know about, but there's one lady I've never so much as heard of."

Interesting. "What's her name? I'd love to check into it."

"I can't recall offhand, but I'll log in later and send it to you."

That suited Dez fine. He needed to move on to the tricky question. He hoped Amelia was comfortable enough with him to not be offended when he asked.

"You're aware we're looking into the death of Warren Malcolm, and I think you know about the break-in and assault that led to his dying," Dez said.

"I am. And I'm a bit worried you're going to suggest my grandfather might have been behind it."

Dez held her eye. "Was he, do you think?"

"Of course not. By all accounts, he was a very kind and level-headed man—not the sort to commit murder."

"Even if he found out his wife had a child with another man while he was overseas serving his country?"

Amelia nodded. "Even if."

"What about PTSD—shell shock, they would have probably called it then. That changes people. One of my great-grandfathers, I was told, went into these states where he'd think he was back in the war. His wife and kids had to hide from him. Otherwise, he was a pleasant guy, apparently. It was like Jekyll and Hyde."

"I've never heard any account of Grandpa Frank suffering from shell shock. When I say he was known to be kind and level-headed, I mean all the time. He wasn't cruel or abusive, intentionally or otherwise. I wasn't very old when he died, so I didn't know him overly well, admittedly. But all the memories I do have of him are fond ones. My older siblings say the same, and they knew him better than I did."

Dez puzzled this out a moment before continuing with another thought. "What about the baby—Paulette? If you don't recognize the photos, it either means something bad happened to her or she was placed for adoption."

Amelia tipped her head to the side. So far, nothing about her suggested she'd been offended by the questioning, "Well, it was a different time, wasn't it? While I don't for a moment believe he would have done anything to harm the child, he couldn't easily take her in as his own. Far too many questions would have resulted, and my grandmother would have been shunned along with their children. It was seen as a terrible thing back then for a married woman to have a child with another man. Now, as you said, two things could have happened. They could have placed the baby up for adoption. Or possibly the baby died as the result of an illness. Child mortality was much higher in the early nineteen hundreds, particularly once the Spanish flu started."

Dez hadn't thought of this bad-case scenario. It was certainly possible if Paulette had died, it had been a natural death. But surely, there would still be a record of it if so. Unless, of course, there was never any record of the baby's existence to start with.

Too many questions, still too few answers.

"One other thing," Dez said. "Your grandmother became pregnant while your grandfather was away. Pretty hard to hide something like that. People would have seen and wondered about it."

Amelia shook her head. "My mom and her siblings would have been very young at the time. I recall her telling me that while her father was away serving, her mom took them away from town and moved in for a while with her aunt in the country. I suppose she could have treated the move as what was once termed a confinement, remaining there until she had her baby. If she did, my mom didn't know about it, but as I say, the kids were very young. It could well be they weren't aware or didn't pay much attention. And not all women show heavily. Especially with the large skirts in fashion those days. Who's to say? There's certainly no one left to ask."

And they still faced the main problem of piecing together a historical crime. If Frank Lomax had been the one who'd savagely beaten Malcolm, it might be they'd never find out for sure.

"Thank you for talking to me," Dez said. "I know it's a difficult topic. I want you to know my intention isn't to run anyone's family name through the mud, only to uncover the truth about what happened."

Amelia smiled. "I understand. If you could avoid making your theories public unless you find definitive proof, though, I'd appreciate it. Because, the thing is, I'm certain you won't find such proof. Although it certainly seems true my grandmother had an affair, I don't see any evidence my grandfather did anything terrible as a result."

As of now, given what he had to work with, Dez was unable to argue. Where that left the investigation was anyone's guess.

24

It felt strange riding with Mr. Grin while possessing no sense of the ghost. Yet that was what Sully experienced as he rode shotgun in Lachlan's car, the lockbox containing Mr. Grin stashed inside the trunk.

It was possible the ghost haunting the dummy had fled, was even now floating around somewhere and searching for a way to victimize some poor unsuspecting person. If so, Sully might not know about it until it was too late, but he was banking on something much different. After Sarah had stopped the attack, the presence felt lessened—muffled, almost. It thrummed like a heartbeat beneath flesh and bone covered by a heavy layer of clothing. Real and present, but not easily detectable.

If it managed to escape again, he would know—if not simply by the feeling it would give off, then by the fact it would, no doubt, come after him again.

The fact he couldn't feel it now told him the iron-lined box was doing the trick, which gave him a massive measure of relief—temporary though it might be until the spirit was dealt with.

But that was a problem for another moment.

"You all right?" Lachlan asked.

Sully rubbed at his eyes. "Tired. Long night."

Lachlan smirked. "Not for a good reason, though, huh?"

"Nope. Not good at all. I want to make something clear: I'm not opposed to June seeing Mr. Grin. But not now. It's safe where it is, locked in the box. The second I take it out, all hell could break loose."

"She really wants to see it."

"It was at the museum. She could have gone there."

Lachlan shrugged. "They only recently put it on display, and she hadn't been made aware."

"Tough." The word had come out harsher than Sully had intended. He put it down to being tired and sore.

Lachlan chuckled. "Well, well, well. Remind me not to mess with you when you've been beaten to hell by a doll."

"I mean it, Lachlan."

Lachlan caught his eye before returning full attention to the road. "I know. I'm not arguing with you. Far as I'm concerned, when it comes to investigative tactics and details, you defer to me given my lifetime's worth of experience. When it comes to this crazy, spooky nonsense, that's all you. You're the expert. You want the thing left in the box, it stays in the box. Just telling you she'll want to see it eventually."

Sully had imagined having to debate this with both June and Lachlan. Having Lachlan onside helped. "Thanks. I appreciate that. And I promise, as soon as I can clear this thing, she can spend as much time with Mr. Grin as she wants."

Lachlan's smile hadn't quite faded, making Sully suspect something else was waiting to be said.

"What?" Sully asked, careful to keep the question light.

"I hear your lady friend kicked some ass, huh? Plus, she ran some decent background for us. If you ever get bored working for me, maybe you can see if she'll come fill your job."

Sully shook his head. "I'll let her know."

Despite the humour behind it, Lachlan's comment wasn't without some truth. Sarah *had* kicked ass. She'd been afraid, sure; so had Sully. Impossible not to be when faced with the scenario they'd dealt with. But she'd handled it. She'd faced down the fear, and she'd given Sully the sort of backup he'd largely only been able to count on from Dez.

Last night had proven more than what Sarah was capable of. It had shown Sully how wrong he'd been to believe his role was to shelter her. She was stronger than that, smarter and far more capable than he'd given her credit for.

She could handle his world, so he could meet her in the middle and share hers. And he now knew without a doubt he could do it without fear.

"You're quiet," Lachlan said.

"I'm always quiet."

Lachlan cast him a glance. "You sure you're good?"

Sully met him with a smile. "Yeah," he said, "I'm good."

JUNE MALCOLM LIVED ALONE in a large house on the northwest side of town, within an older neighbourhood called Crestview. Once its own town—one populated by wealthier, white-collar workers who wished to be near the city but not within it—Kimotan Rapids had since swelled to encompass it. The homes—many of them classic brick-and-stone structures—had held their value, and it remained a sought-after location to this day.

June's home was a two-storey brick with windows suggesting it possessed the sort of full attic many people had taken to turning into a bonus space, a master suite or a rental apartment.

As they pulled up next to the property on the street—no

driveway given homes of this era typically had garages off the back alley—Sully cast a doubtful eye toward the back of the vehicle.

Lachlan appeared to pick up on it. "What do you want to do with the dummy? And no, I wasn't talking about your brother."

Sully figured Lachlan was angling for a laugh, so he gave him a quick one before getting back to business. "I hate leaving it here, but lugging it into the house doesn't make much sense." Not just because he didn't want the dummy around anyone else either. The safe wasn't oversized at all, but its weight sure made it seem like it.

Lachlan ducked his head, the better to see the house out the passenger-side window. "I'm not fond of leaving a pricy historic artifact unattended. Tell you what: let's see if she's up for having a chat on her veranda there. The weather's nice enough today, and we could keep an eye on the car."

Sully liked the plan, and it turned out June wasn't opposed to it either.

"I hate to waste a nice spring day indoors," she said. "I can get us some tea. It will ward off the chill."

Sully was about to politely refuse the offer when Lachlan overruled him. "Tea would be wonderful," Lachlan said.

June was gone less than five minutes, suggesting she'd already had tea and snacks in the works before her company arrived. She returned with a tray laden with a teapot, cups and saucers, sugar, cream, spoons and a plate of cookies. Sully immediately assisted with the tray, placing it carefully atop a small, dust-covered table between a pair of wicker chairs.

"Hope you're all right with oatmeal cookies," June said. "They're all I had on hand. I'm diabetic, so I don't buy sweets very often."

"Oatmeal's fine," Lachlan said, proving it by shoving half of one into his mouth.

Lachlan had already taken one of the chairs, and Sully waved away June's attempt to usher him into the other.

"I'm fine standing," he told her. "I sat all the way here."

June smiled appreciatively as she lowered herself into the remaining seat. She was on the heavier side, and the way she'd been moving, Sully suspected she needed a knee replacement.

"This is a beautiful home," Lachlan said once he'd swallowed the cookie and chased it down with a swig of cream-cooled tea.

"Thank you. It's been in my family for a while. There aren't many of us left—there weren't really many of us to start with—so it meant I inherited a fair bit from my parents, including the house."

"I understand you're a descendant of Warren Malcolm's brother," Lachlan said.

June clasped her hands over one of her knees—the one Sully had seen her favouring. "I am. Lawrence Malcolm—Uncle Warren's brother—was my grandfather. Warren would be my great-uncle." She leaned forward. "Do you have Mr. Grin with you?"

The request Sully had been dreading. He was attempting to mentally formulate a response when Lachlan spoke up.

"Bit of a difficult issue," he said. "My associate here will no doubt explain it better than I ever could, but we have some safety concerns regarding the dummy."

Sully blinked as he regarded Lachlan. He'd expected his boss to invent an excuse; he hadn't expected him to offer a toned-down truth.

Then again, Lachlan had mentioned June was eager to meet Sully. Could be she had already expressed interest in the paranormal. If so, why shield her from the truth, even as ugly as it was? Anyway, given her family's history, she had to be well-versed already in ugly truths.

Her eyes held a question as she turned to Sully, so he went

about answering it. "We were initially called to investigate because the museum that was bequeathed Mr. Grin was having some trouble with it. Truth be told, it's—"

June held up a hand to stop him. "Haunted. I'm aware."

Sully lifted a brow. "How did you know?"

She tilted her head. "It's a bit strange. I had a visit a while back from the fellow who purchased Mr. Grin at auction. James Holmes. Incidentally, he also bought Uncle Warren's old house."

"We know," Sully said. "The place has some issues of its own."

June gave a grim smile. "Oh yes. I actually went there at James's request to speak to him about Mr. Grin. I had a terrible feeling the whole time I was there. Couldn't wait to get out, honestly."

"Why did he call you in the first place?" Lachlan asked.

June paused for a long sip of tea. She swallowed a little heavily, and although he'd only just met her, Sully could see the discomfort in her expression.

She set the cup down before answering. "He told me he believed there was something unusual about Mr. Grin. He said he'd done some research on my family, which was how he found me. He wondered whether I'd ever heard any stories about the dummy—more specifically, whether it was reputedly possessed."

Sully leaned back carefully against the railing, ensuring it would support his weight before sitting atop it. "Had you?"

"Actually, yes, I had. When I was a little girl, Uncle Warren absolutely fascinated me. Part of the reason, I suppose, was because my grandfather steadfastly refused to discuss him with his children. Lawrence and Warren had a sister, though—my great-aunt Edith—and she was far more willing to speak about Uncle Warren. Unfortunately, my grandfather had a difficult relationship with his brother. Jealousy, I understand. Warren was talented, handsome and, as a result of his act with Mr. Grin, very wealthy.

"It didn't matter to my grandfather that Warren neither sought out fame nor particularly enjoyed it. If anything, Uncle Warren shrank from it. He was a very private person, I was told. I think he set out to make some money doing what he loved but ended up with far more than he'd bargained for."

All very interesting, and likely important to know, but June hadn't quite answered the question.

"What about the dummy?" Lachlan asked.

June grimaced and gave an embarrassed giggle. "I'm sorry. I do tend to get off track. Anyway, yes, the dummy. Well, after Uncle Warren died, his property was divided equally between my grandfather and my aunt. Their parents had already passed away, you see, and Warren had no wife or children."

Sully held his tongue for now. There would be time for questions later.

"Neither my grandfather nor Edith wanted the house, not after what happened there. They agreed to sell it and split the profits. I'm sure you can guess they made a pretty princely sum. My grandfather used the money to buy this house. As for the rest of the property, they divided it between them. My grandfather ended up with Mr. Grin and a few other things."

Sully and Lachlan exchanged a glance.

"Hold on," Lachlan said. "Our understanding was that Mr. Grin was stolen following the attack on Warren."

June flushed. "Oh. Oh dear. I suppose I shouldn't have said anything."

"Why is that?"

"Well, I only know what I was told by my aunt, you understand. But I believe my grandfather was concerned Mr. Grin could be stolen from Warren's house and privately sold by someone looking to make some money—even by a police officer, potentially. My grandfather attended the house in the aftermath of the attack, and he took Mr. Grin with him. The police believed the dummy had been stolen, and I'm afraid no one in my family corrected this assumption. It's very possible the police would have taken the dummy as evidence, and the family didn't want that. It would have been extremely easy for some unscrupulous person to make off with it. My grandfather wanted to keep Mr. Grin in the family."

She paused for another sip of tea. Sully suspected Lachlan was chomping at the bit to ask her to keep going, but he wisely kept his mouth shut.

June swallowed, this time keeping the cup in her hands, wrapping her fingers around it as if to warm them. "It wasn't long after Warren died that my grandfather met a bad end. Something else my family doesn't talk about, really. I don't know how to explain it—he went mad. Despite him not being close to Warren, he was apparently badly impacted by his brother's death. He was an absolute bear with his wife and kids, and he began accusing Edith and her husband of trying to take more of the estate than was their right. Edith and her husband, my uncle Roger, took in a baby girl named Beth shortly after Warren's death. Edith never told me why, but she said she believed Beth had a claim to Warren's property. I have no proof of this, mind you, but I've always wondered whether Beth was actually Warren's."

The pieces had started to fold together in Sully's mind, a truth dawning he hadn't anticipated when they'd come here.

"How did Mr. Grin end up at the train station?" he asked June. "Do you have any idea?"

"It was my Aunt Edith, actually. I mentioned Mr. Grin was haunted. I think the automatic assumption would be that it was my uncle Warren, but I think it was my grandfather. My aunt told me that before his death, Lawrence became obsessed with Mr. Grin. He'd started taking it everywhere with him. He watched it endlessly. Sometimes she'd even catch him staring into its eyes, as if he were in a trance. And he'd mutter things like, 'He knows.' It was as if he'd become convinced Mr. Grin was alive."

"Could it be it was haunted already?" Lachlan asked.

"My aunt never saw any evidence of such a thing, not before Lawrence died. Afterward was a different story. She took Mr. Grin, but she didn't keep it for long. One night, she awoke and went to check on Beth. Mr. Grin was inside the crib, looming over the baby. She wasn't harmed, but Aunt Edith had no doubt in her mind as to the threat. She never said what she did with Mr. Grin. Refused to tell me, actually. Said it was safer no one ever find it.

"In retrospect, it makes sense. Roger was a porter at the train station. As I understand it, the area where they found the trunk was the old lost property section. Roger spent a long career at the station and was still alive when it closed. He would have been in a position to watch over it and make sure Mr. Grin was never found."

"You said you believed your grandfather is the one haunting Mr. Grin," Sully said. "What makes you say that?"

June peered down into her cup. "I feel terrible even saying it out loud."

"Please," Sully said. "It's important."

June met Sully's eye. While she didn't immediately reply, she didn't look away either. Finally, she drew in a breath.

"My aunt said Lawrence came over one day with Mr. Grin. Aunt Edith thought he wanted to play with Beth. But when she walked into Beth's nursery, Lawrence was trying to suffocate her. She screamed, and he ran. He tried to kill Beth, and I think it was because he worried she'd someday lay claim to Uncle Warren's estate. You see, Uncle Warren had left everything to his siblings, but only if he didn't have children to inherit.

"Now, given he wasn't married, it would have been a great scandal at the time, him having a child. So I believe that's how my aunt and uncle ended up taking her in. They would have kept her identity a secret to protect her, of course, but there would always have been a chance it would have become known one day. As soon as that happened, I suppose Lawrence would have lost everything—this house, Mr. Grin, money he inherited. All of it would have been gone."

"What happened to Beth?" Lachlan asked. "Did she stay with your aunt and uncle?"

June shook her head. "Not after that. After the attempt on Beth's life, my aunt and uncle took steps to protect her. They didn't just conceal Mr. Grin. They concealed Beth. All I was told is they gave her to some trusted friends to raise, along with a promise they'd turn over her share of the inheritance once she came of age. I think their worry was that Lawrence might find a way to come back. If Mr. Grin escaped the trunk, Beth might suffer the consequences—unless, of course, he was unable to discover where she was."

"And you don't know anything more about her?" Sully asked.

"No, nothing. They kept her new identity a secret, even from other members of their family. Considering it was a family member who'd targeted her in the first place, who can blame them?"

The vision came back to Sully, the image of the jewel-adorned cane. "Did your grandfather happen to use a walking stick?"

June's brows lifted. "Why, yes, he did. He was shot while serving in the First World War. The injury was debilitating enough he couldn't return to the Front. He was sent home and used a cane until he died."

"Do you happen to have a photo of him with this cane?" Sully asked.

"I believe I do." June placed her cup on the tray, then used the chair's armrests to heave herself to her feet.

Lachlan waited until she'd limped back inside. "What are you thinking?"

"I had a vision. I think I know what happened to Warren."

Once June returned with the photo, Sully's theory was proven. Though he hadn't seen the face of the killer, he'd seen his cane. The one held in Lawrence's lap in this photo was unquestionably the same cane.

Granted, it could have been wielded by someone else, but given the nature of Lawrence's injury and his permanent need for the cane, Sully doubted it would have left his side.

"You said James Holmes asked you over," Sully reminded June.

She nodded. "He thought it was my uncle haunting the dummy. He hoped as a member of the family, I could reason with him, help put him to rest. I did my best, but I don't think I was much help." Her eyes misted over. "I feel responsible somehow for what happened to that poor man. He was so scared, and he wanted me to help. I can't help wondering if my grandfather had something to do with what happened to him. I heard he died falling down the stairs in that house."

Sully nodded. "He did, but it's not your fault, all right? None of it is your fault."

"Maybe I can help prevent something bad happening to someone else. Maybe if I try harder or find the right thing to say, I can fix this. This all originated with my family. Maybe it needs to end with us. Maybe it needs to end with *me*."

Sully forced a smile, one he intended to show he was sympathetic to what she was experiencing. "You're putting way too much on yourself, June. Ghosts are just like any other person. They have motives of their own, and they sometimes find ways to act on them. If a person doesn't listen to family members when they're alive, they won't be any more willing to listen once they're dead—not unless it's going to benefit them in some way or if they've grown enough to grasp a different sort of reality. Lawrence hasn't grown. If anything, he's only become more bitter. Lawrence figured out how to use Mr. Grin to achieve his own ends. He would have followed through on his intentions no matter what you did."

"Why Mr. Holmes though? Horrible enough to target a baby, but at least I can grasp a motive—disgusting though it is. Mr. Holmes is another story. What did he ever do to Lawrence?"

Sully thought back to last night's attack. "James tried to control Mr. Grin, which meant he was, without knowing it, trying to control Lawrence. And Lawrence doesn't strike me as the sort of person to sit back while someone else decides his fate."

"Is there anything you can do?" June asked. "Any way you can stop him?"

Sully held her eye, pouring confidence into his gaze. "I'll stop him. One way or another, I'll make sure he won't hurt anyone else."

June released a breath, her shoulders dropping with clear relief. "Thank you. I thought I could try to talk to him through the dummy, but I really dreaded seeing it again, actually. This whole thing has made me so sick. I'm so grateful you found your way to this case."

Sully wasn't nearly as pleased about the situation, but he'd long since grasped the necessity of his involvement.

One more question occurred to him. "June, how did Lawrence die?"

"It happened while he was running from Beth's nursery. Probably his bad leg tripped him up."

June's final statement popped into Sully's brain a moment before she said the words out loud.

"He fell down the stairs."

25

DEZ, Sully and Lachlan regrouped shortly after at their office, one of several businesses located inside what was once a Victorian mansion north of the river.

Dez provided a rundown of what Amelia had told him before listening to Sully and Lachlan's discovery. While he'd begun to question the theory about Frank being the one to kill Warren, Dez hadn't expected this as the solution to their mystery.

"Lawrence Malcolm?" he said, eyes shifting between Sully and Lachlan. "He killed Warren? Why?"

Sully crossed his arms as he leaned back on the desk. "The two of them never got along to begin with. Lawrence was jealous of Warren's success, his fame and his money. And he was mentally unstable, possibly at least in part because of his combat experience."

Lachlan sat forward in his desk chair, settling his elbows atop the desk. "We might never have all the answers. What we do know is Warren's estate was to be divided between his two siblings." He held up an index finger. "As long as Warren had no offspring."

"Only he did," Dez concluded. "And Lawrence apparently caught wind of it."

"Precisely," Lachlan said. "Now, I don't know whether Lawrence would have been told from the start or if he found out by accident. What we do know is Paulette was taken in by Warren's sister Edith. The baby was renamed Beth before she was handed over to another couple to raise. We don't know the names of the couple, so no way to know what became of Beth."

"She never inherited as she was meant to?"

Lachlan leaned back, his chair protesting the movement with a noisy squeak. He threaded his fingers behind his head before answering. "In a roundabout way, she did. Edith and Roger held the bulk of their share of Warren's money in trust for Beth until she came of age. While June couldn't say for sure what happened, it's likely Edith and Roger found a way to get the money to Beth—probably via the adoptive parents to ensure Beth didn't discover anything she shouldn't. All for her protection, it would seem."

Dez, seated in one of the room's other chairs, pinched at his lower lip. "What about Lawrence's share? What happened to that money?"

"Stayed with Lawrence's family," Sully said. "Edith didn't want to deprive Lawrence's own kids, especially since she was close to them too. Given the amount they made on Warren's house and its contents, Edith and Roger had enough to live on even after putting Beth's money away for her. They weren't greedy about it."

Lachlan's eyes strayed to the lockbox containing the dummy. "Not like that Lawrence bastard."

"Still don't understand why he killed Warren," Dez said. "I mean, he would have been jealous a long time without acting on it. What pushed him over the edge?"

Sully glanced at the box before focusing back on Dez. "Maybe I can find out if I open myself up to another vision."

"No," Dez said firmly. "Not that important."

"I've got a theory," Lachlan said.

Naturally, Dez thought.

Lachlan went on without waiting for anyone to ask. "It's little more than a guess, mind you, but you said the brothers were arguing, Sully. Correct?"

Sully peered at Lachlan. "Definitely. Warren was really pissed off. And the hate coming off Lawrence was off the charts."

"Right. Well, I think it might be Lawrence found out about Paulette—or Beth, I guess. He would have wanted to know where he stood insofar as any bequeathals. The brothers already disliked each other—"

Dez cut in. "If they didn't like each other, why wouldn't Warren have simply cut Lawrence out of the will?"

"June Malcolm actually had a copy of the will," Lachlan said. "Turns out it was made years before Warren's death. He was still a relatively young man when he died. Common for people to neglect to update their wills when they don't feel they have a pressing reason. Hell, I think my will still names my ex-wife as my beneficiary. Guess I should do something about that. Anyway"—he cast Dez a pointed glare as an apparent warning to let him finish—"money was already a sore spot. Likely Lawrence put up with a certain amount of frustration given he figured he stood to inherit in the event of Warren's death. But with this baby suddenly in the mix, it changed things. Big time. Maybe Lawrence went over to ask Warren to alter the will to include his siblings as well as any offspring. Maybe he just went to air his grievances or to confront Warren about his indiscretions with this married woman. Whatever it was, it's clear a heated argument occurred. I mean, you don't remark on a man's child and expect he won't react."

It made sense to Dez, as much as homicide would ever make sense. "And the cane? You're sure it's the same one, Sully?"

Sully nodded. "Positive. It was a distinctive cane. June said she heard Warren bought it for Lawrence after he was shipped back home with his injury. Seemed like Warren spared no expense. And yeah, I thought about the possibility someone else could have used it to kill Warren, but I doubt it. Between the cost of the thing and the fact Lawrence needed it for mobility, I doubt he would have—or even *could* have—let someone borrow it."

Dez frowned. "So Lawrence beat his brother to death with the same cane Warren bought to help him. Nice guy."

Lachlan leaned forward, causing another creak from his chair. "If we've answered all your questions, Braddock, there's something I'm wondering about." He turned to Sully. "We strongly suspect it was a combination of greed and mental illness which led Lawrence to kill Warren and attempt to murder Beth. What I don't get is why he still seems so bent on killing people. Where's the motive now?"

"Like I mentioned to June, I don't get the impression Lawrence likes being controlled by others.," Sully said. "He spent years locked away thanks to Edith and Roger. He would have come out of the trunk wanting to make someone pay."

"So much so he'd go after anyone?"

"Anyone he sees as a threat. Edith and Roger aren't around anymore, and no one can tell us what happened to Beth. Lawrence can't target any of them. What he can do is try to keep himself from being locked away ever again. Lawrence formed some sort of a weird bond with Mr. Grin before he died. Treated it as if it were alive. I think his spirit attached itself to the dummy afterward, maybe for no better reason than his desire to follow through on killing Beth. It wouldn't have been about the money for him, not anymore. I think he was already bent on revenge. It was why Edith and Roger were smart to give Beth up."

Dez dropped his elbows onto his chair's armrests and steepled his fingers beneath his chin. "So he killed James Holmes because he locked up Mr. Grin, and he's going after the people at the museum—and Sully for that matter—for doing the same. What's the fix? We can't just let him out of the box and say, 'Here you go, buddy, enjoy your freedom.'"

"No," Sully said. "I need to draw him out and send him over. Problem is, I think I need to take care of the entity at the Holmes estate at the same time. It's where Lawrence is drawing his power."

Dez tapped on Sully's knee. "Hey, no offence, but it sounds like a terrible idea to me. You take Mr. Grin and Lawrence back inside with that demon-type thing, and who's to say how they might feed off each other? We think Mr. Grin's a problem now—might turn out we ain't seen nothing yet."

Sully sighed. "I see your point. I guess I can try to pull him out here, force him to cross over."

Lachlan cleared his throat. "Not in my office. You want to do your exorcist thing, you take it elsewhere. The building owner's still not happy with having me as a tenant thanks to that time years back when I was attacked in here. We end up in some epic paranormal struggle, we'll be out on our asses in the mud inside of five minutes. Take it elsewhere."

Dez met Sully's eye. "Any ideas?"

Sully shrugged. "I don't know, but we'd better come up with something quick."

Dez considered this. "What about a large, walk-in safe, if we can find one? That way, when we open the lockbox, Mr. Grin won't be able to get away on us."

"No good," Sully said. "If spirit can't pass through iron, I don't think I'd be able to open a doorway and send him through that way. Even worse, I think I'm going to have to release it from the chain. It acts as a barrier too."

Dez grimaced. "Bloody hell." He rubbed at the corners of his eyes, pinching back building pressure. "This sucks."

"Tell me about it," Sully said. "I'm going to need to be quick if I'm going to get this done without anyone getting hurt."

Dez closed his eyes, thinking it through further before offering additional thought. "Okay, how about this? If we're going to maintain the upper hand, the element of surprise might be useful. Maybe we need to pick our location. The Holmes estate is too dangerous, so maybe we go somewhere else meaningful to Lawrence."

Lachlan lifted his brows and jabbed a finger toward Dez, suggesting he'd followed Dez's train of thought. "June Malcolm."

Dez nodded. "She lives in Lawrence's old house. Taking him back there and letting him see it might be enough to give us a few seconds to get a leg up on him."

Sully lowered his brows, thoughts playing out across his face. "I had a hard time getting a grasp on the ghost inside the dummy before. I think Mr. Grin acts as a sort of fortress for him or something. I think I can do it, but it might take a bit longer than a few seconds."

"Do we have longer than a few seconds?"

Sully looked to be forcing a smile. "Guess we won't know until we try."

26

SULLY SAT in the passenger seat of Dez's SUV as they made their way to June Malcolm's.

While he knew Dez better than almost anyone, he figured even a stranger could sense the bundle of nerves fraying inside Dez as they drove.

"I don't like this." Dez barely cast Sully a glance as he said it, his eyes fixed on the road ahead, knuckles white as he clenched the steering wheel.

"Me neither," Sully said. "Not like we have much of a choice though."

"Well aware." Dez passed a hand over his face. "You know, sometimes I get really sick of ghosts determining our lives for us. Would be nice if they'd do things on our terms once in a while."

Sully slouched in his seat, training his gaze out the window. "Story of my life."

They drove the rest of the way in silence, Dez turning up the music en route. Lachlan had elected to remain behind, which Sully thought was a good idea. The fewer people around as possible while he dealt with Lawrence and Mr. Grin, the better.

When they pulled up in front of her home, June was in the window as if watching for their arrival.

"Think we can convince her to leave while we deal with this?" Dez asked.

Sully's lips pressed into a straight line as he eyed the living room window and the woman awaiting them inside. "Gonna try my damnedest."

Dez turned his gaze on Sully. "What about Mr. Grin? Think we need to wrestle the lockbox inside, or should we remove him here?"

"Not that I want to make more work for us, but I'm going to suggest the lockbox. I'd rather Lawrence not clue in as to where he is until I'm absolutely ready for him."

Dez gave a tight nod and bailed out of the vehicle.

The two of them grunted, teeth gritted, as they lugged the safe toward the house. It hadn't gotten any lighter. They'd moved it around a couple of times today already, and Sully already couldn't wait to see the back of this thing.

With luck, they'd be done with it very soon.

By the time they arrived at the door, June was waiting for them.

"Is that him?" Her voice came out slightly hushed, her eyes fixed to the lockbox in Sully and Dez's hands.

"Yeah," Dez said. "Okay for us to bring this inside?"

She nodded rather than answering audibly, holding the door open for them to pass.

"Don't worry about your boots," she said. "Where would you like to do this?"

"Here's fine," Sully said, using his chin to nod toward a spot near the base of the stairs in the entry hall. Though he and Dez set the safe down as carefully as possible, it still landed with a heavy thunk.

June stood with her arms hugging her body. "Now that it's here, I'm not so sure I want to see it."

Although June hadn't asked for one, Sully made a quick introduction, ensuring she knew Dez was working with him. Preliminaries out of the way, he acknowledged her most recent comment.

"You don't have to see Mr. Grin," he told her. "In fact, I'd kind of rather you don't. If it's okay with you, I was going to suggest you head to a neighbour's while we deal with this."

Her lips formed a tight smile. "I don't really know my neighbours anymore, I'm afraid. Not well enough to simply drop in on them. Anyway, I think I should stay. I wasn't able to help James, but maybe I'll be able to do something to help you."

Sully doubted it. Often when people who didn't understand the paranormal tried to work with it—good intentions or not—they failed to accomplish anything. Worst case scenario, they made the situation worse.

"It could get kind of hairy," Sully said.

"Sully told me James had asked you to go and see him about Mr. Grin," Dez said. "Didn't you see the dummy then?"

She shook her head. "He had it locked away at the time, he told me. He refused to take it out. I spoke through a wall at it." Her eyes once again dropped to the box and stayed there, staring. "Where would you like me to be?"

Preferably, another city until this was over, Sully thought. Out loud, all he said was, "Stay away from the entry hall, out of direct sight of the dummy. I don't think Lawrence should have any issues with you, but I don't want to take chances."

Dez raised a brow, silently mouthing, "Upstairs?"

Sully shook his head. He'd thought about asking June to move either upstairs or to another room but decided he'd feel better if he could see her. God forbid Mr. Grin got away from them and got to June before they could.

He waited until June obeyed his instructions, settling herself rigidly into a chair in a sitting room off the hall. Then Sully met Dez's eye, silently exchanging thoughts about their upcoming move.

Sully raised a brow. Dez raised one back, then set his jaw and nodded. He was ready.

Sully would need to be ready too.

He took a moment, centring himself, ensuring he was as calm as he could be. With calm came strength and power. Fear and anxiety would give the ghost something to latch onto.

Once his heart rate and breathing settled, he knelt next to the lockbox.

Dez remained standing, a formidable presence at Sully's right shoulder as Sully worked the lock open. He took a breath before flipping open the lid, ignoring the way it hit the stair banister a little too hard.

Sully didn't delay. He reached into the box and withdrew the still-chained dummy. A sharp intake of breath came from June behind him, and he instantly regretted not insisting she find somewhere else to be. Too late now.

"When I take off the chain, be ready," Sully told Dez as he stood with the dummy. The words, he knew, were unnecessary, Dez's posture revealing he was far from relaxed.

Sully steeled himself and pulled the chain free.

The emotion rolling off Lawrence was palpable. Surprise, confusion, anger—everything competing. Sully took the emotions in, allowing the unpleasant connection in order to get a hold of Lawrence.

Lawrence who had already started to control the dummy. Its eyes flashed wide, head snapping to the side to focus on the staircase. These weren't the stairs on which he'd met his end, but they were stairs nonetheless. Lawrence had both died and killed on staircases; they carried meaning for him.

Rage filled Lawrence—rage he desperately wished to sate. Locked onto him, Sully knew this easily, felt it as if it were his own.

All of this within just a few short seconds.

"Sully," Dez said. The word was a warning to move.

Sully moved. Psychically, he grabbed hold of Lawrence, pushing past Mr. Grin's physical walls to get there. His eyes fixed on Mr. Grin's, holding there as if by looking into those hideous orbs, he might see into Lawrence's soul.

He pulled, felt Lawrence's shock as he was gradually pulled from the dummy.

But the connection was strong, fortified by decades of attachment to this unlikely object. Lawrence tugged back, and for a moment, Sully nearly released him. Lawrence was stronger than expected. Much stronger. The reason came to Sully in a flash.

The Holmes estate entity.

Lawrence possessed a connection to the entity, one that remained firm even now, miles away from the source. He'd found new strength there, and he'd never let go.

The element of surprise Sully had counted on was failing.

"Chain," he managed to get out. He sensed Dez moving, bending to reach the chain Sully had laid on the floor.

Lawrence sensed it too. Mr. Grin's head whipped toward Dez, mouth working.

Behind Sully, June screamed.

The sound startled Sully, set his nerves on edge, breaking his calm. Into this, Lawrence pushed.

Sully saw himself in the closet, curled on the floor, surrounded by boxes and recycling. He held a box containing the slow cooker over his head and shoulders to protect himself, but his body started and writhed with each painful blow from the baseball bat.

Over and over, he was hit. And with each pained grunt from Sully, Lawrence's excitement—his bloodlust—grew.

•

"Sully!"

The strangled shout from Dez cut through the vision. Or rather—as Sully abruptly discovered—Lawrence released him from the vision. He was busy with something else.

He was busy with Dez.

The chain Dez had been trying to rebind Mr. Grin with was now wrapped around his neck.

Fear gripped Sully as he dashed toward Dez, who was writhing on the floor, hands scrabbling at the chain in an attempt to pull it free. Sully crouched, his own fingers fighting for purchase on the chain.

But it was tight. Too tight for either of them to budge. The flesh of Dez's neck pinched beneath the chain, his face reddening with trapped blood as he kicked blindly at the floor.

"Lawrence!" June cried out. "Stop this! Stop it now!"

Sully thought he heard her moving nearer. The temporary distraction was enough to bring him back to himself a little.

Get Mr. Grin, he reminded himself.

He forced himself away from Dez to turn back to the dummy, intending to lock back onto the ghost inside. June was already there. Her lower joints weren't good, but she managed a solid kick nonetheless, booting the dummy down the hall.

Sully felt the release almost immediately as Lawrence lost his grip on them. Sully spun back toward Dez, and together, they pulled the chain free.

Dez curled onto his side, one hand keeping his upper body partially lifted as he wheezed and hacked. Sully gripped his shoulder, setting himself up as a barrier between Dez and the last place he'd seen Mr. Grin. The chain lay curled on the floor, and Sully picked it up before returning to Dez's side.

"You okay, D?" he asked.

Still coughing, Dez managed a nod.

Sully's eyes made the short journey from June to the spot

down the hall where Mr. Grin had landed. A spot no longer occupied by the dummy.

"You didn't happen to move it, did you?" Sully asked her.

June, clearly rattled, gave her head a quick shake. "I didn't go near it again." Already pale, she lost another shade. "Do you want me to look for it?"

"Not yet," Sully said. "We'll go together as soon as Dez is feeling better."

Dez batted at Sully's thigh. "Dez is feeling better. Give me a hand up."

Sully did as asked, tugging him to his feet. Dez was shaking, but then, so was Sully.

Dez rubbed at his throat, where an ugly red line had formed across his skin. In a couple of spots, the skin was scraped and scratched. While Dez would bear physical evidence of the attack for at least a few days, he was alive. To Sully, nothing was more important.

With Dez set, Sully picked up the chain, and they started down the hall, June pulling up the rear.

"Stay close," he told her over his shoulder. At this point, he was going with the safety in numbers approach. "By the way, thank you."

"No need," she said. She didn't add to it, the tension in her tone evident.

Dez pressed near to Sully. "That room at the end, what is it?"

"Rear parlour," June said. "I've been using it as an office."

"Does it connect to anything?"

"There's no other way in or out. Except the window, I suppose, but I don't think it even opens anymore. It needs fixed."

"How many potential hiding places would there be for Mr. Grin?" Sully asked.

"A few, I guess. Under the desk. On the far side of the bookshelf. I have a few boxes in there, but they're full of stuff, so no room in them for something his size."

The room proved to be neat, June seemingly not one for clutter. It took less than a minute to ascertain Mr. Grin was no longer in there.

"Oh God," Dez muttered.

Sully didn't ask him to elaborate on his thoughts. He was certain their minds had gone to the same place.

"Where is it?" June asked. "I know I kicked it down this way. It couldn't be anywhere else."

Sully wasn't sure how much he wanted to tell her. The truth wouldn't make her feel better.

Except he didn't really have a choice. Not anymore.

"It's going to sound weird," he said. "But ghosts can move around between locations. I can't explain why because I don't really understand it myself, but sometimes ghosts are able to do the same thing with physical objects."

"Move them between places?" she asked. "You're right. It sounds weird. Weird and terrifying. You're telling me this thing could be anywhere inside my house right now?"

"We won't leave until we find it," Sully assured her.

But already, he had his doubts. Whatever had happened, his connection to Lawrence and Mr. Grin had faded. He didn't feel the ghost at all now, the same as it had been when Mr. Grin was locked away inside the gun safe. He hated to think why.

With June between them for safety, Sully and Dez spent the next twenty minutes searching the house. They moved methodically, covering first the entirety of the ground floor before heading to the upper floor. To Dez's dismay, they swept the basement and the dusty and cramped attic as well. Throughout the search, Sully kept himself open to the spirit, reaching out for any psychic sign of it.

Nothing.

Lawrence was gone, Mr. Grin with him.

Back on the ground floor, Sully pinched at the bridge of his nose and gritted his teeth. He muttered a curse word under his breath, resisting the urge to kick the now-useless lockbox. He'd already lost Mr. Grin. Finding it again would only be more difficult with a broken toe.

Dez landed a hand on Sully's back, giving it a solid pat. "Hey. We'll find him."

Before Sully could debate the truth of the statement, Dez's phone rang.

Dez fished it from his pocket, grimacing as he met Sully's eye. "It's Evelyn. What should I tell her?"

Sully had no idea. How were they going to explain having lost a valuable historical artifact, let alone the fact it had managed to slip away of its own accord?

Dez answered. "Dez here."

Even though Dez had the phone to his ear, Sully could easily hear Evelyn.

She was frantic.

Dez clicked the speaker button for Sully's benefit, holding the phone between them as he tried to cut into her panic. "Evelyn—Evelyn—slow down. I'm with Sully now. I need you to calm down and tell us what's happening."

She stopped, took a breath. She sounded shaky, even tearful.

"Please," she said. "Help me. Please."

"What's wrong?" Sully asked. "Where are you?"

"At the Holmes estate—Bob and I. Mr. Grin just showed up. I just saw it. It came at me. Please."

Sully and Dez exchanged a wide-eyed look.

"What do you mean, it came at you?" Sully asked.

"I was on the second floor, near the staircase. It jumped out of the shadows. It—oh God—I think it did something to Bob. He won't answer. And now it's—" She broke off in a sob, heaved a breath in a bid to get out the rest of what she needed to say.

Sully knew what she was going to say before she said it. It didn't make her words any less shocking.

"It tried to push me. Please come. Please! It's trying to kill me!"

27

Sully and Dez were rushing out to Dez's SUV when the call with Evelyn cut out. When Dez tried to get her back, the call went immediately to voicemail. Two more attempts garnered the same result.

Dez jammed his phone back into his pocket. "Shit."

"It doesn't have to mean anything horrible," Sully said. "Ghosts drain batteries, remember? Could be what happened."

He'd meant the words as much to make himself feel better as he'd intended them to comfort Dez. It didn't work.

At the passenger-side door, Sully paused to catch Dez's eye over the roof. "Maybe I could see if June has a car I could borrow. I can go to the Holmes estate on my own, and you can go find Dad, Jack and Aiden."

"No. It's too far. You'd get to the estate way before I could make it even halfway to Edge Creek. You're not doing this alone, Sully. Not even for five minutes."

Dez yanked open the driver's side door and got into the SUV, forcing Sully to do the same on his side. Sully clipped in his seat-belt while Dez steered back onto the road and sped down the block, eyes scanning endlessly for potential hazards the way he would have learned during his policing days.

Dez didn't take his eyes from the road as he continued with his statement. "You can handle this, Sull. I know it seems like a lot, but you can do it."

Sully wasn't so sure. "I know I said I had to face this down if I wanted a life with Sarah, but I don't know now. It tossed us around like we didn't weigh anything. What if I can't do this?"

"You can."

Sully's gaze shot to the side of Dez's head. "No, I mean it. What if I can't? It's not just Sarah, Dez. It's you too. It's our clients. If I fail to stop this thing, and someone gets hurt because of it, I won't be able to handle it."

Dez risked a glance at Sully, catching his eye before returning his visual attention to the road. "You can do this. And you know how I know? You're the strongest person I've ever known. You need to stop worrying about everything and everyone else and focus. That's all. Focus. You can't let yourself get distracted. Trust me to take care of myself and our clients. I can handle it. You take care of your part. If we can work as a team, we'll get this done. We're partners, Sull. Equal partners. If we each do what we do best, we'll make it through this."

Despite the situation, Sully felt a smile plucking at his lips. "Sarah kind of told me the same thing."

"And she kicked ass. I know I've had my ass handed to me a couple times since we took this job, but I'm still good to go here. Homicidal puppet or not."

Sully chuckled. "Okay. Okay, I hear you. Partners. We've got this."

Though still not convinced, he had the rest of the drive to work himself up to believing it.

He'd need to believe it if they were going to beat this thing.

THE GATE WAS UNLOCKED when they arrived. Evelyn hadn't told them why they were at the estate, nor had she mentioned having a key, but he supposed they'd been given one by a lawyer involved. Probably Jill. Wouldn't surprise Sully she'd be in no hurry to return here, not even with the museum officials.

"Why'd they come here?" Dez grumbled as he ate up the rest of the distance to the house.

Sully didn't respond. He didn't have the answer, and Dez probably wasn't looking for one. Not from Sully, anyway.

Dez jammed his foot on the brake as they neared the house, pulling to a stop next to a half-ton truck with the museum's insignia on the side.

No sign outside of either Bob or Evelyn.

Dez shut off the SUV, and he and Sully bailed out, racing to the front door. Dez made it there first, taking the steps in one bound. By the time Sully regained his side, Dez had the front door open.

Sully pushed past him, entering the shadowy interior. The place was eerily quiet. So quiet, Sully's thoughts travelled to dark places as he envisioned what fate might have met their clients.

The silence was alive, sentient and evil all on its own. It pressed down on Sully as if it intended to suffocate. He tried twice before managing to draw in a full breath. He used the moment to centre himself, to work himself up toward shattering the silence. He had no choice but to shatter it.

"Evelyn? Bob?" His shout in the dark seemed to him like a rock through a window. "Where are you?"

Nothing.

Not at first.

Then Dez grabbed his arm. "Hear that?"

"Hear what?"

"Evelyn! She's screaming for help! Bob's hurt."

Sully hadn't heard anything. "You sure? I didn't—"

Dez had yet to release him. He tugged hard as he started off. "Sounds like it's coming from the back of the house! Come on!"

Sully still hadn't heard anything, and for him, it meant one thing.

Ghost.

Damn it. Did it mean they were already too late? Or was it something else?

They hadn't been to the kitchen before, but Sully had seen it in the vision. He thought it must be toward the back of the main floor, which was the direction Dez was taking them.

Sully didn't recall seeing any other doorways leading from the hall beside the stairs. Instead, he ducked into a room to the left from the entryway, using his cellphone flash to prevent their crashing into furniture. They passed a sitting room, then a large dining room before coming to a set of pocket doors that had been drawn shut.

"Evelyn?" Sully called out.

Still, he didn't hear anything. But Dez, fingers tightening painfully, clearly had.

"She's on the other side of these doors," he said.

While Sully couldn't hear what Dez had, he could sure as hell feel something. It was here, uncomfortably close, a whirlwind of negative energy pulsing from the entity. Just beyond these doors.

Waiting for them.

Sully paused, hand on door as he turned toward Dez. "It's here, in the next room. When we push these open, I need you to look after Evelyn and Bob if they're in there. If you want me to focus on this thing and put everything else out of mind, you need to do the same. Focus on them, not on me. You hear me?"

Dez blinked. "Sully—"

"We've got a job to do. Our clients' safety comes first. I'll hold it off. You get them safe."

Dez's mouth formed a straight line, lips pressed together, jaw set hard. He obviously wasn't happy about this, but he nodded anyway.

Sully nodded back.

With his palm flat against one of the doors, he pushed it open.

28

DEZ WASN'T PSYCHIC. Though he'd seen spirits a couple of times while close to death, he'd rarely been able to experience the paranormal using one of his five senses.

But as he pushed through with Sully into the kitchen of the Holmes mansion, the evil felt thick enough to chew. He tried for a breath, but it got caught halfway, making it more a gasp than an inhalation.

Sully took another step forward, putting him next to a dusty table. "Evelyn?" He'd been shouting earlier, but this time, it came out as a whisper. The change in tone made sense. If Dez could feel the evil in here, Sully had to be drowning in it.

A groan came to Dez's ears. Not a woman's but a man's.

Dez pushed past Sully, circling the table until he reached a newer island.

A pair of shoes came into view followed by legs.

Dez took a final step forward, giving himself a full view of the person lying on the floor.

Bob.

"Sully," Dez said as he closed the remaining distance to Bob.

With Sully's reassuring presence next to him, Dez crouched to examine the semi-conscious man.

Bob was bleeding badly from the head, an open wound on the left side of his forehead.

Dez reached down, examining the injury, careful to keep his touch light. Despite not being fully conscious, Bob reacted violently, grasping blindly at Dez's hand.

"Bob, Bob, it's okay. It's Dez and Sully. You're going to be all right. I'm going to get you out of here."

"Ev," Bob moaned out. "Ev."

The name served as a reminder. Dez's head snapped up as he scanned the kitchen. "Where is she?"

Sully shook his head without otherwise replying.

"Sully, I heard her. Where is she?"

"It wasn't her." The three words formed the extent of Sully's answer.

Dez's stomach knotted. Even with his limited understanding of the spirit world, the meaning was horrifically clear. If it wasn't Evelyn he'd heard, it had been something imitating her voice. And the only reason he could come up with was that something had intended to lure them back here.

Not good.

"Ev," Bob groaned again.

Dez returned his gaze to the man's face and spoke fast. "We'll find her. Right now, let's focus on getting you out of here, all right?"

Bob gave a subtle nod.

"Can you carry him outside?" Sully asked.

"Ordinarily, I'd prefer not to move him until I'm clear on the extent of his injuries. But—"

Sully cut in. "If you don't get him out now, his injuries will be even worse."

Dez's own mind had already gone to the same place. At the

confirmation from Sully, Dez sprang into action. Wanting to avoid undue pressure to the head, he decided against the firearm's carry, opting instead to lift Bob in a cradle.

"Where's the ghost?" Dez asked as he carried Bob from the kitchen.

Sully's response didn't ease Dez's worries. "Everywhere."

With Sully bringing up the rear, Dez pushed forward through the house. Behind him, came the sound of something heavy and metallic.

"What's that?" he asked.

"The chain."

Dez put it down to tension that he hadn't earlier noticed the thing jangling inside Sully's coat.

Dez entered the entry hall, front door now within sight. "You can't exactly tie the thing up, can you?"

"I was figuring on using it more as a weapon. Better than nothing, right?"

Dez didn't respond. The doorway stood now in front of him, welcome light flowing through the space. A few more long strides and he'd have Bob safely outside.

The door slammed shut.

Dez jumped. "Goddammit! What the hell?"

He turned back toward the house's interior in time to see Sully put his back to him. He had wrapped half the chain around his right hand and wrist, leaving a decent length of it free, swishing it back and forth like an angry cat's tail.

"Try to get the door open," Sully told Dez.

Dez did as asked, leaving Sully for the moment to handle the entity. Sully was right. They needed to get their clients safe.

Dez shifted Bob until he was certain he wouldn't drop him once he released his grip on his legs. He used his now-spare hand to grip the doorknob. It twisted easily, but the door refused to budge.

"It's stuck," Dez said.

"Not stuck," Sully said. "This thing is keeping it shut." He raised his voice, setting Dez's nerves on edge as he called into the house, "Come on, you bastard! You want me, come and get me!"

Dez felt the change, a heavy electricity like a severe thunderstorm. Behind him, came the sound of the chain whistling through air. Once. Twice. Again.

The heaviness abated.

"Go," Sully said.

Dez tried the handle again. This time, the door opened.

He wasted no time, rushing through the opening with Bob. He nearly tripped on the steps as he ran but managed to stay upright until he'd reached the truck. The doors were unlocked, allowing Dez to settle Bob onto the back seat.

Dez turned, expecting to find Sully behind him.

He wasn't there.

Worse, the front door was again shut.

"Ah hell," Dez groaned.

He stared at the closed front door, praying to see Sully emerge.

He didn't.

Dez forced away fear, needing to focus for the moment on Bob. He eyed the wound while dialling nine-one-one with his other hand.

"I need EMS to Twenty-Four Packham Lane, east of Rocky Creek. I have an adult male, semi-conscious and breathing, with a head injury."

With Bob fading in and out, Dez recognized the signs of concussion. He could only hope he hadn't also suffered a skull fracture. With Bob's legs hanging outside the truck, Dez maneuvered himself inside the cab and leaned over the older man, eyes fixed on his face, free hand turning Bob's head to search for any injuries he might have missed. Luckily, nothing else revealed itself.

Dez answered the operator's questions as best he could given he hadn't seen how Bob had acquired the injury. With the operator holding the line, Dez focused fully on Bob, hoping to drag him back to full consciousness—at least long enough to get some answers.

"Bob, I need you to try to wake up. Come on, man." Dez took one of Bob's hands and squeezed his index finger, hoping to use pain response to bring the man around.

Bob groaned. His eyes fluttered open.

"Hey," Dez said. "It's okay. I brought you outside. You're safe." At least he hoped so. "I need you to talk to me. Can you tell me what happened?"

Bob's eyes weren't entirely focusing, but he was trying. "Where's Ev?"

"Sully's inside, looking for her." Again, Dez hoped so. "Where did you last see her?"

"I can't … um, I think … I think the front hall." His words came out slow and slurred. "Get Mr. Holmes's things. Something on her mind. Mind changed. Besides the collection."

Dez tilted his head, not sure if he caught the meaning. "She didn't say what she was thinking?"

"No. She was fine. Fine, troubled. Seemed troubled."

"Okay. And you don't have any idea which part of the house she went to?"

Bob tried for a head shake but ended up grimacing at the movement.

"Okay," Dez said. "We'll find her. I want you to stay in the truck. Ordinarily, I'd tell you to lock the doors, but under the circumstances, I'd rather you didn't. I want you to try really hard to stay awake until EMS arrives. Can you do that for me?"

"Try," Bob said, eyes doing a slow blink. The word came out

mumbled, leaving Dez without much hope for Bob's ability to do as requested.

Dez returned to the operator. "Catch all that?"

"Yes. You believe there might be a second victim?"

"Potentially. My brother's inside, searching. I need to join him. How far out is the EMS crew?"

"A few minutes. I've dispatched a couple of police units as well. I'd like you to stay on the line until they get there."

"Negative," Dez said. "I need to get inside. If there's a threat, my brother needs backup. I'll call back with any additional info."

He didn't wait for the response before disconnecting. Nine-one-one operators typically wanted, for obvious reasons, to keep callers on the line until emergency crews arrived. But Dez couldn't afford to have his attention diverted, not by anything. Having someone on the phone wanting answers counted as a significant distraction. Besides, he wanted his line free in case Sully called him.

Dez pushed Bob's legs inside the truck and shut the door before sprinting back to the house. He gripped the doorknob and shoved. Again, the door refused to budge.

He growled low, backed up a step and put his boot to it, kicking hard against the wood near the lock. While he felt the vibration of the impact, the door refused to budge.

Dez released tension through a shouted curse, then gave it one more try.

Still nothing.

He dragged hands through his hair, trying to force his mind past the growing panic.

At least one other door was at the back of the house, he reminded himself. If that didn't work, he'd find a way through a window. Failing that, he'd drive his vehicle through the wall. He was getting inside this damn house one way or another.

He ran, mind on nothing but reaching the back door and, from there, Sully.

He was fighting his way through a tangle of grass and weeds at the side of the house when his phone rang. Though he didn't recognize the number, he knew if it was the nine-one-one operator, it would show up as an unknown caller ID. He debated not answering but decided he'd better. If it wasn't immediately important, he could simply hang up.

"Dez Braddock," he huffed into his handset, still on the move.

"Oh, hello. It's Amelia Friedmann?" The statement spoken as a question as if uncertain whether he'd remember her.

He was about to suggest he'd call her back, but she continued before he could say as much.

"You asked about the DNA test I did on the ancestry site. You wanted the name of the lady I discovered on there I'm apparently related to."

Dez recalled. He still didn't think this was the time. Again, he'd been about to say so but was cut off.

"Well, to be honest, I wanted to check with the lady before I passed along her name. I didn't want her to be surprised to find a private investigator on her doorstep. I did a little research and located some information about her. I was able to connect with her and discuss our family history. You'll never guess."

Dez wasn't in the mood to guess. He'd just made it to the back of the house and was dismayed to see the back door was completely covered by overgrown rosebushes. With no machete at his disposal, he had his work cut out for him.

Even so, something about Amelia's tone gave him pause. He had the impression she wanted him to ask. "What did you find out?"

"Well, you remember how we talked about Paulette—how she'd been given to another family whose identity we were never told? Well, between me and this lady I spoke with, we figured it out. Paulette was this lady's grandmother. Can you believe it? Of course, she wasn't named Paulette. She was renamed Henrietta—Etta for short. But it all fits! Paulette didn't die. She lived a very full and happy life. This lady sent me a photo of her grandmother as a baby. It's the same baby, without a doubt. Isn't it incredible?"

It was. Or it would have been were Dez in any other situation. As things stood, he had only one question. "Did she give permission to pass along her name?"

"Well, there's the other amazing detail. She already knows you."

Despite the situation, Dez froze. "What? Who is it?"

"Her name is Evelyn Harlow."

29

SULLY MOVED THROUGH THE HOUSE, walking as fast as he could while ensuring he wouldn't miss evidence of Evelyn's presence.

Given the state in which they'd found Bob, Sully worried he'd also find Evelyn injured. He could only hope she hadn't been hurt so badly she was beyond help.

While he'd intended to leave the house with Dez, his instincts stopped him at the threshold. He hesitated long enough to see Dez move safely off the steps. Then the door slammed shut in Sully's face.

He guessed he was now trapped inside, but he felt a measure of relief knowing Dez and Bob were safe from the entity for the time being. Ordinarily, Sully would have worried Lawrence might remain a threat to Dez and Bob even outside, but he was certain the ghost was now firmly inside the house. Sully had felt it, the subtle yet noticeable increase to the big entity's power, as if it had regrown a needed limb with the return of Mr. Grin and Lawrence. Unfortunately, good news for the entity meant bad news for Sully.

And Evelyn.

Sully called her name for what felt like the hundredth time. Again, he received no response.

He'd finished checking what he could of the main floor and was making his way toward the stairs leading up when his phone rang.

Dez.

"Sully? Where are you? You good?"

"Yeah. Still trying to find Evelyn. How's Bob?"

"Hanging in there. Concussion for sure, maybe worse. Won't know until someone does a proper check. EMS and police are on the way."

Sully wasn't sure what to think about that. While he was glad medical help was coming, he didn't want anyone else inside the house until he'd managed to make the place safe.

At the moment, it felt more like a big if than a when.

"Why were they here?" he asked Dez. "Did Bob tell you anything?"

"I think it was Evelyn's idea to come here. Plan was to go through more of Holmes's things, but something seemed to be bothering her. She wouldn't tell him what was going on."

"Maybe she was anxious about coming, given what she'd dealt with earlier with Mr. Grin."

"No, listen, I think I know what it is. I heard back from Amelia Friedmann—you know, the Lomaxes' descendant? Anyway, she said she found the name for me of the lady she discovered through DNA was a blood relative of hers."

Sully guessed before Dez could finish the thought. "Evelyn."

"Bingo. The two talked a short time ago, and I think it upset Evelyn. She probably went there looking for answers or hoping to settle something. It must have been a shock for her."

Sully scrubbed a hand over his face. "I wish she'd called us first."

"Me too, but like I said, she was probably in shock."

Sully understood completely. He'd once been in the situation himself of having the secrets of his blood family sprung on him. Difference was, in Evelyn's case, it seemed she came from largely good people. In Sully's case, finding out about his birth family made him only more grateful for the people who'd adopted him.

Didn't matter now. They had the situation they had, and they'd need to make the best of it. If Sully could find Evelyn, he could help her through this.

"Stay with Bob," Sully said. "I'm going to keep looking."

"No way in hell. He'll be okay until EMS arrives. I'm trying to find a way in. Wait for me."

"Dez—"

A scream pierced the air, cutting Sully off and making him jump.

"What was that?" Dez demanded.

"I think it was Evelyn."

"Actually Evelyn, or the ghost pretending to be Evelyn?"

Sully peered up into the darkness overhead. The dangers it held were clear, but nothing else at the moment seemed certain. "Well. Given I heard it too, it must have been her. But I need to check."

"Wait, okay? I'll be there right away."

"I can't wait. Not if it means something bad happening. I need to find her. Please, don't come in here."

Dez sighed heavily. "Quit fighting me on this. You know I'm not backing down. I'm at the rear door now. How am I supposed to find you once I'm inside?"

Sully echoed Dez's sigh. Dez wasn't going to take no for an answer, a fact Sully knew as well as he knew himself.

"Okay, hang on. I'm coming toward the back of the house." He disconnected with Dez, hoping to save as much of his battery as possible. Already, it was draining, and it would no doubt drop even quicker as he continued to confront the ghosts haunting this place.

Sully couldn't deny he felt anxious about responding immediately to the scream. With the entity's strength, and the way the entire house seemed to thrum with its power, there was something to be said about safety in numbers—not just for Sully but for Dez too. Dez would eventually find a way in, and Sully didn't want him facing this thing down by himself.

Sully rushed through the house, back into the kitchen. A chill hit him, one telling him the entity was reforming itself, sucking energy and warmth from the air. Two more steps, and it was like running into a psychic wall.

Sully took a step back and swung the chain in a wild arc, once high, a second time lower.

The feeling faded, and he ran forward, past the spot where the entity had been hovering. It would be back, without question. He needed to be ready.

But first, he had to try to get Dez inside.

An opening on the far side of the kitchen led to what appeared to be an old mudroom. Into this Sully passed, using his cellphone's flashlight to locate a door, presumably leading outside. He heard a series of thuds against it, no doubt Dez trying to kick it down. Dez's actions were prevented by a single solid board nailed across the doorway, so Sully searched the area for something he could use.

Though nothing immediately showed itself, he had an idea, one that would hopefully serve more than one purpose. He'd passed a fireplace in the front sitting room. Where there were fireplaces, there were usually fireplace tools.

He sprinted back toward the front of the house, passing and whipping at another cold spot as he ran. In the sitting room, he dashed to the fireplace and was rewarded, as hoped, with a set of tools. Hefting a poker, he received even more good news.

It was heavy and solid.

Iron.

Sully took both the poker and a spade, then ran back toward the house's rear. Again reaching the back door—still under siege by Dez's boot—Sully dialled his brother.

"Give me a minute," he said once Dez picked up. "I need to pry off a board."

Sully set down the chain and the spade, using the poker to pry at the heavy board. He'd nearly succeeded with one side when the sensation of icy cold behind him had him spinning. He lashed out with the poker, effectively impaling the spirit and once again forcing it to dissipate.

Another few seconds, and Sully succeeded in prying the nails from one side of the wall. The other side remained fixed, but Sully suspected Dez would make short work of it. And he'd need to. The door both locked and unlocked with a key, leaving no way to simply open it, even from the inside.

"Okay," Sully said into his phone. "You should be clear."

Sully had just enough time to pick up the chain and fireplace tools and step back. A moment later, the door crashed inward. Backlit by daylight, Dez was a bear, heaving breath and tensed posture taking nothing away from his intimidating presence.

Sully was thrilled to see him.

"Doing okay?" Dez asked.

Sully handed him the poker, then opted to give him the chain as well. "Good to see you."

Dez managed a tight smile. "Back at ya."

Leaving the back door open, Sully led Dez through the main floor to the base of the stairs. Sully spared Dez a glance before redirecting his gaze to the shadows overhead. "This thing's come at me a few times, but I've been able to drive it off by hitting it with iron. Stay right behind me—*right* behind me—and just keep swinging, all right? I'll tell you when I feel it getting close."

Sully started up the stairs, Dez immediately on his heels. Midway up, cellphone flashlight raised to light the way, Sully kicked away pieces of bannister he'd earlier shattered with his body.

As they moved, the entity's rage roiled around them. It was like being in the middle of a tornado. Sully's breath caught, and he had to pause for a moment to steady himself.

Dez's hand on his back was reassuring stability. "Almost there, bro. Hold it together."

Sully wasn't sure he'd count them as almost there, but he did what he could to obey Dez's ask. He was dizzy and slightly nauseated, the way he felt when he'd spent too long enjoying carnival rides. Without the wall and Dez to use for balance, he thought he might have tumbled down the stairs like James Holmes.

"Don't let it get to you," Dez said. "Block it out if you need to."

"I can't," Sully said. "I need to stay connected so I know when it gets close."

"I can feel it too. No idea how you're managing this."

If it was strong enough Dez could feel it, Sully wasn't sure how he was managing it either.

They made it to the top of the stairs. There, Sully used a wall for support while playing his cellphone flashlight beam down the hall.

"Evelyn?" Dez called out. "Can you hear me?"

Sully didn't speak, straining to hear a hoped-for reply. The silence was deafening, possessing the same sort of cotton-wool effect as a heavy countryside snowfall. It was the sort of silence that stifled sound, held and gagged it.

Wherever she was, Evelyn might not hear them. Sully knew they had to keep trying.

He inhaled, about to give it another go when a sound came to his ears. Quiet and muffled, it seemed to come from somewhere ahead.

"Hear that?" Dez asked.

"Yeah. Sounds like thudding. And I thought I heard a voice too."

"If you heard a voice, it's not a ghost. Not this time."

Sully hoped he'd finally found some reason to hope. "What do you think? Closet maybe?"

Dez's eyes strayed forward and up. "I don't think so."

Sully followed his sightline until he sighted what Dez had. A hatch in the ceiling.

"Had to be an attic," Dez grumbled.

Sully plucked at Dez's sleeve to get him moving. "Come on. You try to get it open; I'll keep watch."

A rope hung down from a handle this side, but Dez—having set down the implements he'd been carrying—used his height to grasp the handle itself. A heaviness had settled once again, and Sully suspected it was the reason Dez was struggling to tug open the hatch. Sully stepped forward and swung with the spade, repeating the process on the other side of Dez. He was rewarded by the sound of the hatch grinding open.

A shriek overhead was decidedly Evelyn's. Not pain but terror.

"It's okay," Sully said. "Evelyn, it's Sully and Dez. Can you find the opening?"

A few seconds and some fumbling noises later, Evelyn's pale face appeared.

"Oh! Oh, thank God. Thank God!"

Dez had unfolded a ladder built into the hatch. "Think you can climb down?"

Evelyn gave a rapid nod, then turned to navigate the ladder. Dez waited, arms at the ready to catch her should she fall. Meanwhile, Sully remained on guard, alert for the entity's return.

As soon as her feet hit the floor, Evelyn threw herself at Dez, grabbing him in a hug. "I've never been so happy to see anyone in all my life!"

Dez gently took her arm to guide her away. "What are you doing here?" he asked as they started for the stairs.

Evelyn began a rambling explanation, talking about her surprise conversation with Amelia. "I knew my grandmother was adopted, but I had no idea. No idea! Once I realized who her birth parents were, I had to come. I was drawn here. I meant to come on my own. When I told Bob I wanted to pick through some things here, he wouldn't let me come alone. Bob! Oh! He's hurt. I know he's hurt. I heard him scream, but the hatch slammed shut and I couldn't get out. We need to find him!"

"Already did," Dez told her. "I took him outside. EMS is on the way."

"Is he okay?"

"He will be."

Sully picked up on the subtle placating tone in Dez's voice. He wasn't convinced about Bob being okay, but now wasn't the time to tell Evelyn that. They needed to focus on getting her out, and it would be easier if she had one less thing to fuel her panic.

Sully led the way back down to the main floor, keeping their pace slower for Evelyn's sake. He took them first to the front door, not surprised to find it shut tight. This time, no matter what he and Dez tried, they couldn't budge it.

Sully took them next to the back, where they again met a closed and sealed door.

"You mean we can't get out?" Evelyn asked.

Sully gave up on the back door and addressed her. "We'll get out. We might just need to fight our way there."

Her eyes flashed wide. "What? How?"

Sully faced her fully. "You said you felt drawn here. What did you mean?"

Panic swirled in her eyes, but she seemed to be trying hard to stave it off. As she drew in a breath and set her jaw, the fear seemed to ebb. "It was a feeling. A strong feeling. Like a piece of myself was here and I needed to find it. I've never been as scared as I was when Mr. Grin turned up at my house, and I knew I had to face this down. If an ancestor of mine is causing this, I need to deal with it. I need to face the fear." Giving her head a shake, she dropped her gaze to the floor. " I don't think I'm making sense."

Sully put a hand on her shoulder. "I get what you're trying to say, but I think there's more to it. I think once you learned who you are—who you really are—a door opened inside you. It allowed a connection to form, one that pulled you here. What you don't necessarily know is how dangerous it is. It's not your grandparents who brought you here. It's your great-uncle. He's the one possessing Mr. Grin. And he's not a nice guy."

Sully held back on his final thought. It wouldn't help matters for Evelyn to know exactly how much danger she was in.

Lawrence Malcolm had set out to do away with baby Paulette, the single biggest threat to his inheriting a fortune from his brother. Despite dying in the course of it, he hadn't given up on his murderous aims. Only now, it wasn't about the money. It was revenge he was after.

Only, the family members who'd locked him away for decades were long dead. All he had left was Paulette's sole descendant.

If he couldn't take his revenge on those he deemed directly responsible for his downfall and death, he'd find the next best person.

"He's after me, isn't he?" Evelyn asked.

Sully debated lying but decided against it. He nodded.

"How did he know who I was? I didn't even know."

"I don't know. Sometimes, I think spirits can sense things we can't. Or it might be he recognized something in you that belonged to Warren or Paulette. Maybe there's no point wondering. Fact is, he knows. And we need to stop him."

"How are we supposed to do that, exactly?" Dez asked. "The bastard's supercharged."

Sully had been giving it some thought as he moved through the house. Taking the entity on would be hard. Really hard. But he thought he might have figured out a way to make it easier.

"I have an idea," Sully said. "But we'll need Evelyn's help."

30

The three of them moved through the house, each armed with an iron implement.

Sully maintained the lead, focused on staying alert for signs the entity was attempting to form near them.

"We need to stay on guard," he told Dez and Evelyn. "Once it figures out what we're up to, it's going to be pissed."

Evelyn's arm appeared in Sully's peripheral vision, finger pointing toward an open door on the main floor. "There's the library. It contains a book James Holmes had in his possession. It was signed by a serial killer eventually killed in self-defence by a would-be victim. Mr. Holmes willed us the book, but for what I feel are obvious reasons, we didn't take it."

Thankfully, the library wasn't as big as Sully had dreaded. While plenty of books lined the shelves, the various bequeathed items had been set aside—likely by Holmes's lawyer as she'd attempted to organize his things—it didn't take long to locate it.

"Do you have your lighter on you?" Sully asked Evelyn.

Her eyes widened. "You want to burn it?"

"That a problem?"

She eyed the book. "Ordinarily, I don't go in for book burning. But under the circumstances, I'm willing to overlook it."

Evelyn picked up the book and carried it toward the fireplace inside the library. Behind her, Sully and Dez formed a wall with their bodies, each facing into the room.

"Be ready," Sully told Dez. "If I'm right about this, as soon as the book starts to burn, things could get hairy."

Dez nodded.

Sully listened without watching as Evelyn flicked the lighter. A few seconds passed before he heard what he was waiting on: the crackle of paper burning.

"What now?" she asked.

"Stay behind me."

Sully kept himself open and ready, alert to approaching energy. He didn't have long to wait.

If the serial killer in question remained connected to this book, it would respond to the burning as a direct attack. Sully had hoped it would come alone though he wasn't surprised to feel the entire massive entity respond. It was like an army, moving as one to respond to a threat.

But like an army, it was made up of individuals. And this individual—railing against the maltreatment of its prized possession—made itself known. Despite it remaining a part of the larger being, Sully could easily pick it out.

He reached out psychically, seizing hold of it, dragging it from the mass. He felt the killer's energy writhing in his hold, but it wasn't going anywhere. Even if controlling the large entity was too much for him at this moment, this much he could do.

He towed the killer toward himself and to the right. A moment later, the large entity rushed forward.

"Dez!" Sully yelled.

Dez swung, blindly slicing through the middle of the entity with the poker. The entity vanished, presumably to regroup.

It was all Sully needed.

He focused on opening a doorway, envisioning it the way he'd previously been taught. It took only seconds. Then only a couple more to fling the killer's spirit through the opening and seal it shut.

"Sully?" Dez asked.

Sully cast him a smile. "One down."

Dez flashed a tight smile and gave Sully an awkward fist bump. "How many more to go?"

"No idea. But it'll get easier as we go. One at a time, right?" He peered back at Evelyn. "What's next? Anything else in this room you know of?"

"There's a set of thumbscrews. I think they're supposed to be in here somewhere."

With Sully keeping his focus entirely on any approaching threat, Dez and Evelyn went through the library, searching for the item in question.

"Got it," Dez said a minute later. "At least, I think these are thumbscrews."

Sully and Evelyn joined him at a glass case containing a variety of items. Though far from an expert on medieval torture, Sully thought Dez was likely right.

"How are we supposed to destroy these?" Evelyn asked. "We can't burn them, and they'll be tough to break."

"We don't have to destroy them," Sully said. "We only need any attached spirits to think we're trying to."

Dez glared at the item. "Good enough for me."

The case was locked, but Dez made short work of it, using the pointed end of the poker to pry open the door. He pulled out the thumbscrews and dropped them on the floor before lifting his gaze back to Sully. Dez raised his brows in question.

Ready?

Sully nodded once.

Ready.

Dez returned his gaze to the item on the floor. Then he lifted the poker and drove it, sharp end down, against the device. Once, twice, three times.

The entity returned. Again, Sully sensed a part of it connected to the item. Not a victim, but a torturer.

Despite the tension of the situation, Sully felt a smile spreading. He'd enjoy sending the sick bastard into the next realm. He had a feeling justice would be awaiting him.

As before, Sully seized hold of the ghost, hauling it free of the larger entity.

"Evelyn, swing!" Sully yelled as the entity sprang toward them.

She swung her acquired spade in a wide arc, unknowingly scattering the larger spirit while Sully kept hold of the individual one. Again, he created a doorway and shoved the ghost through.

"Get it?" Dez asked.

"Two down. Anything else in the library, Evelyn?"

"Don't think so. There's a bedroom on the upper floor with some things in the closet. One is a suit worn by a gangster when he was shot by police."

"Nothing else on this floor?"

"Might be, but I don't have the list Mr. Holmes's lawyer gave me, unfortunately. I'm going by memory at this point."

Better than nothing. Anyway, the more individual spirits they sent packing, the easier it would hopefully be to tackle the large entity. With luck, he wouldn't need Evelyn's help for long in tracking down individual possessed items.

"We still haven't found Mr. Grin," Dez pointed out.

"He's here somewhere," Evelyn said. "I'm not psychic or anything, but I can feel it. He's here—and he knows we are too."

Though Sully agreed, he remained silent. His acknowledgment wouldn't make anyone feel better.

They moved together through the library and, from there, into the hall. The stairs loomed ahead, shadows blocking the upper half from view.

Sully settled his nerves and led the way, taking each step as quickly as he could while ensuring he remained alert for threats overhead and physical hazards underfoot.

Unable to shake the feeling of being watched, he was grateful they made it to the top without incident.

"Which bedroom?" Dez asked.

"I was told it was in the opposite wing from Mr. Holmes's," Evelyn said. "Warren Malcolm's old bedroom."

"Holmes didn't sleep in the master?" Sully asked.

Dez snorted. "Hey, if I moved into a house where a dude was murdered, I wouldn't sleep in his bedroom either."

With Evelyn guiding them, they entered a large bedroom overlooking the expansive rear gardens. While these windows were also covered, gaps had been left between the boards, providing some light.

Sully followed Evelyn to the closet and stayed next to her as she picked a garment bag from off the rack. A label dangled from the hanger, marked "KR Historical Museum—Edmund Rivers suit."

Evelyn unzipped the bag. A suit lay inside. She removed it, carried it to the bedroom's fireplace and dropped it inside.

They repeated the procedure they'd used for the book, Evelyn using her lighter to burn the clothing while Sully and Dez prepared to do battle.

The entity's rage was clear as it charged, so fast this time, Sully barely had time to lock onto Rivers before calling on Dez to swing the iron poker. A few seconds later, the entity was momentarily out of commission and Rivers was gone forever.

Three ghosts down now. Sully had the impression the entity was weakened, but like a wounded animal backed into in a corner, it had plenty of claw and bite left in it. Another one or two ghosts, and hopefully he could tackle the big one.

"What's left?" he asked Evelyn.

"Probably lots, but I'm blanking on stuff in the house. One of the things I do recall was the car driven by the Kelso brothers, the one in which they were fatally shot. It's in the garage. How are we going to wreck it?"

"Trust me," Sully said. "Dez can do a lot of damage in a short time."

He sensed Dez's eye roll without needing to look.

They rushed from the bedroom, making their way back to the staircase. Given the problems they'd encountered previously with getting locked inside the house, Sully wasn't sure whether they'd face a similar issue, but they'd deal with it if needed. For now, he focused on navigating the stairs, keeping a slow enough pace to ensure everyone's safety.

They were nearly halfway down when a distant sound came to his ears.

Sirens.

Damn. Whether it was EMS or police, Sully knew he was very shortly going to have more people on hand to protect.

"Sully!" Evelyn cried.

The sound had left him momentarily distracted. It had been enough.

He spun in the direction of Evelyn's voice, in time to see Mr. Grin lunge at her from the shadows. She screamed and backed away—directly toward the opening made previously by Sully's body.

Dez sprung for her, grabbing hold and trying to pull her back. But Mr. Grin was no longer being controlled by just Lawrence. The entity was behind it, and it had plenty of juice left.

Mr. Grin hammered into Evelyn's body, sending her backward, through the opening and down.

Dez, arms still wrapped around her, went with her.

Sully gave a strangled cry but otherwise pushed through the shock as he ran down the stairs, not caring now about potential obstacles. Gripping the banister, he swung himself around at the bottom and closed the distance to Dez and Evelyn.

Dez was already stirring as Sully gripped his arm. "Dez, you okay?"

"I'm getting really bloody sick of being tossed around. How's Evelyn?"

Good question. With Dez sitting up and in apparently okay condition, Sully focused his attention to their client. She moaned as he touched her shoulder. He knew from its appearance it was either dislocated or broken.

"Evelyn?"

"God, my shoulder."

Sully peered up, into the shadows surrounding them. There was no sign of the dummy now. Despite this, Sully could feel the entity watching, knew it was building strength for another attack.

"We need to move," Sully said. "Now."

Dez didn't delay, scooping Evelyn into his arms and rushing her to the nearby front door. Sully grabbed the fireplace tools dropped by Dez and Evelyn as they landed, then made his way out as well.

This time, the route through the door remained unbarred.

"It's getting weaker," Sully told Dez as they dashed with Evelyn toward the truck where, earlier, Dez had left Bob.

"Not weak enough," came Dez's reply.

Bob had sat up, but the flesh of his face had taken on a greenish cast. Already, he'd left a puddle of vomit next to the truck, and he appeared close to adding to it. Despite that, his eyes wobbled to Evelyn as Dez carried her over.

"Oh God," he ground out. "Is she—?"

"She'll be okay," Sully said. "Can you look after her while we take care of something? The sirens you hear are EMS and police. They should be here in a minute or two."

Bob gave a slight nod. Any more head movement was likely to cause a bigger problem.

With Evelyn settled on the front seat, Sully touched Dez's arm as indication for him to join him.

Evelyn caught Sully's sleeve with her good arm. "If you find Mr. Grin, you nail that little bastard, you hear me? Don't worry about its value. Just toast him for me."

Sully grinned. "You got it."

Then he and Dez sprinted across the front yard to the detached garage.

31

The garage was awash in darkness when they cracked open the door. Thankfully, it was sealed by a pair of doors which swung outward and latched. Having dragged them fully open, Sully and Dez were able to flood the garage with natural light.

This was far from a standard garage, more a large shed providing parking and protection from the elements for up to seven or eight vehicles. A couple of spaces were empty, and Sully was reminded the museum had already taken a couple of Model Ts. What they had remaining were a couple more modern cars as well as a small collection of vehicles dating between the nineteen forties and eighties.

"The Kelso brothers," Sully said. "Which car? I don't know the story."

Dez frowned. "They were shot by police while in the car, right? Look for bullet holes."

Sully started with what appeared to be the oldest car while Dez took the next one over. They'd left the iron spade with Evelyn for protection, leaving Dez to wield the poker in a two-handed grip as he moved.

Dez vibrated with tension; Sully could see it even from a

short distance away. But he was holding it together, which was all Sully could ask.

"Where are we looking for bullet holes, do you think?" Sully asked.

"My guess is along the side panels. Could be either driver or passenger-side. Maybe both—hang on."

Sully glanced up from his search. "What?"

"Got something here. Look."

Sully rounded the car he was checking, joining Dez next to his. He followed Dez's pointed index finger to a hole punched in the black metal. Sully's gaze travelled downward, where he spotted and pointed out a second hole. Below that and a little nearer the engine side of the car, a third.

Sully circled the vehicle to the passenger side. "Dez, there are a whole bunch of bullet holes over here. This is it."

Dez stepped forward, putting him next to the windshield. "All right. Ready?"

"Hang on." Sully stepped toward the rear of the car, near the garage doors. One set of sirens had already reached the house and had cut out. From here, Sully could see a paramedic attending to Bob. He didn't see Evelyn but supposed she could already be in the ambulance.

Now to make sure they'd stay safe.

Sully turned back toward Dez. "Do it."

Dez lifted the poker, bringing it down hard against the windshield glass. He gritted his teeth at the impact, but he repeated the move again and again. Finally, the glass broke.

"Damn it!" Dez exclaimed a moment later. "Poker's stuck."

Sully tossed Dez the chain. "Go after the headlights or the sideview mirrors. Whatever you can break, do it."

Dez obeyed, whipping at the vehicle with the end of the chain.

Sully felt two spirits this time, combined with the larger entity.

"It's here," he said for Dez's benefit. Then he focused, dragging the Kelso brothers from the mass while Dez lashed at the air between himself and Sully. Dez wasn't hitting anything, but his movements provided the distraction Sully needed. He sent the Kelso brothers across, sealing the door behind them.

Five down. No idea how many more to go.

A thud and a grunt from Dez had Sully's attention snapping back to the side of the vehicle. The driver's side door was open, and Dez lay on the ground next to the neighbouring vehicle, apparently having been struck.

Sully went rigid as he watched for movement. "Dez!"

Dez sat up a little, stalling there, eyes widening as they focused on something inside the car.

"Mr. Grin," he said. "Sully, it's him."

Sully tracked Dez's stare until he too saw it.

Mr. Grin sat behind the wheel, its head turning completely around, until its eyes fully met Sully's.

Then the engine started.

Sully took a step back but couldn't get out of the way in time. The back end of the car hammered into him, knocking him to the ground in the weed-dotted gravel outside the garage door. He had just enough sense left to tuck in his limbs as he fell, but while he managed to avoid the tires, he felt painful pressure as the guts of the undercarriage dragged across his sternum and stopped there.

Dez screamed his name, and Sully could only hope he didn't need help too. Trapped under the car, he could do nothing for him.

Sully sucked in a breath, trying to relieve some pressure on his midsection. With luck, he'd be able to squirm free.

He estimated he'd made it less than a foot when a different

sort of pressure struck him. In the first couple of seconds, it reminded him of the tight feeling he got when his throat swelled with a cold. From there, it intensified, the pressure mounting and tightening, until he gasped for air.

He had to get out from under the car, but the more he struggled, the worse it got. Nothing physical was around his throat; he slapped at his neck to make sure of it. Yet something—something evidently not of this world—had wrapped around him and was squeezing.

He was being strangled.

He tried to call out to Dez, but no sound escaped. Nothing beyond the desperate sound of his own choking. Dez called for him again but had yet to appear. Possibly he was being held back by the same force as was attacking Sully.

Estimating he had only a few seconds left before he began to lose consciousness, Sully sought calm, needing it to gain control over this thing. But with death so close, calm proved elusive.

His body reacted on his own, fingers of one hand scrabbling at his throat, palm of the other shoving ineffectually against the undercarriage of the car.

The car didn't budge. Neither did the pressure at his throat.

His vision, already swimming, began to blacken. His heart thudded hard and rapidly enough to burst. Blood pounding through his head drowned out everything else.

Through the pinhole of vision remaining, he spotted movement to his left. Feet. Not Dez's.

He heard one of the car's doors being wrenched open. A primal yell—Evelyn's—sounded. A moment later, Mr. Grin landed on the flattened weeds next to the car.

The pressure against Sully's throat released, leaving him gasping and hacking, chest scraping the bottom of the chassis with each tortured cough. For a moment, his watering eyes locked with the dummy's. He watched as the blade of the iron spade came down twice, severing the head from the body.

Sully felt Lawrence's shock as if he himself had been beheaded. Lawrence's rage at Evelyn was so heavy Sully could almost taste it. He wanted to kill her, and he was damn well going to try.

"Not this time, you asshole," Sully wheezed. He felt the change, the weakening of the ghost as it separated from the damaged dummy. He pressed into that weakness, psychically grabbing Lawrence and hauling him away before he could reach Evelyn. He opened a doorway, pressing the struggling spirit toward it.

"If there's a hell, I hope it's waiting for you," Sully said. Then he shoved Lawrence the rest of the way through and sealed the door.

Six ghosts gone. The entity was still here. Sully could feel it. But it wasn't just wounded.

It was dying.

Dying and dangerous.

The sound of an exploding tire told him the threat was far from gone. Already crammed between chassis and cold, hard ground, Sully would be crushed if the car dropped fully onto him.

The vehicle had fallen at the front passenger side, nearest Sully's right foot. He shifted his leg aside far enough to prevent a broken foot, then managed to awkwardly maneuver his legs out of the way as the second front tire exploded.

The ghost was toying with him. Once the tires at the back went, he'd be toast.

He had to end this first.

Sully lay back and closed his eyes. He pressed past his fear, past his pain. All that mattered now was the entity.

He allowed no space for doubt as he seized hold of the spirit mass. He felt it writhing, felt its power within his psychic grasp. It wasn't defeated. It might be weakened, but it wasn't weak.

Neither was he.

He held on harder, finding strength in thoughts of Sarah and Dez, of his other loved ones, of the clients counting on him to keep them safe. He could do this.

He *was* doing this.

Sully held firm, relying on his own power to maintain his hold as he opened another portal.

The entity fought, squirmed against him. If he could hear it, he knew it would be screaming.

He had it now. One more push.

Then it was gone.

Sully lay back, trying to drag in a breath past the continued press of the undercarriage. Dez called for him again, but he didn't answer. Not yet. He took another moment, reaching out with his mind, searching for anything he'd missed. He'd check the house over again later, but for now, he received the answer he'd been hoping for.

They were safe.

"Sully? Sully, talk to me, damn it!"

Sully turned his head, found Dez flattened out next to the car and peering beneath it.

Sully met his eye. "I'm okay. Just get this damn thing off me, okay?"

Dez released his breath in a whoosh and laughed. "You got it, bro."

32

Two days later

Sully rubbed his ribcage as he stared at the facade of James Holmes's mansion.

While he'd been spared fractured ribs—thankfully—he'd come away with an unpleasant case of road rash.

All in all, he supposed they'd gotten away lucky.

Except it had nothing to do with luck.

Sully turned to the woman standing next to him, his eyes dropping to her shoulder. Evelyn wore a sling, and she bore a few bruises on her face and hands. But overall, she appeared to be well.

Better than well, in fact. She looked to be both calm and stoic as she regarded the house. As she turned to meet Sully's eye, a smile formed on her lips.

"You doing all right?" Sully asked. "Shoulder's okay?"

She indicated the shoulder with a jut of her chin. "This old thing? Ah, it'll be fine."

"And Bob?"

"He'll recover. Concussion, but I'll make sure he gets through it fine."

"You're looking after him?"

"He's staying with me, yes." Her smile broadened. "It's been nice, actually."

Sully grinned. "How nice?"

She chuckled without otherwise responding. Sully figured it was answer enough.

Her gaze returned to the house, then to the garage. "I can't believe I did that."

"Cutting off Mr. Grin's head? Yeah, you kind of rocked."

"It's a valuable item. More than my job's worth, quite frankly." She laughed again. "Little bastard had it coming. Anyway, no damage that can't be fixed." She tilted her head as she regarded Sully. "What about you? You doing all right?"

"Definitely. All good. Between Dez, my girlfriend and my mom, I've got all the people fussing over me I'll ever need." He wiped the smile from his face, ensuring Evelyn would know a serious statement was coming up. "I owe you big time. Thank you for doing what you did."

She snorted. "Are you kidding me? After everything you helped me with, it's the very least I could do. I wasn't going to stand by like a wimp and let it hurt you or Dez worse than it already had. I wasn't sure how bad you were injured. I thought for a minute maybe you ..." She took a deep breath. "Thank God I was wrong."

Her eyes drifted back to the house. "You know, it's weird. I never knew where I came from. I had this whole part of my family I didn't know about. I did the DNA test a while ago, hoping I could find out a little more about my family history. When I found out—" She peered at Sully from the corner of her eye before returning her gaze to the house. "Well, I couldn't believe it, really. I think part of me needed to finish this, to help send Lawrence to whatever justice awaits him on the other side. It's like things have come full circle. Like I've helped my biological family find some justice."

Sully crossed his arms and quirked an eyebrow at Evelyn. "So—safe to say you've changed your views on ghosts and the afterlife?"

She laughed. "Safe to say." She touched his arm. "I know I've said this a few times already, but thank you."

He patted her on the back nearest her good shoulder. "Don't mention it."

Dez, Lachlan, Forbes Raynor and Jill—James Holmes's lawyer—emerged from the house and made their way over. Forbes had wanted a walkthrough of the house as part of the process of reopening the investigation. He'd already had forensic identification officers take possession of the despatch box and its contents. Mr. Grin, too, was back in police custody. This time, Sully knew, the dummy would be staying put without the need for added measures.

"I'm going to need you to provide a statement," Forbes said as he reached Sully and Evelyn. "Both of you."

"You sure you want the full rundown on the record?" Sully asked.

Forbes frowned. "You can tell it to me first. Maybe we'll forego a few of the creepier details." He turned his attention to Evelyn. "As for the dummy, it might be in police possession for a little while—at least until we officially wrap the case. Obviously, we won't be laying charges, but we still need to answer as many questions as we can. Someone will let you know when we're done."

Evelyn raised a brow. "I know acquiring Mr. Grin was big win for the museum. But honestly, if I never see the dummy again, it'll be too soon."

Sully stood in the middle of his tiny apartment above the Golden Hand pawn shop, eyes sweeping over the items inside.

"You're not seriously thinking about taking any of this crap with you."

Sully turned at Dez's words, finding him standing with his arms crossed and gaze judgmental as he eyed the place. Dez had a right to his opinion. Most of this stuff had once been his as the original renter of the place.

"Not much, no," Sully said. "Anyway, I'm not giving the place up for a while. I needed to give a full month's notice, and I wanted to make sure Emily's niece was close to moving in before I left completely." Sully once again passed his gaze over the place. "We've been through a few things in this apartment, haven't we?"

Dez harrumphed. "Most of them not good." He turned to meet Sully's eye. "So you're officially over your whole worry thing?"

"About moving in with Sarah, you mean?" Sully nodded. "Yeah. Much as I hate saying the words out loud and risk swelling your ego, you were right."

Dez smirked. "Told you. I'm always right."

Sully nudged him. "I know the furniture belongs to the apartment, but is there anything you brought here you want to take?"

Dez shook his head. "I'm just happy to see the back of it."

Sully understood Dez's feelings on the matter. It didn't represent anything good for him. For Sully, though, the apartment had been largely the opposite.

"I got my life back here," he said.

Dez acknowledged the statement with a nod and a smile. "Yeah. I guess you did. But you're taking new and better steps with your life now, Sull. And you're getting a new and better place to do it in." Dez's turn to nudge Sully. "I hope we'll still see you around sometimes—once you're settled in with Sarah, I mean."

Sully peered up at Dez. A lot of thoughts went through his head, most of them about how so many of the jobs they worked served as reminders of how lucky Sully had been in the adoptive family he'd stumbled into. Like Paulette, Sully had escaped a horrific situation and found peace and happiness in a new family.

But he'd said it all before. Dez knew his thoughts without his needing to air them. Instead, all Sully replied was, "You kidding? We'll be around your place so much, you'll be sick of us. Sarah likes you more than I do."

Dez laughed. "Told you she's a smart lady. I'm happy for you."

"Thanks, D. Listen, I know you've got to get back soon, but I wondered if you might want to stay a bit. We could watch something on TV and order a pizza. Old time's sake, you know?"

Dez grinned at him. "Long as I get to pick the place, I'm all over that plan."

AFTERWORD

Thanks so much for reading. I am continuing to work on the next Dez and Sully books, and would be pleased to keep you updated on future projects and release dates if you would like to join my mailing list. As an added bonus, a growing anthology of short stories, entitled *Haunted: The Ghosts of Sullivan Gray,* is available as a gift to subscribers. Visit my website at lpbayne.com to sign up and grab the current version of *Haunted.*

The books in *The Braddock & Gray Case Files* are intended as standalone books, so they can be read independently of each other and from the preceding *The Sullivan Gray Series. Braddock & Gray* follows the events of *Sullivan Gray,* so those who have read the previous series will find a few cookies scattered here and there. I will include links below to the books in *The Sullivan Gray Series* should you wish to check them out (if you haven't already, of course).

The books in *The Sullivan Gray Series* can also be read as standalones to some extent, each containing a plot that wraps itself up by book's end. But there is a deeper plot that threads throughout the seven novels, so for that reason, I always suggest they're best read in the following order (click the titles to check them out on Amazon):

Black Candle

Harbinger

The Dule Tree

Crawl

Hollow Road

Second Son

Spirit Caller

As mentioned, the books in *The Braddock & Gray Case Files* can be read as standalone novels, but for those interested, here's the publishing order:

The Edge Creek Light

The Haunting of Thornview Hall

The Wynne Witch

The Blake Ghost

Dead Man's Lake

The Hanged Man

Twitch

Mr. Grin

As always, I wanted to take a moment to thank my family and friends for their incredible support. I am so appreciative of all the people in my life who have been at my side throughout this journey.

A big, Dez-sized thanks also to my brilliant editor Hannah Sullivan and to my absolutely stellar team of advance readers, all of whom ensure each of the books is all it can be and more. And thank you as well to my subscribers and my followers on Facebook, especially the Sully's Spirits among you. I am incredibly grateful to you all.

And, of course, a huge thank you to everyone who's picked up this and other Sully books. I thank you from the bottom of my heart for making my author dreams come true.

ABOUT THE AUTHOR

Fascinated by ghost stories and crime fiction, H.P. has been writing both for well over two decades, drawing on more than fifteen years in a career in a criminal justice setting. Raised on a farm on the Canadian Prairies, H.P. enjoys reading, portrait drawing, travel and spending time with family and friends.

For more information, visit H.P.'s website at hpbayne.com.

ALSO BY H.P. BAYNE

Books in The Sullivan Gray Series (best read in the following order):

Black Candle

Harbinger

The Dule Tree

Crawl

Hollow Road

Second Son

Spirit Caller

Or pick up the box sets:

The Sullivan Gray Series Box Set 1

The Sullivan Gray Series Box Set 2

Books in The Braddock & Gray Case Files (can be read in order or as standalone novels):

The Edge Creek Light

The Haunting of Thornview Hall

The Wynne Witch

The Blake Ghost

Dead Man's Lake

The Hanged Man

Twitch

Mr. Grin

Printed in Great Britain
by Amazon

58337979R00158